N. SINGH

Legends of the Gnomish Persuasion

The Well of Stars

Contents

Chapter One

A Promise Made

Villains and heroes come and go as the eras turn, as ages pass. Some are remembered, most are forgotten. And for fewer yet, we know of how their stories began. How did they embark on their paths to villainy or heroics? What pulled them to the dizzying heights of greatness? Was it that old dullard Fate with its predetermined paths, written ends and oh-so-rote air of inevitability? Or was it that sly minstrel Chance who tugged at the strings of time and place to set in motion events that careened into dark unknowns? We never truly know. At best, we make our judgments based on the legends and tales they leave in their wake. Yet...every now and then, this world bequeaths to us a legend that, if not told in its entirety, would be chalked up to myth and fireside musings.

One such tale begins in a quiet corner of a stormy seaside town known as Port Caradin.

Rain battered at the high windows of the old shop. The ancient glass rattled in its frame as raindrops the size of juniper pellets drummed away their dreary beats. Black haired, bronze skinned and diminutive like the rest of his kind, Thimble stood at the shorter half of the shop's two-height counter grinding away with the mortar and pestle in his hands. He looked up as a loud rattle of rain struck the door, but alas, no one stepped through.

Thimble sighed. The gentle scents from the crumbling ingredients between the stones tugged at his eyelids. *Wait, which one's the mortar again?* He thought to himself. *I think the stone grindy thing is the mortar...but then, that would make the bowl the pestle. That can't be right. The stone looks more like a pestle...gods I'm bored.*

The door flew inward and crashed into the shelves lining the front of the shop before rebounding. Thimble stood frozen for a long moment, if only to ensure his soul hadn't left his body, before looking toward what had caused the racket. A massive figure framed the doorway, rain matted hair plastered to his face, the downpour continuing unabated behind him.

"PENNYWHISTLE!" the man's voice thrummed through the little shop. He stomped his way inside, slamming the door behind himself and wiping away the hair in his eyes.

Thimble's shock quelled a bit as he recognized one of the townsfolk. Egon Vomer was a large man, even for a human. His bulk made the shop seem even smaller than it already was.

"Ah, Mister Vomer," Thimble said as amicably as he could. He set aside his work and ascended the step ladder behind the tall counter until he stood almost eye level with the big man.

"Don't *Mr. Vomer* me you little shite!" Vomer said as he thumped his way to the counter.

Little's a bit on the nose, but I'll let it slide. "Can I help you with something?" Thimble asked.

"What were you *thinking*?" Vomer slammed his giant hands on the countertop. Thimble's mortar and pestle tumbled to the floor from the jolt.

"Come on!" Thimble lost his composure. "I've been mortar or pestling that for two hours!"

"I don't give a thoran's last arse hair! Why did you sell my son a growth potion?"

Thimble watched the undulating veins on the man's forehead as he tried to remember what in the world he was talking about. "Oh, right. Well, it's an *embiggening* potion first of all. And the boy said your crops were coming in a little thin this year. He wanted something that could help."

Vomer rubbed at his temples with a hand. "And you believed him?"

Thimble shrugged. "Why wouldn't I?"

"Thimble," Vomer ran his hand down his face. Much of his ire had turned into quiet exasperation. "Dewin is a sixteen year old boy. What do you *think* he did with it?"

"How am I supposed to know what a teenage human...oh..." realization dawned on Thimble in one horrible wave. "Oh *no.*"

"Yeah, yeah, *yeah,*" Vomer stared daggers through him. "You're coming with me, and you're setting it right."

Thimble shook his head. "What? *Eugh,* I don't want to see that. Wait here," Thimble hopped off the step ladder and hurried into the back room of the shop. He pulled open drawers and cupboards filled with ingredients, reagents, finished bottles of something-or-others until he came across what he was looking for. He snatched the small vial of brown-orange liquid and hurried back into the shop proper.

"Here," Thimble said, climbing the steps once more. "This is a de-scaling salve. He didn't use the whole bottle did he?"

Vomer nodded, eyes closed.

"Oh, brother. Use the whole vial then. Um...*things*...should be back to normal within a minute."

Without another word Vomer snatched the bottle from Thimble's hand and pounded his way out the store.

"That'll be three gold!" Thimble yelled after him. Vomer slammed the door hard enough to rattle the jars and bottles on every wall. "Great."

He climbed down from the tall counter and grabbed a broom for the mess at his feet. "Actually managed to *lose* money today," he muttered to himself, sweeping up the fine grains of wasted ingredients from the stone below. "Some caretaker you are, Thimble."

Thimble's grampa, Sibelius, was the true alchemist in the family. Thimble had decided to watch over his grandfather's shop, and became something of an understudy after the old Gnome fell ill. The arrangement worked for a while though lately, stores had begun to dwindle and customers followed suit. Though Thimble had picked up a handful of things, he wasn't a master of the craft like Sibelius.

"Ah, forget it. I'm done," Thimble stowed the last of the ingredients and equipment back into their respective cupboards and chucked the broom into the back room. Grabbing his hooded cloak, Thimble stepped out into the drenched cobblestone of Port Caradin.

Grampa Sibs' shop sat in a small nook on the eastern side of town. Flanked on either side by a bait and tackle shop and a butcher, Penny's Pots and Pains was easy enough to miss. The usual bustle of the docks just beyond the square was thinned to the occasional dashing silhouette as one person or another braved the downpour for home or elsewhere. Thimble quickly locked up the Penny and hurried his own way home.

Grampa Sibs' house sat south of the Port overlooking the poorer side of town on a quiet out of the way hill, on the edge of a quiet out of the way village. Lights glimmered in the windows of the little abode as Thimble approached, his thoughts already set on a hot meal and hotter bath. He pushed open the old door and closed it quickly behind, sighing in relief in the dim quiet. He stripped out of his waterlogged cloak and hung it beside the crackling hearth.

"Grampa Sibs? I'm home."

A thin voice floated out of one of the two open doors to his left. "Thimble, is that you my boy? I hope you don't mind me staying in bed. My legs don't seem to want to cooperate at the moment."

"No worries, Gramps. Can I get you anything?" Thimble pulled off his boots and set them against the warm bricks of the fireplace.

"Some tea would be grand."

"Tea. I'll join you in that," Thimble made his way to the small kitchen just to the right of the entrance. He pulled an ancient clay pot and two mugs from one of the cupboards. "At least the catcher'll be topped off for a while," he said, filling up the pot from the spigot set into the wall above a rounded stone basin.

"True, true. How was your day anyhow?"

Thimble placed a metal grille over the dark iron oven. He took a pinch of firesand from a small jar beside the stovetop and scattered it under the grille muttering "*Salen*" under his breath. A merry crackling fire sprang forth from

4

where the firesand touched iron. He set the pot down on the grille and set about looking for the tea leaves. "Not terribly exciting," he said. "Until Egon Vomer showed up all blustery and loud."

"Did something happen?"

"I sold his son a vial of embiggening potion a few days ag–"

"You sold embiggening potion to a teenage human *boy*?" Sibelius said.

Thimble scattered finely chopped leaves into the pot with an exasperated sigh. "And apparently *I'm* the only one who didn't know that was a bad idea."

"Bah, it's all right son. These things happen. Did I ever tell you about Jean Bartok?"

Thimble stuck his hand into the narrow cupboard under the basin and felt around for the stickiest jar of the lot. "I don't think so."

"Well that's my bad then. Something similar happened with him when I was about your age. Problem was, I hadn't learned how to make a descaling salve yet."

"Woof," Thimble pulled the jar of honey from the cupboard and set it near the fire to get the contents melting. "That can *not* have ended well."

"I still feel bad about it. Hope he found someone who could help. Although... whenever I need a good laugh, I just remember old Jean hobbling his way out of town." A series of mirthful cackles echoed from Sibelius' room followed by a round of hacking coughs. Thimble grinned and shook his head.

"So what happened?" Sibelius asked as the coughing fit ended. "I imagine Egon wasn't too happy. He didn't threaten you did he?"

"No, just the usual thumping and thundering. You know how tallfolk are."

"What have I told you to do when someone threatens you, Thimble?"

"He didn't threaten me, Grampa," Thimble said, a bit louder than he meant. He stirred the tea with a thin wooden spoon. "And I'm not going to use the shrinking powder–"

"Ah ah! Call it by its name!"

Thimble slumped his shoulders. "I'm not going to use the *Taste of Gnome* just to prove a point. Besides, he wasn't that bad. I gave him the descaler. The boy should be fine soon. Honey?"

"Lots."

Thimble spooned a bit of honey into one cup and too much into the other. As the tea began to simmer, he took the pot off the flames and poured into each cup, mixing the honey into the amber liquid.

"I've been looking over the ledger you left me this morning," Sibelius said, his voice pensive.

Thimble set the two cups aside to cool from boiling and busied himself with washing the old pot. His heart sank a little and a twinge of guilt left a bitter taste on his tongue. "Oh yeah? What does it say?" he asked, knowing the answer.

"It doesn't look good, son. The Pennys' costing more to keep open than it's bringing in. I think it might be time to shutter her for good."

Thimble swirled clean water into the dregs at the bottom of the pot, his attention not quite there. "I'm sorry, Grampa," he said. "If I'd been able to learn a bit more from you, things might be different."

"Sorry?" Sibelius' incredulity brought about another round of coughs. "Don't you dare say sorry! You left your life, your job, *everything* to come look after me. Besides, this work isn't for everyone. If it didn't take, it didn't take. No harm."

"Still." Thimble turned the pot over onto a drying rack beside the basin. "I know how much the store meant to you and Grama Ethel." He scooped both cups and made his way into his grampa's room.

Sibelius sat in his bed with the covers pulled over his feet. Papers with numbers and calculations lay strewn about him, some tangling with the old blue nightgown hanging from his slim frame. A pair of round spectacles sat perched at the end of a spotted nose and slid ever-so-slightly down everytime the old Gnome moved.

Sibelius looked up as Thimble entered and smiled wide. His once impressive mustache drooped at the ends and his wispy white shock of hair bobbed at the motion. "Ah, thank you, son." He took the cup from Thimble into both hands and sipped lightly at the warm liquid. "Ooh, that's nice." He looked at Thimble over his glasses, a hint of sadness touched the understanding reflected in brown irises. "I think Ethel would be proud of what we built. And even she'd admit it was about time. Nothing lasts forever, unfortunately."

Thimble pulled the chair from under the writing desk on the far wall and moved it beside the bed. "We could always ask Dad for some money," he said, sipping his tea.

Sibelius shot him an annoyed look. "I'm not asking my son for a loan, Thimble. It's not gonna matter soon anyhow."

"What do you mean?"

"You *know* what I mean."

He did. The pair sat sipping in silence for a moment.

"How *is* Grumble anyway?" Sibelius said. "Have you heard from him lately?"

Thimble nodded. "Got a letter from him yesterday, actually. Forgot to mention. He's...he sold the house."

Sibelius raised a brow. "Oh? How come?"

Thimble shrugged. "After I left, it was just him and Mum for a long time. They always said how noticeable the quiet was." Thimble looked at his feet, a lump rising in his throat. "Then after Mum passed...it took two years but, I think the silence got a bit too loud for him, you know?"

Sibelius reached over and patted Thimble's knee, a sad smile on his lips. "I know how hard Frida's death was on both of you, son. I can't blame him for his choice."

Thimble cleared his throat, blinking wetness out of his eyes. "What do you think he'll do now?"

"Knowing Grumble?" Sibelius sat back and crossed his arms. "He'll probably go for a long walk. The boy always did love to wander. Surprised me when he chose to settle down all those years ago."

"I remember the stories," Thimble said. "Still, I wish he'd take it easy at his age."

Sibelius snorted. "Bah, what is he just over ninety? Got plenty of good decades in front of him, don't you worry about that. Taught *you* everything you know, didn't he? He'll be fine."

Thimble nodded, a bit of his concern subsiding. The pair sat sipping for a while in comfortable silence. Raindrops pattered away on the wood and stone of the old abode in hypnotic beats.

"You give any more thought to opening up a bureau here? Like your old one?" Sibelius asked.

Thimble sighed. *This again.* "I don't know, Grampa. I don't know if I can go back to that."

Sibelius held up his hands. "Hey, it's your call son. I don't mean to nag. I just think it would be good for you to get back to what you enjoy again. You were a hell of a sleuthhound and, while it's no Veppen, I think you could still make some decent coin here."

Thimble stood and held his hand out to retrieve Sibelius' empty cup. "Finished?"

Sibelius handed it to him with a smile, gentle and understanding. "Thank you, my boy. I feel much better now."

Thimble returned to the kitchen alcove, his mind on his past. And his future. He'd come to Port Caradin to look after Sibelius a little under two years ago. With nothing better to do with his time, his old job far behind him in his home city, he'd picked up what he could of the alchemist trade from his grampa; to help with the store if nothing else. Now, with the store about to go under and his grampa approaching the end, Thimble wondered what would become of him moving forward. *Could* he return to his old job? He shook himself of the thought. No. That part of his life was over.

The sound of breaking glass from Sibelius' room made Thimble whip around. "Grampa?" Thimble hurried into the room, panic and worry rising in equal measure.

Sibelius sat leaned against the foot of his bed, his bedside mirror lay in pieces beside him. His hair was plastered to his head with sweat and his nightgown twisted around his frame.

"Grampa!" Thimble hurdled the glass and crouched beside the old Gnome.

Sibelius' breaths came ragged and pained. "Oh. I thought I'd come out to sit by the fire, but...I don't think this old body agreed, my boy."

"W-what can I do?" Thimble asked, panic beginning to set in. He'd never seen his grampa look so frail.

"I think it's time, son."

"N-no no no that's...m-maybe we can try a health tincture or...or one of the *old* recipes," Thimble's mind raced. Potion after salve after mixture flashed through his mind, anything to prolong Sibelius' life a little longer.

Sibelius placed a hand over his. "It's alright. It was only a matter of time."

Thimble shook his head. "It's too soon," he whimpered. "It's too *soon*."

Thimble stared at the old Gnome. *How is this happening again?* He scolded himself. *Everything you've learned, everything you've done until now, what was the point? To sit by and*

do nothing?

Sibelius sighed. "I see that look." He pushed himself straighter, groaning with the motion, his breath becoming more and more strained. He patted the space beside him. "Come here, son."

Thimble sank onto his bottom beside his grandfather. A hazy numbness had fallen over him. *Not again...not again.*

Sibelius leaned his head back against the bed frame. "I know things have been hard for you, Thimble. And I know this won't make things any easier. But you're so much stronger than you let yourself believe. You went out of your way to help me when you yourself were barely keeping it together and I'm so, *so* grateful."

Helpless. Moisture crept into the corners of Thimble's eyes. "It's just not fair."

Sibelius laughed weakly. "Things rarely are. Do me a favor would you?"

"Of course, anything."

Sibelius lifted a shaky finger and pointed. "There's an envelope in that dresser. Bring it here."

Useless. Thimble obeyed. He pushed aside a stack of old cloaks until his hand brushed against a rough bit of parchment folded neatly in threes. He turned the envelope over in his hands and found his father's name written on the front.

"Send that to him if you could," Sibelius said, his voice now little more than a whisper. "So many things I wish I'd had the time to say." His eyes fluttered closed. "I love you, son." Tears rolled over wrinkled skin as his breathing slowed.

Worthless. Thimble nestled himself beside his grampa, resting the old

Gnome's head on his shoulder, his own breath choked by strangled sobs. He gripped Sibelius' weakening hand in his own; like he had his mother's only a few years before. His mind raced back, forcing image after image of that damned day to the front of his thoughts, the pain and grief of two times wrenching his heart in twain between then and now.

No. He wouldn't let it happen again. Not again. He shot to his feet.

"Thimble...don't..." his grandfather's voice faded in the distance as he tore through the little house. There was a chance. A slim one, a risky one. The only one.

Reckless.

Chapter Two

Undercity Rardell

The taffrail pressed against Thimble's stomach, the old sodden wood helping to push the last of his breakfast into the rapidly lightening sea. The morning fog had yet to burn off and a thick layer of grey clung to the ship. He was grateful for that at least. Somehow, he felt a view of the horizon would make things much worse. He let his arms hang over the edge and hooked his feet to the underside of the flat railing. Maybe if they hit a stiff wave, he would find peace in the watery grave waiting below.

"Ho there! Thimble!" a familiar shout carried over lapping waves. Captain Hawthorne was a rotund brute of a man. A gaudy tricorn with a long parakeet feather sat atop his sun darkened head. His hand length black beard was wired through with bits of white, and it was difficult to tell where the nose hair ended and the curling moustache began. A broad toothy smile poked through the tangled whiskers as he approached. "Sorry 'bout the mornin' swells there, son. The approach into Rardell ain't ever smooth."

"Mmhuh", Thimble replied.

Hawthorne snorted. "I told you to take it easy on those sickness draughts, but..." he trailed off, smug.

"I hope you get scurvy," Thimble managed to get out before another dry heave cut at his words.

The Captain chuckled and leaned against the rail beside him. He straightened the cuffs of his maroon long coat. "Bah, you'll be fine. You survived three weeks. What's 'nother hour? You out of ingredients too?"

"Mm."

"*Tsk*. How it is sometimes. Still, must be bad for you to be riskin' your neck. I know how your kind feels about water."

Thimble hauled himself up to sit despite the protests from his stomach. "We don't *feel* any way about water. It's *deep* water that's the problem. Turns out short arms and legs aren't the best for swimming."

Hawthorne snorted. The pair stood for a long moment watching the deckhands bustle to and fro attending to their duties. "So," the Captain said after a while. "You ever been to Rardell before?"

Thimble shook his head. "I haven't even been on the *continent* before. My family, a lot of families really, left Baesalt a little under a century ago. The rest that didn't make it are still remembered where I'm from."

The Captain nodded. A light flush crept into his cheeks as he stared across the deck into the mist.

Thimble smirked. "Don't start getting all red on me, Captain. You're no more responsible for the Culling than I am. Or...what was it they called it again...ahh, the '*Smallfolk Uprising*'. Ha!"

Hawthorne cleared his throat and gave a gruff nod. "Well, should know a lot of the old feelin's haven' quite faded. Hidden. Masked behind gritted smiles. A lot of the Old Families still think what they did was right."

"I guess I'll have to stay away from the Old Families then."

"And the Anvil."

"Anvil?" Thimble said. "'I think I've heard that before. What is it?"

"Forgemaster's Anvil. Paladin order based outta Atolon. Branch in every major city o' the Reiksal Dominion. Like to think o' themselves as peacekeepers. Imagine the ego. Nothin' good can come from minglin' with that lot, I tell you. Smallfolk or no."

"I see."

"Why're you comin' all the way out here anyway?"

Thimble reached into an inside pocket of his dark green coat and withdrew his Almost Unending Pouch of Things. He rummaged for a moment, his mind on a specific item, and withdrew the short folded letter. He shook out the parchment and began to read aloud.

Dear Mister Pennywhistle,

My name is Ema de Erek Profs, third granddaughter of the late Lady Annabeth de Evoire, an old friend of yours if her stories were anything to believe. I know this is presumptuous of me, but I must request your assistance with a matter. Something strange is happening in our fair city Rardell. Something everyone seems to be paying no mind to. I've tried again and again to bring it to attention, but I have been stalled, rebuffed and rebuked at every turn. The Anvil pretends to take note, then does nothing. My family is terrified of ostracism were they to cause any upset. I have no one else to turn to. Please, Mister Pennywhistle. If there was ever any love between yourself and my beloved grandmother, please help me.

Lady Ema de Erek Profs.

Fourteenth day of Midsun.

Thimble folded and placed the letter back into his Pouch.

The Captain, who had listened intently throughout, eyed him sideways. "*How* old are you?"

"Twenty-four."

"And you...and this girl's grandmother..."

Thimble waved an impatient hand. "No damn it. I found this letter addressed to my grandfather at the post a few days after he...passed. So, I'm going in his place. As a sort of final favor."

Hawthorne let out a quiet whistle. "Guess my advice is in the wind. Still, it sounds like she's from an Old Family. Why reach out to your grandfather?"

Thimble shrugged. "Don't know. Grampa Sibs never really spoke about his time before leaving the Dominion. Part of me coming was hopefully finding out what the hells that man was all about."

Hawthorne was denied another question by the arrival of his first mate. First Mate Delsin wasn't quite as hefty as the Captain, but cut an impressive figure nonetheless. His braided dark hair was tied back with a heavy orange band; each braid set with thick golden rings spread evenly along the length. A long coat of deep blue and orange draped over his shoulders hiding a curved sword on his left hip. Thick corded muscle wound its way down his dark arms and weighty gold and silver bangles decorated his wrists. When he spoke, his accent rolled and pitched like the sea.

"Captain. Harbor's a mile out," he said. "Fog's burning off quick."

Hawthorne nodded. "Bring us in, Delsin."

Delsin grunted in reply and stalked off barking orders. The lounging deckhands hopped to action, climbing sails and tightening ropes with practiced fluidity.

The Captain turned back toward the larboard railing and leaned his elbows against it. "I'm jealous. I remember my first sight o' Rardell. I...well...you'll see."

Thimble spun in his seat until his legs dangled over the open ocean and looked out into the thinning mist. He could just about make out the outline of a massive cliff face stretching out to either side, haloed by the eastward rising sun beyond. As the mist rose, it gave a first glimpse at a wide harbor that stretched for hundreds of yards lined with row upon row of docks of varying size and their resident vessels in port. Workers, passengers and the like milled about their vessels exiting, entering, loading, and unloading. The harbor was set back into the cliff face for a hundred yards at most ending in solid rock. There didn't seem to be buildings or shops or anything of the sort along the entire length of the harbor.

His question was answered as the mist rose further. Vast circular disks of some glimmering metal descended from the mist above carrying loads of people and cargo. Upon each disk stood a figure in robes of deep purple and a matching black brimmed hat with white fabric gliding gently down their necks to the small of their backs. These figures stood ushering people onto and off of the disks before, with simple hand motions, setting the disks to rise into the mist once more.

"Where are they going?" Thimble wondered aloud.

Hawthorne grinned. "Oh, just you wait."

As their ship approached, their path was darkened by the looming colossal cliff above. Thimble looked up as more of the mist washed away and noticed the strangest, blocky looking stalactites he had ever seen. The mist receded showing more and more of these odd formations. Some glittered with a metal-like shine around the borders while some flashed like mirrors in soft light. Thimble's heart skipped a beat as he realized what he was looking at. Buildings. Buildings of stone, glass, metal, thatch and everything in between loomed downward from the cliff base above. Domiciles and towers, shops and inns, streets upon streets of structures of all sizes and shapes stared down at him from above. An impossibility.

The last of the mist burned away revealing cobbled streets as far as the eye could see. There were people, just *walking*. Upside down without a care as if the sea wasn't lapping onto the rocks hundreds of yards above their heads. He saw carriages drawn by horses, wagons pulled by teams of oxen. Children played in the parks and ponds all far, far above his head. He stood there, unaware of how long, mouth agape. *How?* He marveled. *Well magic, obviously, but who? And...how?* The kind of spellcraft that could achieve such an infeasibility wouldn't even lead to a trial in his home country. The caster and his head would be parted soon as the headsman was roused. He snapped out of it as the ship bumped gently into the dock.

The Captain clapped a heavy hand onto his shoulder, a broad grin stretched his features at Thimble's reaction. "Welcome to Undercity Rardell."

Chapter Three

Cold Welcomes

It took Thimble only a few moments to gather his things from below decks. When he emerged, the Captain stood waiting by the lowered gangplank. Thimble extended his hand towards Hawthorne. "Well, Captain. I can't say it was pleasure to be aboard your ship these past few weeks, but I am grateful for the passage. Thank you."

Hawthorne dropped to one knee to reach his hand and clasped it. "Can't blame you, son. I owed your old dad a favor's all. We'll just call it even, eh?"

They shook and broke apart. The Captain rose to his full height and gazed up toward the city. "How're you plannin' on gettin' back home?"

Thimble shrugged and followed his gaze. "Dunno. Don't even know *when*, never mind *how*."

"Mm. Well we come by here every three months or so. If you're ever in town and want a ship back, there's space on board for you. Have to pay next time, o' course."

Thimble smirked and stepped onto the gangplank. "Of course. I appreciate it, Captain. I'll keep it in mind."

"Oh, 'fore I forget. If you're needin' a place to stay, keep an eye out for Gloen's Getaway. Run by an old mate o' mine out in the Merchant Ward. Crotchety old bastard, but he'll look after you. A good place to get away from the eyes. Just tell 'em Hawthorne sent you."

Thimble nodded over his shoulder and raised a hand as he made his way off the ship. "Safe journeys, Captain."

A myriad of expressions greeted him as he stepped onto solid land, open and staring. Some showed surprise or shock. Others confusion or curiosity. Dotted here and there were the ones that truly stood out through narrowed brows. Disgust, contempt, suspicion, revulsion, indifference, and malice warred in more than one set of eyes.

Thimble ignored the heated gazes and wound his way through the milling crowd toward a cluster of people loosely queued in front of one of the circular disks he had seen earlier. The disk itself was made of marble, inlaid with patterns of silver. The silver curled in separate but intertwining whirlpools of odd runes and letters that all met in the middle where a grapefruit sized violet gem sat pulsing a gentle lavender light. Thimble surfed the crowd aboard and found himself standing beside a man in the familiar purple robes.

"No more please!" he called to his partner, a woman dressed in similar robes standing just off the platform. She nodded and stuck out a hand, holding back a surly looking older gentleman who turned an amusing shade of scarlett.

The man in purple braced his feet and swirled his hands in front of him as if gathering dandelion fruits on the breeze. He brought his hands together, opened them and raised his upturned palms toward his chest. With a rumble and jerk, the platform began to move skyward.

The ground-sky hurtled towards them at an alarming speed. The tallest building tops whisked by first, followed by smaller towers, then flagpoles, finally rooftops. A few hundred yards from the ground, Thimble felt the smallest shift. His hair suddenly pitched upwards and a strange sense of relief gripped him as the weight lifted off his body. For a bare instant, he went from bracing against the speeding platform, to a stomach turning realization that he was now falling. His feet left the platform as his heart finally caught onto what was happening. He wanted to shout, but sudden terror squeezed his throat with frigid fingers.

Thimble gaped toward the man in purple as a full panic set in and saw him standing serene as ever, eyes focused, robes billowing from the sudden shift.

He stood still for another terrifying moment, then turned both of his hands over in a swift motion to face the now falling platform. The world turned over in an instant; the platform swung a rapid about-face with its passengers still aboard. Thimble smacked hard onto his bottom as up became the new down. A smattering of derisive chuckles rose from the surrounding crowd who, he noticed, had managed to stay standing through the whole ordeal. A flush creeped up his cheeks. He decided to stay seated in case he embarrassed himself any further.

A handful of seconds later, the platform bumped gently into place in the middle of a bustling street. The purple man pushed himself to the edge of the platform. "Orderly please!" His words came snippy, annoyed. "For all new to Rardell, please visit the intake port over to the right," he gestured toward a stall built into the wall of a much larger building where a pair of older women sat chatting in officious looking green coats. "For all else, feel free to go about your business. Welcome to Rardell."

Thimble picked himself up as the passengers departed and followed a portly gentleman scrabbling toward the stall. Standing there amid the bustle and hum of this hanging city, he felt...odd. Buildings flanked the street on either side. Shops, food stalls, the occasional inn and bar – just like any other city. Then he looked up, into the lapping waves of a sea disappearing into the horizon where sky met it from below.

"Next please! Excuse me, sir? Are you alright?" One of the green-clad women stared at Thimble with a raised eyebrow. He caught himself hunched, his knees bent as if bracing for gravity to come to its senses at any second.

"Oh! Ahem, right," Thimble willed his legs toward the stall, forcing his thoughts away from the "sky". "Ah, hello," he said as he approached.

The woman stood and stooped over the stone countertop to keep him in sight. Sharp yellow eyes, bagged and tired, bore into him, taking in his every detail. "Name?" she said after a moment, picking up a sheaf of parchment and a quill.

"Thimble. Thimble Pennywhistle."

The woman scratched something onto her parchment. "Hmm," she sniffed. "Reason for visit?"

"Visiting, actually. Oh," he stuck his arm into his Pouch and pulled out the letter. "I'm here by invitation to see Miss Ema...erm...I'm not even going to try with that surname."

The woman hesitated for an instant before snatching the letter from his hand. Her eyes flew over the letter and paused for a long moment on the signature at the end. "Jenna," she said to her partner, her eyes trained on Thimble. "Read this."

Thimble's eyes flashed between the pair. Deep unease tickled the back of his neck.

Jenna took the letter and paused in much the same way at the bottom. She gave Thimble a quick eye, then traded a few quiet comments with her partner. Without another word, Jenna's partner stood and swept into the larger building through a rough door in the back of the stall.

Jenna smiled. "If you could kindly wait just a moment please, Ren will be right back."

"Is there a problem?" Thimble asked.

"Not at all, sir. Just confirming something."

He sighed and stepped aside to allow the queue to continue. "*That's* not ominous at all," he muttered to himself. He leaned against the wall and returned to staring at the sea above. "And *that's* going to take some getting used to."

Thimble stood lost in the crashing waves above for almost an hour. The entire time, that odd sense of standing at a precipice, one wrong step from a long fall never dissipated. In his mind's eye, he imagined himself falling into the waves and rocks above again and again. He wondered how long it would take. What the water would feel like on impact.

Thimble tore his eyes from the mesmerizing sight before his mind got carried away. In the hubbub of the busy thoroughfare, the occasional glance and grimace his way didn't go unnoticed. Though, for all the eyes that stared, *and* the ones that didn't, he noticed an odd sluggishness to their gazes. Too slow by half to look away as they noticed him watching, too lagging the drop and rise of heavy lids. And in a sea of multihued complexions, he spied the same sickly pallor on every face that crossed his sight. *Odd.*

"Mister Pennywhistle?" The voice brought him back from his musing.

The speaker was a woman in her younger years with short, chin length black hair and sun darkened skin. She wore an intricate set of silver and white plate armor that gleamed even in the dim light of the undercity. A longsword rested on her left hip and a deep blue cloak drifted from her shoulders. She stood flanked by two similarly armored and cloaked others. A young man likely in his early twenties, and a much older man with a nasty scar that ran from the top of his escaping hairline down one side of his neck. Ren stood to the side of the trio, still holding the letter in her hand.

Thimble straightened from his stiff lean with a groan. "Yes. That's me."

"Follow me," the armored woman turned and stalked off down the street, plucking the letter from Ren's hands as she went. Scar joined her as they disappeared into the crowd.

Tallfolk had a habit of walking off and expecting everyone to keep pace whether or not they were physically able. It was annoying at the best of times. Thimble stood staring into the crowd with his arms raised to his side. "Follow?"

He glanced to his right and noticed the younger man smiling in his direction. "Apologies," he said. His voice rumbled deep and his tongue rolled an odd accent. "Warden Thelia is a bit...on edge as of late. She's not alone, I'm afraid. You may come with me if you like." His short cropped dark hair faded to stubble down the sides and a thick curling moustache made his smile double in size. A round shield sat on his right shoulder in place of a pauldron and a sword clung to his right hip.

"Um. Who in the hells *are* you?" Thimble asked, irritated.

The young man looked taken aback. "Oh! Apologies. My name is Odion Grey. I'm with the Forgemanster's Anvil here in Rardell. As are my departed companions."

"Do I have any kind of choice in this, Odion?"

"Ah, I'm afraid not Mister..."

"Thimble. Just Thimble"

"Thimble. It would be best for you to cooperate for the time being."

Thimble glanced down the bustling streets spider webbing from this point.

He could disappear into the crowd easily enough, though he wondered how long a running Gnome would last here. He eyed the *feet* of steel strapped to Odion's side. *I don't like this.* Thimble shrugged. "Lead the way then."

Chapter Four

The Anvil

Odion fell into step beside him as they started up the street, slowing his pace to match. The path took them through a mercantile quarter of some sort. The salty sting of the sea followed crates upon crates of goods unloaded from ships below and mingled with myriad spices drifting on the breeze. Shops and stalls lined the streets, each overflowing with heaps of goods he'd never laid eyes on. Here a stall carried bright pink and blue fish that changed hues as the keeper turned them this way and that to the scrutiny of his customers. There, a man with a bristling moustache busied himself with a knife, chopping the life out of a strange spiked fruit and mixing the mush with something out of a darkened bottle. Across from him, a couple stood flourishing in radiant fabrics and supple cloth in front of massive bolts of the same material spun taut, their movements labored, their smiles forced.

Thimble found himself staring into a window where a sheaf of velum sat stretched against a board. An inch-wide almost-perfect circle of red on the far right-center caught his eye. An inch more to either side were short lines of spikes from north to south. Small black dots sat marked on the inside of these lines each marked with a word: *Labria* to the west; *Perconos* to the east. To the north of there, little forked stalks peppered the valley between a vast mount and the coast, fading gradually to the east. West of there curved a flowing coastline. Near the midpoint, a simple dot touched the coast with the word *Rardell* scrawled beside it.

"Thimble?" Odion snapped him out of his trance-like poring.

"Hm? Oh...right, sorry."

Odion walked up beside him and peered through the glass at the map. "I take it this is your first time in the Dominion?"

"Yeah, something like that," Thimble said absentmindedly. His gaze had fallen once more on the red spot to the east. The natural cracks and lines in the bleached velum gave an odd effect in the light. The spot appeared to writhe and pulse as if some great mass of worms festered just below the surface. He caught himself rubbing his arms, as if trying to wipe away some unseen oozing filth.

"Draws you in, doesn't it?" Odion asked.

"What is it?"

Odion quirked an eyebrow. "You haven't heard?"

Thimble shook his head.

"Hm. No I guess you wouldn't have. There was a conflict, around three centuries ago. One that everyone saw coming. Nobody calls it a war, because it didn't last long enough." He pointed to the two dots either side of the red spot. "Labria and Perconos. Sister cities, founded around the same time, so the stories say. So, naturally, they hated one another. Tensions brewed until one day the two leading families decided they'd had enough. Each fielded an army led by the eldest son of their family. How long do you think the battle lasted, eh?"

Thimble shrugged. "You said not long, so...few days?"

Odion smirked. "Heh. Try few *minutes*. The stories say the two armies charged with the sons at the head. The moment the two joined swords, a wave of force, so terrifyingly massive emanated from their clash that both armies were obliterated in an instant. Nothing remained of the soldiers or sons. Nothing but a sea of blood: the Blood Well." He gestured to the red spot.

Thimble eyed him for a moment. "Bullshit," he snorted.

Odion chuckled and shrugged. "That's the story anyway." He stepped off back down the path. "Best not keep the others waiting."

Thimble tore his eyes from the Blood Well and followed, casting a quick glance at the shop name in case he needed to return: *Scrolls and Atolls*. He chuckled under his breath at the absurd story as he walked. *Still*, he wondered. *What would be the point of adding something from a myth to a map?*

Odion led them through the merchant's quarter toward the center of the city where shops lessened and homes rose in their place. As the sun "set", Thimble became aware of a dull violet glow emanating from somewhere up ahead.

"What's that light?" he asked Odion.

"That would be the Attrangem. Actually," he checked to his left as they emerged into an empty intersection, "ah there it is. See for yourself."

Thimble gazed down the street toward the city center and his eyes widened. At least a hundred paces across and half as tall, a colossal violet gem sat placed into the ground in the center of the city square. The glow coming off the gem was strong enough to bathe the not-so-close buildings around it in the bright violet pulsing light.

"Wow," Thimble breathed. "Attrangem—wait!" His eyes lit up as name greased the cogs in his head. "Is *that* what keeps the city up?"

Odion nodded, impressed. "Very, very astute. Without it, all this would fall. Or...maybe *it* wouldn't, but *we* would,".

"I think I saw something similar on the platforms that brought us up here," said Thimble, remembering the harrowing trip.

Odion nodded and beckoned for him to follow. "Good eye. Those were made, while this one was found...or so the story goes. The Reader's train to be able to control the effects of the stones; the purple robed people you saw. Ah, here we are."

Thimble was forestalled another question by their arrival. They stood in front of what was ostensibly a cathedral. A small courtyard of grass and stone paths rested inside a broad, spiked iron gate. Men and women in much the same apparel and armor as Odion either gathered around one of the few fountains and benches, or flowed into and out of the tall towered building. The structure extended for a few streets either side and stood a few hundred yards tall at least. Painted windows decorated much of the exterior of the building forming a pleasant colorful contrast with the white-grey stone.

Odion led Thimble through the front doors, where more than a few sets of eyes turned to regard the shorter of the pair. The immediate interior opened into an immense hall with doors and hallways set into every wall and a grand sweeping staircase rising from the left of the hall to the second floor. Another staircase rose from the second floor along the right wall, and another to a fourth floor beyond that. Thimble hurried along behind, trying his best to catch a glimpse of everything. They entered a corridor to the right and swept through a door standing open to the left. Thimble found himself in a spacious chamber that stood mostly empty except for a long table on a raised dais at the far end. Five high-backed chairs sat at the table facing outward, though only the center one was occupied.

A matron with steel-grey hair piled high sat poring over something in front of her from behind a pair of round spectacles. To the right and off the dais, stood Thelia and Scar. Thelia shot a hot glare at Odion who held his hands up in a placating manner.

"Warden Grey, so kind of you to join us," the matron spoke without raising her eyes. Her voice was low and smooth, holding the faintest accent similar to Odion's. "Step forward."

Odion nodded to Thimble and led the way toward the center of the room. "High Inquisitor Rhythe," he gave a short bow. "This is Thimble Pennywhistle," he waved a hand toward Thimble. Thimble dipped an awkward half-nod, half-bow. "Before you begin, High Inquisitor, may I make a request?"

The High Inquisitor laid aside her spectacles and stared down her sharp nose toward the pair. "You may."

"I would ask that we forgo the use of the Circle for today's proceedings."

As Odion spoke, Thimble's eyes alighted on a large circle set into the center of the floor before the dais. Runes carved in gold and amber formed the outer ring and similar carvings in silver and sapphire formed a larger pattern in the center. A sense of unease blossomed in his stomach at the sight.

The High Inquisitor sighed. "You have made your position on the matter clear in the past, Warden. Your request is heard and your objections noted.

We will continue as intended."

A small clatter from behind made Thimble glance over his shoulder. The unease in his stomach deepened as four more armed and armored Wardens slid into the room, flanking the door on either side. *What in the world is going on?*

"High Inquisitor, Thimble is a guest of the city and a newcomer to the continent. It's not the Anvil's way to assume the worst—"

"Warden," the High Inquisitor's voice cut through Odion's words. Her dark eyes shone like thunderclouds. "I am well aware of the Anvil's ways having sat this seat for the past fifty years. Do not presume your new cloak gives you the right to lecture *me* on the bylaws. Your objections are noted. Stand aside."

Odion hesitated for a moment, as if wanting to say more, then stalked off to lean against the leftmost wall.

"Thimble Pennywhistle," the High Inquisitor called. "Step into the circle if you would be so kind."

Thimble edged into the runes and felt a bit foolish as nothing happened.

The High Inquisitor folded her hands in front of her, her expression a stoic mask. The softest touch of dark circles cupped her eyes. "Mister Pennywhistle, my name is Samara Rhythe. I am High Inquisitor of the Forgemaster's Anvil here in Rardell. Frankly, in matters such as these, I would typically be joined by my colleagues the High Warden, The Archbishop, The Keeper of Writ, and the Knight Commander," she motioned to each empty seat in turn, "but they are all away on business which leaves the task to me alone. I hope—"

"Um, sorry, High Inquisitor?" Thimble raised a hand. His interruption earned an almost imperceptible growl from Thelia, but he couldn't wait. "'Matters such as these'? I'm unaware what matters you're speaking of. This all happened a bit quickly and I'm still *very* confused."

Samara raised an eyebrow at the interruption. "There were some questions raised by the letter you gave to the entrance recipient. Questions I would have rather asked in person. I hope you don't mind answering a few."

It wasn't a question. Thimble shrugged and braced himself for whatever was coming.

"Thank you. Could you please tell us what your relationship is to Ema de Erek Profs?"

"Is that how you say that? Yikes. Um, none. That letter was the first I've heard of her."

Samara nodded. She picked up a sheaf of parchment from the table in front of her. Thimble recognized it as Ema's letter. "And the Mister Pennywhistle mentioned in this letter is..."

"My grandfather."

"Ah. I see. What would his relationship be with the de Erek Profs and de Evoire families?"

Thimble shrugged. "I'd say 'you'd have to ask him', but that's quite impossible now."

Samara studied him for a moment. "I see. I am sorry for your loss and any ill feeling my questions may have brought."

Thimble frowned at the stately Inquisitor. Her words sounded...genuine.

"What is your profession, Mister Pennywhistle?"

Thimble was taken aback by the change in tack. "My, um...profession?"

"Yes. What do you do as an occupation?"

"I'm an alchemist," Thimble said. The runes beneath his feet flared for an instant and a gentle, invisible pressure squeezed the sides of his throat before relaxing. Thimble stood wide-eyed, his heart hammering a dancing rhythm.

Samara quirked an eyebrow down at him. The others in the hall tensed the smallest amount. "An alchemist?" she said. "Is that all?"

"Um...yes," was what he meant to say. Before the last word could leave his lips, the runes beneath him flared in golden brilliance and his throat clamped shut as if held in the tightening fist of an ogre. Thimble sputtered and struggled, clawing at the invisible force that held him, before the grip on his throat lessened a few seconds later. As he doubled over, attempting to catch his breath, he understood the purpose of the runed circle.

He straightened after a long moment and found all eyes narrowed in his direction. Except for Odion, who seemed more curious, all held accusations. "Oh dear," Samara said from atop her perch. "Shall we try once more? Mister

Pennywhistle, what is your occupation? And do be aware that half truths don't work here."

Thimble's breathing eased bit by bit. "I'm also...an investigator...of sorts."

Samara frowned. "An investigator? Could you elaborate?"

Thimble shrugged. "It's not really specific. I help people find things."

"Is that all? Things?"

"Sometimes people." He felt around his throat, the sensation of the phantom fingers not quite gone. "But, I don't do that work anymore. Haven't for a couple of years."

Samara clicked her tongue, staring Thimble up and down. "Any particular reason for wanting to hide this information?"

"No," the runes flared once more. "N-no...really!" Thimble tripped over his words in panic. "I just...you've read the letter, right? That letter makes twice that I've been, let's say *given an idea*, about you and your order. I didn't want you to assume, because of my past work and because of what's in the letter, that I was involved in whatever is going on here, because *clearly* something is, and I definitely *am not*."

Samara watched him ramble with impassive eyes. The others relaxed ever so slightly. "I see," Samara said. "We'll make sure of the last soon enough."

Thimble gulped.

"Are either of your professions profitable?"

"I...guess so. My bureau was successful enough. Veppen, where I'm from, is a pretty big city. A lot like here really. Except, you know, the right way up." Samara placed a finger on her lips, but Thimble caught the twitching at the corners of her mouth. Odion smirked at the ground from his corner. "So, there's always something lost and someone needed to find it. The alchemy, not so much."

"Why the change then?" she asked.

Thimble sighed. "Almost two years ago, my grampa got sick. I moved in with him in Port Caradin to take care of him and help at his apothecary. Picked up a few things so I could keep it going when he couldn't."

"Very kind of you," Samara said, her brow furrowed. He could almost see the gears whirring behind her eyes, though he couldn't begin to guess where he stood in her estimations.

Thimble shrugged. "He's family."

"Were you any good? At your old job?"

Thimble lowered his eyes to the floor. "Not enough." He mumbled. The runes blinked briefly under his feet. "Oh, what do you know?" He hissed, annoyed, under his breath. The High Inquisitor watched on, awaiting an answer. "Yeah," he said aloud after a moment. "I was pretty good." The runes remained inert. Thimble refused to be flattered by carved rocks.

Samara leaned back in her throne-like chair. Fingers steepled, she studied Thimble with a penetrating curiosity. Thimble shuffled where he stood, occasionally casting glances toward Warden Thelia and Scar. Thelia's eyes darted between him and the High Inquisitor, her expression becoming more and more unpleasant as the conversation progressed. Scar stood leaning against the wall, staring off into space. He could feel the presence of the guards behind him, but resisted the urge to look.

Samara leaned forward after a moment. "Mister Pennywhistle, I'm going to ask you a question that I strongly suggest you answer truthfully. The *first* time."

Thimble gulped again. The air in the room thickened. Thelia and Scar, once stood in languid poses, appeared ready to spring at a moment's notice. Even Odion had come away from the wall, his hands on his belt, inches from the sword on his waist. Thimble nodded, his mouth dry. He could almost feel the crackling energy of the spell beneath his feet.

"Do you, or anyone you are affiliated with, have anything to do with the murder of the de Erek Profs and de Evoire families?"

Thimble's jaw touched the floor. "*What?*"

"Answer the question please."

"No! Of course not."

"Do you, or anyone you are affiliated with have any involvement in the abduction of Lady Ema de Erek Profs?"

"No!" Thimble's mind reeled. Murder? Abduction? What in the world was even happening?

Samara sat back in her chair, her demeanor mellowed the slightest bit. She raised a hand and gestured to the armored men and women in the back of the room. Each saluted in turn and began filing out.

Warden Thelia stepped forward, her arms out at her sides. "What? That's it?"

Samara rubbed her eyes. "Yes, Warden. Mister Pennywhistle has answered every question within the confines of the Circle. I believe all that has been disclosed."

"The Circle has been fooled before!"

"Once, Warden. Only once. And that was a *very* long time ago." She turned to address Thimble, "You may step out of the circle if you wish, Mister Pennywhistle. I am grateful for your cooperation and I apologize for the inconvenience."

Thimble let out a long-held breath and inched toward the edge of the circle. A slight buzzing in his ears faded as he withdrew. "Oh, well. It's, ha, it's quite alright. It sounds like you've got a lot on your hands."

Samara nodded, deep in thought. "Tell me. What do you plan to do now that visiting the one who invited you seems...unlikely?"

Thimble scratched his chin. He hadn't considered that. "I guess I'll go back home. The ship that brought me here should still be in port, unless they were in a hurry."

Samara tapped the tabletop with a finger. "How would you feel about being under the employ of the Forgemaster's Anvil?"

Thimble blinked. "Uh...I...what?"

"You have *got* to be joking!" Warden Thelia gave Samara an incredulous look.

"Mind your tone, Warden," Samara snapped, eyes narrowed toward the younger woman. "And no. I am not. His skillset could prove usefu-"

Thelia rounded on Thimble, a cold hatred in her eyes. "Lady Ema was taken the week after sending that letter and you expect us to believe you had no involvement whatsoever? I'm not falling for it...I know what your *people* are like."

The heat rose in Thimble's cheeks. "I don't care what you believe, *Warden*. I've answered your questions, your own High Inquisitor seems to believe me, so you can take your 'thinly' veiled nonsense and piss off!"

Thelia's hand flashed toward the sword at her hip. "You filthy *pint!*"

"WARDEN THELIA!" Samara's voice boomed through the hall. The High Inquisitor shot to her feet, her eyes blazing with a cold fury. "Donning the Anvil's cloak means abiding by its tenets, one of which is leaving your prejudices at the door. If that is too *difficult* for you, feel free to leave your cloak on this table and exit these walls for good."

Thelia hadn't taken her eyes off Thimble. He returned her glare unblinking. The slur stung, but he'd heard the like before. Thelia ground her teeth at Samara's words and, with a huff, swept past the group and out the doors. Scar waited long enough to sweep a small bow toward Samara before following. A strained silence lingered at their departure.

Samara rested back into her seat, fingers massaging the space above her eyebrows. "I...apologize for Warden Thelia's behavior. It's...she's...it's a complicated matter."

"Isn't it always?" Thimble said. "Family matter I assume? Someone wronged by one of my kind decades ago?"

Samara quirked her head to a side. "Quite astute, Mister Pennywhistle."

"Well," Thimble shrugged. "Inherited hatred has a different...*look*...to it. You know what I mean? Always a twinkle of uncertainty behind all of the disdain, but the years of reinforcement keep it from blossoming into doubt. Call me Thimble by the way. 'Mister Pennywhistle' makes me feel ancient and is a drowning mouthful besides."

Samara nodded. "Then you may call me Samara," she shook her head at the closed door and leaned forward in her seat, composed once more. "Well, Thimble. The offer stands. If you would be willing, we would like to hire your services in this matter."

Oh right, that. Thimble had forgotten in the excitement. A nagging deep in the pit of his stomach begged him to refuse outright. His curiosity, as ever, forced its way to the front. "Must be in quite the bind to be asking. There's, what, hundreds of you in the city? Why ask for my help?"

Samara sighed. "Truthfully, we're lost. We've scoured the city, questioned everyone the family would have even a passing association with and turned up absolutely nothing. In my opinion, a fresh set of eyes, specifically one that's entirely unfamiliar with the city and our ways might be what we need. And, however distant, you have some sort of connection with the family, perhaps one even you don't realize yet. This is a risk, mind, and a *massive* one at that but," she frowned, a curious expression on her brow, "it feels right."

Thimble tapped at his chin. The nagging in his stomach grew stronger. He was curious, painfully so. But this was beyond out of his depth. "Murder... abduction...that's not really what I usually dealt with. Sure I've located some people who'd gone missing, but more often than not it's a child running from home, or a fed up spouse looking for a new start. Nothing like this."

"We'll pay you five-thousand gold."

The nagging stopped. "Fi-uh...F-five *thousand?*" Thimble glanced from Samara to Odion. The latter stroked at his moustache, hiding a grin under his hand. "Sure. Yeah. I can ask a few questions."

Samara smiled, the expression brightening her lined face a surprising amount. "Excellent."

"Alright, well. What better time to start, eh?" Thimble rubbed his hands together, mulling all he'd heard so far in his mind. "You say you've scoured the city. I'm assuming that's mainly for the killer? What about the girl, Ema? How can you be sure she's still here?"

Samara opened her mouth to answer, thought for a moment, then closed it. She started once more, only to fall silent again. After a few more start-stops, finally she said, "You'll see soon enough."

"Mhm. Not ominous at all. So, where do you think I should start?" Thimble asked.

Odion stepped forward. "I can show him, High Inquisitor."

"Agreed," Samara nodded. "Odion here will take you to the family estate, Thimble, and he will remain with you during your time in our employ as a liaison and as a guide should you require it." Samara chewed on her lip for a moment. "On second thought, why don't you hold off on your decision to join up until *after* you've visited the estate."

"Um. Works for me, I guess," Thimble said. *I'm beginning to think 'ominous' was an understatement.*

"Excellent," Samara nodded pointedly toward the exit. "Keep us updated on what you find, Thimble. Oh and ah, welcome to Rardell."

Chapter Five

A Family United

"Honestly what do you people do with all the space?" Thimble pressed his cheeks between the bars of a thick iron gate standing twelve hims tall. Through the gate, and adjoined brick walls, a stone path led through a massive grassy courtyard to a manor that stood almost identical in size to the Anvil's cathedral. The cathedral that housed *hundreds* of Anvil members at any given time. He watched two of those members emerge from the front doors and start their lengthy walk to allow them entry. Thimble shook his head. "It's actually going to take them *minutes* to get here. From the *front door.*"

Odion stepped up beside him and looked through the bars himself. A not-so-subtle air of distaste crossed his face. "It's not so much a tallfolk thing than it is a money thing...I think."

Thimble studied him for a moment. "Not too fond of the Old Families, eh?"

Odion shook his head. "It's not that. I'm *from* an old family, actually. It's just...this," he waved a hand at the gallantry before them, "it's all a bit much for me, really. Can I ask you something?"

Thimble nodded, watching the approaching Wardens.

"Don't answer if you don't want to, but I was curious. What Thelia called you back there...p– uh well, you know. What does it mean?"

"Pint?" Thimble chuckled. "Well, you know, people like me are called pint-sized. Like pints you get at any pub or bar."

"Oh," Odion appeared almost disappointed. "Is that all? Innocuous for an insult don't you think?"

"Mm. Back during the Culling, or 'Uprising', Dominion soldiers used to tally how many Gnomes they had killed using pints as a way to 'hide' what they were talking about. 'How many pints have you had today, Flannagan?' 'Oh, I'm three pints deep already, Blathering, how about you?' "Six! I'll be in a right state in the morning!" har, har, har." Thimble rolled his eyes. "Nothing quite as hysterical as genocide, eh?"

Odions ears turned scarlett as Thimble spoke and his eyes looked ready to pop out of place. "Gods," he whispered. "I'm sorry, I–I didn't know."

Thimble waved a hand. "Bah, don't worry about it. If you didn't know, you didn't know. Hells, I wish I didn't know." He stepped back as the closest Warden reached the gate and pushed it open.

He greeted Odion with a nod, his perfectly coiffed hazel colored hair bobbing in the breeze. "Odion," he turned his head toward Thimble and raised an eyebrow. Thimble raised his own in response. "Who is this?" the coiffed man asked.

"Garrett," Odion said. "This is Thimble Pennywhistle. The High Inquisitor has offered him a job to help with the...family matter."

"It's about damn time," another voice spoke up from behind Garrett. The second Warden stepped up to the now open gate and removed his helmet. Thimble's jaw hit the stone.

Pointed ears with tufted fur sprang free from the confined helmet, twitching this way and that at the slightest sound. Piercing blue eyes gazed down a pointed snout filled with what Thimble assumed would be razor sharp teeth and fangs. One strong clawed hand gripped the helmet under his arm while the other rested casually beside a massive longsword belted at his waist. Fur covered clawed feet poked out from under plated greaves in place of boots.

Thimble stared openly at the dark furred wolf-person in a mixture of awe and terror. "Holy *Gougen*!"

The wolf-man barked a laugh. "Ha! More right than you realize. I take it you've never seen a Gougen before?"

Thimble shook his head, his heart still trying to escape his chest. "Nope."

"Well," the Gougen crouched to Thimble's eye level, pushing his sword down with a free hand to keep it from scraping the ground. "We're in the same boat then. Thimble was it? A pleasure to meet you Thimble, my name's Kerrak, an Inquisitor of the Anvil."

Thimble forced calm into his voice. "P-pleasure." He tried anyway. Until a few seconds ago, Gougen had only existed in the stories he'd been told by his family. Wild, violent beast-men from wilds beyond the blighted lands far to the east of the Dominion. Now, a Gougen stood before him, polite as all.

Kerrak seemed not to mind his reaction. He straightened from his crouch and gestured to the other Anvilite. "And this mopey lout is Warden Garrett Lyos." Garrett punched Kerrak in the shoulder, but nodded a greeting to Thimble all the same.

"The High Inquisitor, huh?" Kerrak said to Odion. "What made her change her mind on outside help?"

Odion shrugged. "Luck really. Thimble, or his grandfather rather, received a letter from Lady Ema calling him here. Apparently the grandfather had some sort of relationship with Matron Annabelle in the past."

"Really?" Kerrak's ears twitched some more. Thimble glimpsed the flick of a bushy tail waving behind him. "And your grandfather sent you in his place?"

Thimble nodded. "He wasn't in the traveling mood considering he's dead, so I came as a last favor."

"Ah," Kerrak's ears drooped slightly. "I'm sorry to hear that. Well," he turned and beckoned the pair to follow. "I'm glad to have some help at last. I hope you've got something up your sleeve, Thimble, because we're in a bind."

Thimble watched Garrett close and lock the gates behind them as they entered. "I haven't agreed to anything yet, but the High Inquisitor mentioned you were a bit lost."

Kerrak growled under his breath. "Bit lost is putting it lightly. People know about the murders now as well as Lady Ema. It somehow got out that we've been looking for the culprit for almost a month. Thing is, last time the Anvil failed to hunt down a criminal in this long, the city itself was nearly destroyed."

"Point is," Garrett chimed in, catching up to their slowly advancing party. "People are scared, and getting more so every day. They're afraid something like that may be happening again."

"Nearly destroyed?" Thimble asked. "Wild. This someone I should know about?"

"Just an embarrassing memory for the Anvil. Raliak the Shunned," Odion said. "Sorcerer, or more appropriately, necromancer. Was a Baron of some repute in one of the Old Families here in the city. Story goes, he went missing for a few decades, came back madder than mad. Laid waste to almost his whole family, raised them and about a hundred others from the dead and rampaged through the city tearing down all in his path. Some people say he was looking for something, others think his new abilities took a massive toll on his mind, eventually breaking him entirely."

Thimble shuddered at the images that popped unbidden into his mind. Hands clawing their way out of the dirt. Debilitated, decaying faces staring through his soul as skeletal, hungering claws reached for his flesh. "Who stopped him? How?"

Kerrak grinned, pearly white canines stark in the dimming light. "High Inquisitor Rhythe. Her and a handful of her friends. She hadn't joined the Anvil at that time. She and her friends were the adventurous types. Happened to be in the city. The Anvil helped too of course, but it was them that delivered the final blow. Lucky for us they were here."

Garrett sniffed. "I doubt the High Inquisitor would see it that way. She lost almost all of her friends that day. The rest a few days later when their injuries wouldn't heal. People say she survived through sheer rage at seeing her friends fall. Do us a favor and don't ask her about it."

Thimble held up his hands. "No problem." They reached the doorway just as the sun set fully on the horizon above. They stood for a moment in the distant glow of the gemstone at the city center and the lights coming from within the manor itself. In the next moments, globes of light sprang to life leading down the manor walkway to the streets beyond, evenly spaced, casting a gentle golden light down on the city. "Incredible," Thimble breathed, watching the globes alight down the street and out of sight.

Kerrak approached the door and knocked three times with a closed fist. The thumps on the old wood echoed in the silent courtyard. The massive door swung open a few inches and a tangle of brown-red hair stuck itself through the opening. "What were you picnicking out there? Hurry up, I want to go home tonight." The female Warden...or Inquisitor, Thimble couldn't keep track at this point, opened the door wide and disappeared within.

"Thank you, Alera," Kerrak said into the empty doorway. "Don't mind her, she's itching for a bath apparently." He swept into the darkened hallway within. Garrett followed close behind, but Odion stopped Thimble just before he crossed the threshold.

"One second, Thimble," he said.

Thimble stopped and waited. The trepidation in the young Warden's face raised his hackles.

"How...um...how bad...oh, this is harder than I thought it would be," Odion smoothed his moustache and sighed. "What's the worst thing you've ever seen?"

"Excuse me?"

"The worst thing. Worst thing you've ever seen. In a drawing or in person, it doesn't matter."

Thimble gave the Warden a sidelong eye before casting his mind back. "I did see someone cut open a rotting whale once," Thimble's nose scrunched at the memory, "you wouldn't believe the smell. And maggots the size of my hands. Bleh, no. Can't think about it anymore. I'll vomit."

Odion nodded slowly. "Alright, good. Well not *good*...you know what I mean. What you're about to see in there is tenfold worse. So, prepare yourself."

Thimble found himself bent double after emptying his stomach for the second time that day.

"Are you alright?" Odion's voice echoed into the brass vase, ringing Thimble's ears.

"Sure," Thimble said, head almost entirely inside the deep pot. "Just give me a minute." He heard Odion step away and begin talking to the others.

"You really stepped in it this time, idiot," Thimble whispered to himself. He pulled his head out of the pot and walked over to one of the many windows in one of the many sitting rooms of the manor. He pushed open the window as far as he could reach and took a lungful of fresh sea air. "Alright. Just look at it. Turn around and look at it. You've seen it once. It's still the same." He stayed at the window until his stomach settled. With one final breath, he turned and looked.

The room was adorned with lavish furniture made of wood and silk and cotton encrusted with gems of all shapes and sizes, some bigger than his own fist. A heavy rug dressed the middle of the floor woven out of thin strands of gold and silver hair and felt like clouds on the fingertips. The low fireplace at the far end sat unlit and empty. Above the mantle, a tall painting hung from the wall reaching all the way to the ceiling. Though, it was quite difficult to make out what exactly the painting was of, given what was pinned to it.

The head was old. Very old, and decaying, but only just. Bits of dirt still clung to her iron grey hair where it still flowed. Her mouth, slightly ajar. The torso was of a man. Younger, middle years maybe. Muscular, but not overly so. The left arm and leg were female. The arm slender and short, the leg corded with muscle and older, definitely older. The right arm and leg were male. The arm, strong looking, bulging with muscles of labor; the torso's owner. The leg, thin, almost malnourished. The hands. Thimble blinked, his stomach begging him to tear his eyes away. Tears crept into the corners of his eyes. The hands and feet, all different, were from children.

"Gods," Thimble dropped his head into his hands and fell to his bottom on the soft rug. He heard someone drop to the floor to his left, then his right, and finally in front. He glanced up to see Odion and Garrett on either side of him, Kerrak in front. The Gougen's massive frame blocking the ghastly sight from Thimble's view. Thimble nodded, grateful to the Gougen. Kerrak nodded back, watching Thimble closely through his piercing gaze. Alera, the auburn haired Warden who had allowed them into the manor, stood off to the side, staring toward the fireplace.

Thimble regained some of his composure and studied the others. "So. How long has..." he waved a hand in the direction of the fireplace, "...*that* been there?"

"Just under a month," Kerrak answered.

"A month, eh?" Thimble mulled over the details to keep his mind occupied. He forced down an involuntary sour retch. "*Ugh.* Around the same time as the girl disappearing then?"

"We think so," Odion said.

"So, the same culprit?"

Kerrak sighed. "Honestly, for our sake, we hope so. If we're hunting for more than one person...I don't even want to think about it."

"Well, you've asked around. Any known enemies or rivals? Is there anyone who stands to gain from this?"

"None that we can think of," Kerrak said. "They are...*were* a respected family. One of the very few from the Old Families."

"What about the girl?" Thimble asked. "Maybe she fell in with the wrong crowd?"

Odion shook his head. "At thirteen? I doubt it. She was," he furrowed his brow, "a normal young girl as far as I can recall."

Thimble glanced around at all of the pomp. "I'm assuming a place like this usually has servants?"

"Twenty exactly," Kerrak said.

"And they've already been questioned?"

"Weeks ago."

"In the scary strangle-happy Circle?"

"Correct."

Thimble clucked his tongue. Normally, he'd prefer to question anyone potentially involved himself, face to face. More things than not can be gleaned from a simple conversation, be they by words or the occasional slip of the tongue or – his favorite – an involuntary tremor at the exact right moment. "Do you trust this Circle thing?" He asked.

"Completely," Kerrak said without hesitation. The others nodded in agreement.

"No chance of it being tricked?"

"None."

Thimble recalled Warden Thelia's outburst. "That's not what Warden Angry said. She mentioned it's been fooled before."

Garrett cleared his throat. "That's a fair point, but that was a long time ago. When the Circle was composed of a single enchantment."

"And now?"

"Fourteen. Each of a different faith and deity."

Thimble blew out a low whistle. "Quite the upgrade. Still, that's a lot of faith to be putting on a pile of rocks."

Kerrak grinned. "Comes with the territory."

Thimble snorted. "Well. That's that then." He rose to his feet, steeling himself for what came next. He took a slow measured breath, then stepped around Kerrak. *They're not people anymore*, he told himself. *They're long gone. Just observe.* "No enemies," he said aloud, "no obvious connection to unsavory characters. Then why?"

"Why?" Kerrak and the others turned to watch him.

Thimble gestured toward the monstrous display. "Who is this for? Clearly it was meant to be found and seen. But by whom? Is it a threat? A message? A gloat?"

Alera gave a frustrated sigh. "We don't need more questions. Believe me, we've asked it all already and all we get for an answer is another unanswerable question because anyone who could have answered is either up there or missing."

Fair enough. "Nine," Thumble whispered. "What were their names?"

"Um," Odion began tentatively. "Well, there's Lady Annabeth. Lord Marcos, Lady Frilia and their...their children Ira and Lescot. There's also Lord Anton, Lady Anita and their children Damin and Sybil."

Thimble nodded along. *Nine.* He quietly filed away the names as they came. All of his focus strained to remain detached. He squinted at one of the body segments, something having caught his eye. "Hold on," he pointed. "You said you found this almost a month ago. I don't know much about human corpses, but even dead wildlife turns to mush after a week. This looks...ugh...fresh." Thimble pulled a face at the bitterness the word left in his mouth.

"Yes," Garrett spoke for the first time in a while. He walked up beside and slightly ahead of Thimble. "This," he held his hand up, palm forward, but not outstretched, "is a Time Anchor spell."

"T–time Anchor?" Thimble rattled through the possibilities of what that could mean in his mind, each more outlandish than the last.

"Here," Garrett pointed to a spot a few feet above his head.

Thimble stared at the space for a few moments. The sight came to him in ripples. First, an almost imperceptible set of lines seemed to converge at the spot Garrett pointed out. The lines spread from that point to surround the fireplace and much of the wall where the body hung and from each line fell a barely visible curtain of swirling light. It was almost like he could *see* the buzzing of hundreds of tiny, silent bees. Now that he saw the crate shaped space, Thimble wondered how he could have missed it in the first place.

"Wow," Thimble whispered, reaching his hand toward the wall of cascading luminance.

Garrett's hand shot forth faster than he could see and snapped around his wrist. "I wouldn't do that."

"Why?"

Garrett sighed and released Thimble's hand. "Time Anchor is a spell that slows the time in a given space to a crawl. Just a hair above stopping entirely. It's why the pieces haven't decayed as much, or at all."

"Wow," Thimble said again, impressed. "You can do that?"

"We can. But it takes three of us to cast, and another to maintain once it's up. They just have to stay within a certain distance to keep the mental link. It's an exceptional way to keep something like this as untouched and new as possible until everyone who needs to has examined it."

"Amazing," Thimble whispered. "So why can't I touch it?"

Garrett rolled his eyes at his companions. "Say you stick your hand into the space. Now, everything from your wrist down is moving at a much slower flow of time than everything else. That includes your blood. Your blood inside the space is now moving much slower while your blood outside the space..."

"Is moving as fast as ever," Thimble finished for him. He slowly withdrew his hand and took a step back. "Don't touch the Time Anchor. Got it."

"Well, Thimble," Odion said. "The High Inquisitor requested your answer

42

on joining us once you had seen the extent of what we're dealing with. What is your decision?"

Thimble puffed out a long breath and ran a hand through his unkempt hair. Murder. Kidnapping. A great big corpse *made of corpses*. And a villain who'd eluded the peacekeepers of the realm for almost a month. He was sure he wouldn't find a bigger pile of shit to wade into if he tried for the rest of his lengthy life. Still, there was a part of him that burned with intense curiosity. Also, five-thousand gold was five-thousand gold. Maybe he could revive Penny's when he returned home. Or restart his bureau.

Except...that's not why you're doing this, is it? He brushed aside the intrusive thought. "Alright, I'm in."

Odion let out a sigh of relief, much to Thimble's surprise. "I'm glad to hear you say that. I had orders to detain you within Anvil headquarters until the end of the investigation if you refused. I'm glad I don't have to do so."

Thimble's eyes darted amongst the armored group. "You're joking right?"

"Afraid not," Garrett said. "We wouldn't allow an outsider to see something like this and hear what you've heard then fade into the wind. It would be... irresponsible."

"Ah, well," Thimble shuffled from foot to foot. "That's good to know."

Kerrak bared his fangs in a wide grin. "Takes a steely spine to step up after seeing all this. Respect, Thimble Pennywhistle. Welcome aboard."

"Hear hear," Odion said with a smile. "What do you plan to do next?"

Thimble shrugged. "First, I'm going to find something to settle my stomach. Then, I need to find a place to stay. Gloen's Getaway, I think the Captain said. In the morning, I think I'd like to speak with the other Old Families. See for myself what they have to say. I assume they refused the Circle?"

The gathered Anvilites nodded, a bit guiltily.

"Figures," Thimble said. "The wealthy ones never make it easy for you."

Kerrak snorted. "Good luck getting that lot to give you anything. But, it sounds like a plan. Let us know if you find anything useful."

Odion gestured toward the front door. "I know where Gloen's Getaway is. I'll show you. Apothecary nearby as well. Oh, here," he rummaged through a small satchel at his side and withdrew a heavy looking leather pouch. He dropped it into Thimble's hands with a weighty *thud* and merry clinking.

"What's this?" he asked.

"Half your payment. The other half to be given at the end."

Thimble let out a low whistle and shoved the sack of coins into his own Pouch as he followed Odion out of the manor. The last thing he heard before the door snapped shut behind him was Warden Alera's voice touched with a smirk.

"Sweet dreams."

Chapter Six

Gloen's Getaway

Odion led Thimble out of the Noble Quarter and back into the Merchants'. The dimly lit streets stood mostly abandoned, aside from the occasional wanderer. Thimble walked in silence, mulling over everything he had heard and seen so far. From the sound of things, the Anvil was nowhere near finding the murderer or even a clue as to whom it may be. He doubted he would come up with much else without any sort of lead. No, he would stick to what he knew best. If he found the girl, he would likely turn up anyone who was involved in her abduction. Then the Anvil would have at least two more people to question and he could walk away having done his part. He puffed out a long sigh. He'd been in the city for a handful of hours and he already wanted to go home. Except...he wasn't sure where to call home anymore.

Odion glanced over at the sigh. "You're taking all this a lot better than I imagined."

Thimble snorted. "You'd think so, eh? Except there's this whole other part of me I've decided to bury deep down that's screaming about being the farthest from home I've ever been surrounded by strangers with swords and hammers and all manner of pointy stabby crushy things and, oh right, an insane murdering kidnapper on the loose. Sorry, *hopefully only ONE* insane murdering kidnapper on the loose." He cleared his throat. "Ahem. I guess it's not as buried as I thought."

Odion smirked. "Well, I hope I can help make things a bit easier while you're here. I think I can get you a meeting with at least one person from each Old Family tomorrow. We'll have to go to them, mind, but it's a fair excuse to see the city, get a bit more familiar with your surroundings. Here we are." He stopped in front of an out-of-place building.

The structure was made out of a dark, wet looking wood. Moss grew from between the planks and oozed to the ground in clumps. Small steps led to a home-like porch where numerous plants of different shapes, sizes and colors grew in pots and jars of clay and mud. A small wooden sign hung over the door depicting the faded image of a green phial. A rocking chair sat in a corner of the porch, its occupant curled up in a furry ball for the night.

Thimble raised a questioning brow toward Odion.

"Apothecary," he said. "For your stomach."

"Ah. Right. Thank you," Thimble pulled open the door with some haste and led the way inside.

The interior of the shop smelled distinctly of fertilizer, but not in an unpleasant way. The dank room was divided into two halves by a high counter. Little vials of solvents, flasks of potions, and bowls of ingredients and spices sat on shelves that lined the walls. The faintest scent of perfumes and incense touched the air. For a brief instant, Thimble felt as if he was standing back in his grampa's old shop.

A man in his middle years wearing an apron with little hammers tucked through the loops in his belt stood speaking to a graying old matron behind the counter. The two seemed to be in the middle of an argument.

"Mistress Nira," the man pleaded, sweat beading his thinning hairline. "Please, you have to understand."

Nira threw up bangled hands, exasperated. "I've told you already, young man, I don't have any more. You could try asking across town at Lambert's."

"I've already been there. They're out too," the man said, looking defeated.

Nira placed a gentle hand on the man's shoulder. "I know it's hard," she said. "As soon as I have more ingredients, I'll whip up a fresh batch and hold at least one aside for you, alright?" The man nodded. "Oh, and here," Nira reached below the counter and pulled out a small bottle of dark amber liquid. She pressed the bottle into the man's hands.

The man peered at the bottle and back at Nira. "What kind of tonic is this?"

"It's whiskey, dear. Of my own making. Might not be what you're looking for, but one swig and I doubt you'll remember much the next day. Take it. No cost."

Tears swimming in his weary eyes, the man bobbed a silent bow toward the old woman and trundled out of the shop.

Nira watched the man leave sadly. "Poor thing," she whispered. A moment later, she turned her attention to Odion, as if noticing him for the first time. "Ah! One of the Anvil's finest. What can Old Nira do for you today, Warden Grey?" She held up her hand. "Wait. Before you say anything, I will tell you what I told young Bertrand there," she nodded toward the door. "I do not have any more Draughts of Quiet Slumber nor will I have any for a while."

"Oh," Odion shook his head, taken aback. "No. No, I'm fine, thank you Mistress Nira," he pointed down toward Thimble. "It's actually my friend here who's in need of your services."

Nira leaned over her counter until her eyes found Thimble. Her already bug-like eyes expanded by over-large spectacles. "By Weaver's Loom a *Gnome*! Ha!" Thimble stood shocked at the woman's elated outburst. "Oh, I haven't seen one of your kind in ages!"

Thimble glanced over at Odion who seemed just as shocked. "Aha," he said, cautiously. "Ages? You don't look a century old."

Nira blinked. "What? Oh, no you silly boy," she wagged a finger playfully down at him. "Not *here*. I traveled quite a bit in my younger days, I'll have you know. In fact," she darted off into a side room and hurried back clutching a vial of bluish liquid. "It was one of your people who taught me how to make this!" She uncorked the vial with no small amount of enthusiasm. A soft blue-grey mist billowed forth from the vial, filling the room within seconds. Thimble stood blinded by the mist for a moment, an odd familiar feeling running through his mind. Within moments, the mist began to dissipate until the air lay still and clear once more.

"Now," Nira placed the corked vial under her counter. She turned excitedly from Thimble to Odion. "What do you smell?"

Thimble sniffed at the air and was surprised to find a distinct lack of any scent.

"Um," said Odion. "I don't smell anything."

"Ah," Thimble caught on a moment later. "*Aminaea.*"

"Ho-oh! Got it in one!" cheered Nira. "Aminaea. A solution that removes all smell from the surroundings. Wonderful little thing for when things get a bit too fragrant." She clapped her hands together once more. "Anyway! Got a bit carried away there. What can old Nira do for you?"

"Well," Thimble said. "My stomach doesn't seem to be agreeing with my...experiences of late. Do you have anything to soothe nausea?"

"Oh, you poor thing. Of course, of course," Nira shuffled her way to the back of the shop and began fumbling with the vials and little pots set along the back wall. She returned a moment later holding another small vial, this one with a seafoam green liquid in it. She corked and held it out to Thimble. "Here you are, dear. That is a concoction made of enlovan tears and sipera venom. One drop a day should keep that stomach of yours quiet enough. Should be enough in there to last a month."

Thimble accepted the vial gratefully. "Thank you."

"Of course, dear. Anything else?"

"Yes actually," Thimble dropped the vial into his Pouch. "There's a few things, if you don't mind," he ticked off each one on a finger as he spoke, "three ounces of crushed duran root, two ounces of flint shavings, any small amount of composted earth, two leaves from a thistle mouse, five ounces of kelafi spice, and bark clipped from a sleeping treant, any amount really."

Nira bustled about as Thimble spoke and returned carrying a number of vials and little pouches in her arms. "Oh my," she said, breathless. "Sounds like someone's got a little alchemist in him, hm?"

"Just a bit," Thimble said, taking each little package and dropping them one by one in his Pouch. "How much do I owe you?"

Nira bobbed her head from side to side. "Oh, let's say...ten gold total."

"That's it?" Thimble said, surprised. "That much treant bark should be twenty on its own."

"You brightened my day with your presence, young man," Nira beamed. "Call it a new friend's discount. Promise to come by for some tea some time, I'd love to hear more about where you're from."

"Uh, sure," Thimble handed over the gold from his now considerable sum. "I'm Thimble, by the way. Thimble Pennywhistle."

Nira dipped a small curtsy. "Nira O'Callan. Pleasure to meet you Thimble. Oh, and this one's for you Odion, dear." She handed Odion a small brown parcel. "Could you make sure that reaches young Alera, please? Be careful with it, dracolisk skin can be quite brittle when dry."

Odion took the small package, curiosity on his brow. "Dracolisk skin? What could she possibly need this for? And how did you even get it?"

Nira tapped the end of her nose. "A good shopkeep never reveals her secrets," she giggled at their expressions. "As for Alera," she shrugged, "you'd have to ask her."

Odion nodded and carefully pocketed the parcel. "You have everything you need?" he said to Thimble.

"I'm all set," Thimble said. He hesitated for a moment. "Actually, could I ask you something, Nira?"

"Of course, dear, anything at all."

"Have you," he hesitated once more. *What's the point? Why do I bother?* "Have you ever heard of a sickness that takes away a person's mobility bit by bit? Until...until they're gone?"

Nira's eyes softened. "Oh dear. I haven't seen the like in a very long time, thank the Weaver. But I believe you're talking about Crockle's Wasting Disease. Starts in the hands and legs and moves inwards towards the heart. Terrible. Just terrible."

"Is...is there a cure?" He held his breath and his hopes in a vice. *You know the answer.*

Nira shook her head. "I'm afraid not, dear. None that I know of. Not even magic helps. Does someone you know suffer from this?"

Thimble shook his head. "Not anymore. I figured that'd be your answer, but I thought – new world, new minds, might as well ask."

Nira smiled sadly and nodded. "I understand. I'm sorry."

49

"Not at all. Thank you for everything."

"Of course, dear," Nira waved as they turned to leave. "Come again soon!"

"I think I can genuinely say, this has been the strangest day of my life," Thimble said. He glanced back at the old apothecary fading into the distance.

Odion chuckled. "Old Nira's always been a bit odd. Still, you can rest easy considering it's not likely to get much stranger."

Thimble winced. "Odion my new friend, if you're going to be hanging around me for any amount of time there's one rule we have to follow," he put a finger up, "never tempt the cosmos with words like that."

Odion chuckled some more and held his hands up. The street opened into a broad square. A grand recessed pool dominated much of the center. "Gloen's is right across the way. Quite the assortment you bought back there. Have something special in mind?"

Thimble nodded. "I imagine you all have tried everything in your magical repertoire to find the girl, but I might as well start from scratch anyway. Little ritual of my own." He uncorked the small vial of medicine he had purchased and dripped the smallest drop onto his tongue. A blossoming warmth flowed into his stomach, leaving a soothing stillness in its wake. "That's better. Speaking of which, I'm going to need something from the girl."

"Something?" Odion asked. "Like what? Clothes?"

"That could work. The more sentimental value the better. A gift, a favorite book, you know. Things like that."

"Alright. I'll have something by the morning." Odion came to a dead stop as the door to Gloen's Getaway burst open in front of them. Three young men with terror in their eyes came tumbling through. The group picked themselves up and darted into the distance without a second look. Thimble and Odion exchanged wary looks before pushing into the building.

The main floor of the inn was mostly empty. A bar jutted out from the left side of the room with a swinging door to admit workers. Heavy round tables sat scattered around the room with odd numbered chairs to each. A staircase to the right led off to the second floor where Thimble assumed the rooms were. A hearth crackled against the back wall, and an ornate painting of a red-bearded dwarf with a massive brown hound hung above. The scene would be peaceful, if not merry, on any other day.

In the center of the space, a man in black coveralls lay writhing on one of the tables while another man, white haired with sharp eyebrows, and a brown bearded dwarf pinned him to the surface.

"You two!" the dwarf turned toward the door where the pair stood wide-eyed. "Give us a hand would you?"

Thimble looked around in vain hope he was talking to *anyone* else. "Oh... um..."

"Come on then lads! Don't have a lot of time."

Odion moved toward the struggling duo without hesitation. Thimble forced his legs forward. Sweat plastered snowy hair to the face of the man across from the dwarf. His arms bulged with the effort of restraining the writhing man on the table.

"Here, here," the dwarf gestured for Odion to join him. "Grab his arm just here, below my hand." Odion did so. "Tightly!" the dwarf moved his own hand. The writhing man had a towelette draped over his forearm, covering much between the wrist and elbow. "And the other arm here, just above mine. Hold tight. I mean it!" As soon as the dwarf released the man he twisted, letting loose a wail of agony.

"Hold him still!" the dwarf barked. "You," he pointed at Thimble, "Fireplace. Grab the tongs, bring 'em here. Quickly!"

Thimble bolted toward the blazing hearth, panic quickening his light steps through the forest of chairs. A set of long iron handles wrapped in a thick leather stuck out from the glowing embers. He hauled the weighty tongs from the fireplace and hefted them toward the table.

Odion jumped and clamped his grip down harder. "Uh," he said, his voice shaky and nervous. "I felt something move...".

The dwarf snatched the tongs, its ends glowed bright orange toward a pointed grasping end. "Get up here," he shot at Thimble, kicking out a chair. Thimble clambered up the chair and onto the table. The dwarf pointed at the man's chest. "Sit. Keep him still!"

Thimble traded an incredulous look with Odion who shrugged. He sat on the writhing man's chest and stared at the arm Odion had pinned.

The dwarf whipped off the towelette. Thimble barely contained a scream. Rows of fat, throbbing rings stood out stark on the man's arm, just below the skin. One end tapered to a smooth end and the other, close to the elbow, squirmed to and fro, as if searching. "What in Forgemaster's name is it?" Odion gasped.

"Bile slug," the dwarf replied, his mouth twisted in disgust. "Gotta be quick, now." He pushed the glowing tongs into the man's arm, along the center of the creature. The man jerked and screamed through the gag. It was all Thimble could do to keep from being chucked off. The mass writhed and thrashed sickeningly under the man's skin. Small pinpricks of blood mixed with a foul smelling liquid sprouted from the arm as it moved. "Come on damn you!" the dwarf pushed the tongs in deeper.

With a spout of blood and bile the slug burst from the arm, its three jaws snapping wildly in the air. Thimble yelped and toppled back off the man's chest.

"Here!" with a deft motion the dwarf clamped the tongs around the thing's head and squeezed. It flailed wildly one last time before falling limp. Its head and body slowly blackening with the heat. The dwarf pulled the rest of the slug out of the man's arm while White Hair pulled out a roll of heavy bandages. Thimble backed away, his hands and knees trembling with equal vigor. He watched the dwarf walk to the hearth and thrust both the tongs and the slug into its hottest depths.

White Hair straightened after layering thick bandages onto his now unconscious friend's arm. "Thank you, Gloen. Joran'd be dead without you."

The dwarf, Gloen, turned from the hearth, his face a thundercloud. "Get out."

"Wha-"

"OUT!" a stein came whipping through the air, barely missing both Thimble and Odion. White Hair hauled Joran over his shoulder and hobbled out chased by a string of curses and cutlery. Gloen slammed the door after the departing duo, breathing hard.

He took a moment to gather himself, then turned to the pair as he made his way behind the bar. "Pull up a chair."

Thimble and Odion slid onto curved wooden stools. Gloen pulled out a crystal bottle with dark maroon liquid and a pair of matching glasses. He half filled one glass, quarter filled the other and slid each to Odion and Thimble before taking a swig from the bottle himself.

Thimble shook his head and lifted the heavy glass two-handed toward Odion. "To not tempting the cosmos, eh?"

Odion, puffed out a breath nodding in acquiescence, clinked glasses and the pair downed their drinks.

"Ohh...that's...not alcohol," Thimble said through a choked breath. The liquid, thicker than expected, left an icy trail down his throat. A light taste of metal lingered on his tongue.

"Heh," the dwarf chuckled. "Shade Creeper blood. Good for the nerves. Appreciate the help, gents," he took in each of their appearances, lingering for a moment on Odion. "even from a Blue Cloak. Name's Gloen."

"Odion."

"Thimble." Thimble glanced over his shoulder toward the hearth. "What *was* that?"

Gloen took another swig. "Told you, Bile slug. Been burrowed in that idiot for a couple days apparently. Lucky for him, it woke up here. Alone at home? He would've been dead in minutes." Gloen shuddered. "Nasty things, bile slugs. Eat you from the inside. Start with the fat, then the meat once they're big enough. Nasty. Anyway, what can I do for you?"

Thimble stared at the old dwarf, horrified. "Um... Captain Hawthorne said you'd be the one to talk to about a place to stay."

Gloen's eyebrows climbed and a grin broke across his face. "No shit? Old Hawthorne's still kicking, huh? Haven't seen the dog in almost ten years now." He hopped onto his own stool behind the bar. "So you're from the north, eh? Whereabouts? Mawali? Juddarn?"

"Veppen, actually. And Port Caradin for a few years."

"Oh, so *real* north. Damn. I haven't been to Dunalis in thirty, maybe forty years. Still up their asses about magecraft? I still remember those suppression units back in the day. Rough times."

"No. Not as bad. But still not *good*."

Gloen waved a hand and took another swig. "Ah, who needs 'em. What're you doing down here anyway? Long way from home."

"Ah," Thimble felt Odion's eyes on him. "Visiting."

Gloen combed his fingers through the thick tangles in his beard. "Visiting, eh?" his eyes flashed towards Odion and back. "Well," he finished the last of his bottle and stowed it below the counter. He rummaged for a moment and produced a single iron key. "We've got a room available, but it'll be normal sized. We've got one smaller one, but we can't get the cat out of it. Two gold per day. Or ten for the week."

"No problem," Thimble reached into his pouch and counted out twenty gold. He smirked at himself. How easy it was to part with the coin now that he had an ample amount. "I'll be here a bit longer than I expected, I think," he said, sliding the coins across to Gloen.

Gloen nodded appreciatively, scooping up the gold. "Works for me. You hungry?"

Thimble started to refuse, but his stomach gave a protesting rumble. No longer plagued with nausea, he realized his stomach had been empty for a while. "Starving."

"Oi! Glena!" he turned and called toward the door behind the counter.

The door creaked open and a young dwarven girl stuck her head through, her bright blonde hair tied in a neat bun. "Yes, Da?"

"Heat up the last of that stew and bring it up to the end room, would you dear?"

"Will do, Da," she paused long enough to cast her eyes over Thimble and Odion before ducking back behind the door.

Gloen snatched up the key. "Let me show you to your room."

Odion stood, clearing his throat. "I'll see what I can do about your request, Thimble. I'll meet you here in the morning." He turned to Gloen. "Thank you for the drink, Gloen."

"Yeah, sure," Gloen said, walking around the counter to stand beside Thimble. Thimble only came up to the stout dwarf's middle arm at his tallest.

Odion bobbed one last nod and swept out of the door.

54

Gloen blew out a whistle as the door thudded shut. "Mixed in with the Blue Cloaks, hm? Bold." He waved for Thimble to follow and headed for the stairs.

Thimble hurried to keep up. "Wasn't really a choice. Why? Don't trust them?"

"Nah, not that," Gloen thumped up the stairs, a slight limp on his right leg. "Anvil's got decent people, got bad people too. That boy might be one of 'em. Can't really say which way." The landing divided into two perpendicular paths, each leading to a row of doors. Gloen moved straight ahead from the stairs to the last door on the landing. "Here you are," he swung the door in and stepped aside.

The interior of the room was sparse, yet comfortable looking enough. A large bed sat against the wall beneath a shuttered window dominating much of the room. A tall dresser sat opposite to the bed and a small nightstand beside it. Some sort of animal skin rug covered much of the open floor between the bed and the wall.

"It's not much, but still a place to lay your head when you need it," Gloen said from behind as Thimble took in the room.

"Good enough for me," Thimble said.

"Oh here," Gloen disappeared out the door. Thimble heard him open another door on the landing and the sound of things being tossed around. Gloen returned a minute later carrying a short step ladder. "For the bed," he said, propping it near the foot.

"Much appreciated," Thimble hopped up the steps and sank into the soft bedding. *At least there was no chance at rolling off*, he thought to himself, taking in the too-big surface.

"Here," Gloen tossed him the key.

Thimble caught it with both hands. The iron was heavier than he expected. He examined the grooved surface. The head, about the size of his palm, was carved with intricate patterns. "I've met a few of the Anvil's people now," he said, eyes still on the key. "They seem decent enough, but...something doesn't feel right." He wondered why he'd decided to open up to this dwarf, but there was something...reassuring about him.

Gloen leaned against the door jamb and crossed his arms. "Did you know they're all paladins? The lot of 'em?"

Thimble nodded, remembering Hawthorne's words.

"Things get weird when faith's involved, lad. You'll just have to decide which ones you can trust and hope you're right."

"Which ones do *you* trust?"

Gloen blew out a long breath. "Haven't dealt with many. That boy you came in with is new, I think. Hamann is an honest man, getting up in years. Celia's a kind young woman, helped my Glena out of a bind once. Samara of course."

"You know the High Inquisitor?" Thimble asked.

"Ha!" Gloen barked. "High Inquisitor. I always get a kick outta that. Samara's an old friend of mine."

"Good to know," Thimble felt some small sense of relief at that.

"Well I won't keep you," Gloen said, turning to leave. "I'll have your dinner sent up. We'll leave it by the door if you're out cold by then. Come find me in the morning if you need something."

"Oh!" Thimble said, suddenly remembering. "Could you have a full bottle of brandy sent up too? I'll pay, of course."

Gloen grinned at him over his shoulder. "Heh," he chuckled. "I've had those days. No problem." The door closed behind him.

Thimble ate a heavy stew filled with thick vegetables and meaty fish. It tasted more salty than anything, but it was hot at least. After he finished, he left the bowl and spoon out on the landing and locked his door. Every part of him wanted to sink into the bed and stay there for the foreseeable future, but he needed help. He cleared a space near the foot of the bed under a cracked window. One by one, he removed the components he'd bought earlier from his Pouch. The root, the earth, the leaves, the bark. Next came little clay bowls into which he tipped a bit of each component. He arranged the bowls in a small circle around himself. He pulled a set of short candles from the pouch next. Each candle went into the center of each bowl. With a wave and a snap of his fingers, Thimble lit the candles. Last, he grabbed the hefty bottle of brandy and settled into the center of his little circle.

He placed the bottle in his lap and closed his eyes. As the candles burned, smells from each component rose and mingled in the air, tickling his nose with their earthy scents. He breathed deeply, recalling the words of the incantation his grampa had helped him form. A small knot of doubt formed in his stomach which he crushed immediately. *Just breathe,* he thought to himself.

Breathe in.

"My body, my temple, my shadow, my marrow."

Breathe in.

"My mind, my palace, my bow, my arrow."

Breathe in.

"My time, in time, unwinds, unravels."

Breathe in.

"My place, our place, safe place, I travel."

The shift was subtle. As the last word left his lips, the slightest breeze began to play across Thimble's face. The smell of earth grew stronger and a heavy moisture hung in the air, as if from a recent rainfall. As he opened his eyes, he found himself seated in damp earth surrounded by trees. The tall redwoods soared into the sky out of sight where little holes in the canopy revealed a rainy sky. He hefted himself to his feet, dragging along the brandy bottle that had Traveled with him. The chittering of forest creatures met his ears as he began to move. *Ahead. Always ahead.*

Chapter Seven

Our Place

He walked for what felt like an hour. Maybe two. The forest remained unchanged, everlasting as the trees that inhabited it. A gentle mist lingered just above his head, stretching as far as the eye could see in every direction. He wondered whether he'd done the ritual wrong. Had he used the wrong words? But, he was sure he remembered them correctly. He'd chosen them himself. His rambling thoughts came to a close as the forest finally opened before him into a small clearing. Low, soft, dew-dropped grass ringed the clearing and flowed in the breeze. A narrow cobblestone path rose from the ground before him and followed a slight rise in the clearing toward the center where a small house made of damp stone and straw sat puffing away from its squat chimney. A familiar sight. A comforting sight.

"Finally," Thimble muttered under his breath. Adjusting his grip on the bottle, he started up the slope toward the house. Nearing the midpoint of the path, he glanced around at a new addition to this familiar space. Lining the walkway and spreading for at least fifty yards on either side, flowerbeds rose in double hued unity. Row upon row of violet irises and pink orchids graced his ascent up the path, their gentle scents mingling in the cool air, sending his mind back to a different time. A time he'd rather not remember. A faint light danced above the mossy windowsills and the door stood a crack ajar.

Thimble pushed open the door and peered in. The inside was the small, cozy little home he remembered. A fire burned merrily in the hearth against one wall, a squashy red armchair angled lazily alongside it. A small tea kettle hung over the flame, a gentle steam rising from its curving nose. Flowered curtains hung from the windows, drawn taught to the sides and an oval rug of black and brownish-red fur embraced much of the floor.

"Um," said Thimble, stepping into the little home. "Grampa Sibs?" No response came. He checked both rooms to the left of the entryway and found them empty. Thimble cleared his throat and called louder, "Hello? Grampa Sibs!"

"OH! Is that you, Thimble? I'm out back, son. Come on out!" the reedy voice floated in from the open back door.

Thimble crossed though the house and out the back door. The backyard was little more than all the other sides, except for a decent sized patch of flat earth, fenced by a hoppable wooden barricade. Well, it had been just flat earth the last time Thimble laid eyes on it. The ground had blossomed with plant life of all kinds since then. Rows of vegetables, some he recognized, others he couldn't begin to guess sprouted from the damp soil. Just beside, a small cluster of stunted trees drooped, weighed down by the massive fruits growing on their little branches. A little rustle approached from behind rows of sugarcane and corn alternating in their placement and out spilled Sibelius Pennywhistle.

Grampa Sibs was old for a Gnome, but he no longer looked his age. In fact, he looked almost thirty years younger than he should have. His shock of white hair stuck up much like Thimble's and his moustache was something Odion could only dream of. He wore an old dressing robe of red velvet and slippers of a feathery purple, now stained with moist brown soil. In his arms, he carried a bunch of the biggest carrots Thimble had ever seen.

"Thimble, my boy!" Sibs dropped the carrots and pulled Thimble into a tight hug, made awkward and uncomfortable by the brandy bottle Thimble still carried. "Ow, what is – oh!" Sibs noticed the bottle. "Ahh, you always brought the best gifts, eh? Let me take that off your hands," Sibs grabbed the bottle and started hurrying his way inside. "Come on! I'll make you some tea.

It's been months since I've seen you, son, something interesting *must* have happened by now."

A bit stunned by Sibs' manner, Thimble scooped the forgotten carrots and followed back into the house. Sibs had busied himself by the fire accompanied by the gentle clatter of tea cups.

"Sit down, sit down," he nodded to a second chair, identical to the first that had appeared across from it. Thimble dumped the carrots into an empty basket by the door and sat, savoring in its perfect plush comfort. Sibs pushed a cup and saucer into his hands. "There you are. Tea with honey and ginger. Just how you like it." He sat in the chair opposite with his own cup and sipped. "Oh, that's the good stuff."

Thimble snorted, sipping his own warming cup. He gave Sibelius a sheepish look. "Um. It's good to see you. How've you been?"

"Grand," he said. "This place is actually quite nice. The weather's almost always perfect, all of my plants actually *grow* for a change, and my back doesn't hurt anymore. In fact," he shimmied in his seat, "I don't think my *anything* hurts anymore." He chuckled and sipped from his cup.

Thimble nodded. He glanced about the room, unable to quite meet his grampa's eyes.

Sibelius noticed. "Alright. What's with the looks?"

"I," Thimble began. He wasn't even sure where to start. "I thought you'd be...you know."

"Upset?" Sibelius snorted and shook his head. "It's all in the past, son. Like I told you last time, *I get it.*"

Thimble sighed. He allowed himself to relax the smallest amount. "What did you mean *months*?" he asked.

"What?" Sibs tilted his head.

"Months. You said you haven't seen me in months."

"Well...yes. The last time was five months ago when we first came here, remember? You know, when I *died*?"

"Oh boy," Thimble set his cup on the new side table to his right. "It's only been a month out there Grampa."

"A month?" Sibelius said after a long pause.

"And a bit," Thimble said.

Sibs whistled over his cup. "So time gets a bit loopy here, eh? Interesting." He took a sip. "What about you? How've you been feeling?"

"Mostly fine, I'd say. Nothing out of the ordinary," Thimble sipped from his own cup. The tea flowed warm as ever. The taste, reminiscent of the leaves he'd used for the last few years. He looked around the comfortable space he remembered. He knew in the moment that he was putting off what had to come next. "Things are looking good here. Sharper, more *real*. I'm guessing you've been working on it?"

Sibelius looked around himself. "Fascinating isn't it? My influence is still very limited, but I can change and manipulate a thing or two."

"What about the flowers outside? Those are new."

"Not my doing, son."

Oh. Thimble sniffed, shifting uncomfortably in his seat. "It wasn't on purpose."

"It wasn't a mistake. Things here never are," Sibelius studied him for a moment, sorrow and remorse in his eyes. "They were her favorite, weren't they?"

Thimble nodded. He pressed away the memory of the last time he'd seen the flowers in person. The two sat in silence for a moment, lost in their own thoughts.

Thimble cleared his throat after a minute. "*Ahem.* I think I should tell you what's been going on, Grampa."

Sibelius set his cup aside and leaned forward. "Oh, yes. How is everything at home? I hope the shop hasn't been giving you too much trouble. I've told you it's fine to shutter the thing."

"I did, actually. I closed it up before I left. I'm," he chewed his lip and braced himself. "Um. I'm in Rardell." Silence followed his words. The kind that made him question for a quick moment whether he'd gone deaf. Sibelius stared at him, unmoving, unblinking. "Uh...Grampa?"

Sibelius blinked and shook his head quickly as if warding off a pesky gnat. "I'm sorry, I was never hard of hearing when I had corporeal ears, but things might have changed given the circumstances. I thought you said you're in

Rardell. As in the Rardell in the *Reiksal Dominion.* On *Baesalt.*"

Uh oh. "Erm...that's right."

"Oh," Sibelius said, his voice an octave higher. "Alright. You know how I said I wasn't upset before? Well I am *now!*" His shout carried through the little hut and out the windows.

"Wait a second. I can explain."

"You had damn well better!" Sibs hopped to his feet and began pacing before the hearth. "What have I told you about this place, eh? Do you know how they feel about people like us here?"

"H-hold-here," Thimble reached into his Pouch and pulled Ema's letter from the depths. He skimmed over the words once to ensure they were correct and handed the uncannily real letter to Sibelius.

Sibelius took the letter and read, his expression melting from annoyance to pure shock by the end. He looked back up at Thimble as he finished. "What *is* this?" He whispered.

Thimble drew a hand through his hair. "That arrived about four days after you...you know. I didn't know what else to do. I figured, had you been able to, you would have come out here yourself. So *I* did."

Sibelius glanced at the letter once more. "Are you certain all of this is correct?"

Thimble nodded.

Sibelius sagged back into his seat. "Ah, Thimble, my boy. You've always been impulsive, but this is something else." He rubbed his eyes and took a long draw from his cup. Thimble spied the opened and partially empty brandy bottle beside his chair. "Have you met this Ema? And um," Sibs shuffled uncomfortably. "Annabeth?"

Thimble shook his head. "No, neither. You might want to top yourself off." He launched into an explanation as to what had occurred since they last saw one another sparing little detail, even the more gruesome ones. When he finished, Sibelius sat stunned, his mouth a sliver ajar.

"*Shit.*" Sibs said.

"Yeah." Thimble agreed. "Look, I know I shouldn't have come here, Grampa, but it's too late for that now and I'm stuck in the middle of this whether I like it or not. I need help here. And it sounds like you knew this woman, so..."

Sibelius shook his head, his eyebrows stuck up from disbelief. "I don't know if I *can* help, Thimble. I...Oh," he buried his face into his hands. "Oh Annabeth, what did you get yourself into?"

"Grampa," Thimble said gently. "Who was she to you?"

Sibelius raised his head, his eyes reddened. "Annabeth is...or *was*...your grandmother. Your *actual* grandmother."

Thimble's teacup clattered to the floor where it vanished without a trace. "*What?*"

Sibelius wiped at his cheek and took a long draw from his cup. He said nothing.

His grandmother? But, Ethel was his grandmother...wasn't she? "Wait," Thimble rubbed at his temples, a bizarre connection coming to mind. "Is *that* why Dad's the tallest one in the family?"

Sibelius gave a weak snort. "By a whole hand, too. Always liked to brag about that, the boy."

"Did *he* know about this?"

"No," Sibelius sighed. Something akin to regret touched his eyes. "What would be the point? Ethel had been in his life for as long as he could remember. Annabeth was a distant memory. One that I was content with letting pass with me. Of course, the cosmos had other ideas."

"Did Grama Ethel know?"

Sibelius nodded. "She did. It was long before I met Ethel. But, I don't think it mattered much to her. She loved Grumble the way any mother would her own child. She kept the secret at my request."

Thimble reined in his spiraling mind after a struggle. "So, Annabeth. When did that start?"

Sibelius shrugged. "Almost a century ago. She had your father, in secret, right after the Culling began in truth. She didn't want her family to suffer if our relationship was ever discovered, so..."

"She abandoned you? And dad?"

"She did no such thing!" Sibelius snapped. Thimble flinched at the anger that flashed across Sibelius' eyes. "She saved me, saved *us*. She managed to get us off that accursed rock before we could be thrown into one of those damnable camps," he heaved a heavy sigh. For a brief moment. Sibelius looked his age. "It was a hard time, Thimble. A strange time. And in that time, Annabeth chose to protect. Protect me, protect her son, and her 'real' family. I don't know if I would have been able to do the same in her place." Sibelius paused for a long moment, staring deep into the fire. "You know, she never stopped writing to me," he said, a small sad smile on his lips. "When you go back, go to my house and look for a small box in my old wardrobe. I kept all her letters there. I think I'd like you to know what kind of woman she was. I'd like someone to keep her memory alive, when I no longer can."

The pair sat in silence for a long stretch.

"You have to find the girl, Thimble," Sibelius said. "I'm sorry, I would much rather you packed up and headed home at once. But she's family, even if she doesn't know it, and an innocent child besides. I don't know what comes next, but if I ever meet Annabeth again, I'd like to be able to look her in the eye."

"I'll try, Grampa," Thimble sighed. "I don't know how much more I can do than the Anvil, but I'll try."

"Good," the glint of steely fury returned to his eyes. "And when you find whoever did this...kill them."

Chapter Eight

Sweet Dreams

Stone. Endless stone. Thimble stepped, clambered, crawled, and there was always more stone. Rising up and up in a spiraling nightmare with no end in sight. He couldn't feel his feet anymore. Nor his hands. Time passed...or didn't. What did it matter? He wondered once, maybe twice if he should turn back. Make his way down this terrible tower, but that wasn't an option. He moved forward and up, no will or want to stop him. His mind felt clouded. Thoughts came and went unbidden, never enough substance to stick.

Step...step...step...sob.

Thimble froze. That was new.

He strained his ears, wishing, praying for it to be real. He heard it again. The gentle sounds of a sobbing child reached his ears through the murk. He snapped himself out of his stupor and ran toward the sound. The stairs wound and wound until finally he shot through an iron barred gate.

He stood in a circular room made of the same stone. Small windows sat high on the walls, also barred, and a gentle violet light pulsed from somewhere beyond. At the other end of the room, a small bundle of blankets sat, faced away, rocking with quiet sobs.

"Hello?" Thimble called out, taking a step closer to the bundle. His voice echoed and warbled in the space. The sobs continued unabated. "Hello? Can you hear me?" The figure didn't react. Thimble was almost within reach now. The figure had pulled one of the blankets over their head like a hood.

"Ema?" Thimble breathed.

The figure froze. Pressing silence filled the space.

Slowly, the figure turned toward him. A thin voice came from beneath the hood. "Is someone there?"

Thimble opened his mouth to answer and felt himself wrenched backward through the door. The stairs flew by at blistering speed. Thimble screamed as he was pulled deep into the tower's bowels.

Thimble bolted up shivering and sweating, the over-large bedding wrapped around him in a smothering vice. He struggled, fought himself free, the panic coursing through his veins. He threw himself off the bed and stood in the early morning chill, stark as the day he was born, gasping for each breath like it was his last.

It took him a while to calm down. Once he had feeling enough in his legs, he threw open the window for some blessed fresh air and crawled back into his boat of a bed. He lay staring at the ceiling for a long while. His mind had already been reeling with everything his grandfather told him, and now this dream.... *I think I hate this city,* was his last thought as sleep finally came for him once more.

Thimble woke the next day feeling unrested and sensing the beginnings of a templeache already brewing. A quick wash and a change of clothes later, he was thumping down the stairs into the tavern floor of the inn, full bottle of brandy in tow. He hefted the bottle onto the counter to a suspicious eye from Gloen.

"Uh," Gloen said, turning the bottle with a finger. "Did you piss in it?"

"What?" Thimble said, caught off guard. "No. I just needed it for... something." Gloen blinked slowly at him. "Alright, I know that doesn't sound much better, but I didn't piss in it I swear. Didn't even open it."

"Uh-huh," Gloen popped open the bottle and took a tentative whiff. He paused for a moment, then gave a mostly satisfied grunt and stowed the brandy back below the counter. "Breakfast?"

"Sure."

"You got company," Gloen nodded to a table in a corner of the tavern hidden by the staircase. Odion sat tucking into a deep bowl of something, a sheaf of parchment in front of him, a quill in his non-eating hand. He saw Thimble notice and waved an invitation.

"Thanks," Thimble said, turning toward the Warden.

"We'll have it out in a bit."

Thimble trudged over to the table and hopped into one of the chairs opposite Odion.

"Good morning," Odion said brightly.

"Mmph," the pain in Thimble's head pulsed savagely at the Warden's voice. He let it droop to the table in defeat.

"Sleep well?" Odion said after a minute.

"Screw you," Odion stifled a snort. Another silent moment passed between the two. "You knew about it? All of you?" Thimble said, sitting straight.

"The dream?" Odion nodded. He dipped a spoon into his bowl and shoveled what Thimble hoped was porridge into his mouth. "Yeah, we knew."

"Why didn't you say anything?"

"Let's see, would you have believed, 'we know the girl's in the city because we've all been dreaming about it for the past month.'?"

"Fair point," Thimble scratched at his head. "Alright, who else has had the dream?"

"Everyone."

"What do you mean everyone?"

"He means *everyone*," Gloen thumped up to the table and slid a smaller bowl of porridge in front of Thimble.

Thimble looked from the dwarf to the man. "How often?"

"Every damn night," Gloen rumbled.

"Every night since she went missing is what we think," Odion added. "And I should correct myself, it's *nearly* everyone. Adults only. Children don't seem affected."

"Thank the gods for that." Thimble reached into his Pouch and withdrew a small pinch of greenish-brown powder from the depths. He sprinkled the powder over his porridge. It hissed as it touched the meal and dissolved without a trace.

"My girl's porridge not good enough for you?" Gloen rumbled.

"Gravewillow root," Thimble said, picking up his spoon and pointing it at his head. "For the headache."

Gloen grunted and lumbered back behind the counter where a patron engaged his attention.

Thimble dunked the spoon into the bowl and lifted it into his mouth. Thick, sweet, and hot, the porridge with the Gravewillow was a needed relief. He found himself pleasantly surprised at the layer of stewed blueberries just under the porridge.

Odion scribbled on his parchment as Thimble tucked in for a handful of minutes. "So, what do you make of this new twist?" he asked.

Thimble pushed his bowl aside and gave a satisfied burp. "Is the dream the same for everyone?"

"Let's see," Odion held up a hand and began ticking off fingers. "Endless stone tower. Sobbing bundle of blankets. '*Is someone there?*'."

Thimble nodded along to each tick. "That answers that then. And no one has tried to do anything different while dreaming? I imagine after a month of this, it gets exhausting to the point of wanting anything to happen?"

Odion shook his head. "We're aware that lucidity is a thing, and a lot of us have tried, *really* tried, but the moment the dream starts, it's like a numbing fog falls over your mind and you forget that you were ever there before. Until you get yanked that is. Then you wake up annoyed that nothing different happened and you do this again and again."

"So no one's seen her face?" Thimble asked.

"No. Not possible."

"Then how do we know it's Lady Ema?"

"Well," Odion scratched at his chin, "we can't be sure of course, but there are coincidences and then there's...*this.*"

"And how can this confirm that she's still in the city?"

Odion crossed his arms and pondered. "Well, aside from the glowing purple light too similar to the Attrangem, the Readers have come to the conclusion that this dream is probably some sort of mass spell being cast by whoever took the girl. Something like this would take considerable power. How much power would be lessened by distance."

"Right. So not only are we dealing with a rampaging murderer, they're also a fairly impressive spellcaster," Thimble buried his head into his hands, palms pressing into his eyes. His headache had disappeared after the porridge, but the sheer amount of things pulling in different directions was beginning to take its toll.

Odion watched Thimble yank at his hair for a few moments. "Do me a favor, Thimble?" He said. He put aside his quill and picked up the parchment.

"Why not?"

"I'm writing to my family and I've never been the best with a quill. Do you mind hearing it to see if it sounds...I don't know...normal?"

"I'm not amazing either, but sure. Let's hear it."

Odion cleared his throat and began to read:

Dear Nota, Atan, and Avra,

"That's my mother, father, and little sister."

I apologize for not writing for a while. The last few months of Initiate training has been exhausting, as I'm sure you know. Wonderful news. I passed! They gave me my cloak two weeks ago and I've been assigned a role under Warden Lomar. I can't say much about what I've been asked to do in a letter, but I promise to tell all next time I come home. I know how much you all have supported me through this and it means the world to me. I hope I've made you proud and I promise I will continue to do so. Lots of love and Amitage's grace to you. Odion.

P.S. Please tell Avra that I speak to Ammy every day about her visit. I'm sure it will happen sooner or later.

P.P.S. Please tell Cass

"That's my older sister"

To stop sending me toy swords and stuffed animals. The other Wardens are starting to laugh.

P.P.P.S. Please keep sending those biscuits you made last time, Atan. I get asked about them all the time.

Odion looked up.

Thimble balked at the sudden stop. "Oh, is that...I was expecting another... nevermind. Yeah, that sounds fine to me."

"Great!" Odion carefully folded the letter and slipped it into a pouch on his belt.

Thumble watched the young Warden curiously. "Sounds like a nice family."

Odion shrugged. "I guess so."

"Are they here in the city?"

Odion shook his head. "No. Our home is in Calria. Southwestern-most part of the Dominion, so a fair distance from here. Though, I can't be sure where Cassandra is at the moment. Her last letter was a few months ago after her assignment in Penosia."

"Is she also in the same line of work?"

"Mhm. We all are. Well, my parents are retired now, but they served in the Anvil as well until a few years ago."

"Wow," Thimble said. "A family full of paladins. Sounds...interesting."

Odion snorted. "You don't know the half of it. We all serve the same patron as well. Amitage, *Ammy*," he patted the pouch where the letter lay tucked away, "is what my little sister Avra calls her. She can't wait for her visitation."

Thimble raised his brows. "Visitation? You actually meet your patron?"

Odion nodded. "Amitage visits us in our dreams when we're young and grants us her blessing."

"What's she like?" Thimble leaned in.

Odion sat back and folded his arms, a wistful glaze filmed his eyes as he stared into the distance. "Radiant," he said, barely above a whisper. "Immense. *Present*. It's...hard to describe."

"Wild," Thimble breathed. He'd never had much use for divinity in his life. He'd also never met anyone so immersed within it either, before running into the Anvil. Odions words tugged at his curiosity.

"Let me ask you something," he said.

"Hm?"

"Yesterday, you were against using the circle during my questioning. Later, you agreed with Kerrak that you trusted its judgment completely. I'm a little confused there."

Odion sniffed and stared into the distance. "I do trust its judgment, I do. The Circle isn't just any magic, it's *divine*. It doesn't listen to your breathing or watch for sweat on your brow to see if you're lying. It simply *knows* when you are. It's also why it doesn't immediately do... you know, its thing. It knows when you don't believe what you're saying and gives an opportunity to return to the truth."

Thimble shook his head at the near absurdity of it. "Sounds...I don't know... excessive?"

Odion nodded. "That's my gripe with it. Despite what it is and what it does, it's meant to be a tool. And one to be used as a last resort at that. Ever since all of this with the de Eviore family started, it's become more of a first resort."

"What do your fellows think of your views?"

Odion shrugged. "Most think I'm naive. Which, to be fair, could be true. I've only had this cloak for a short while, but...I don't know. I prefer to put my faith in people. People like you or me or," he glanced around at the few other guests scattered about "anyone here. Faith that we'll do what's right in the end."

Would we? A pang of guilt snaked through Thimble at the words.

"What about you, then?" Odion said. "How's your family?"

"Oh," Thimble waved a hand dismissively. "It was just me and my grampa before he passed."

"And your parents? Siblings?"

He shook his head. "They're not around anymore".

"Oh. I'm sorry to hear that," Odion sounded like he meant it.

"Don't worry about it." Thimble changed subjects quickly. "So, what's the plan for today? Were you able to set up meetings with the old families?"

"Ah, yes," Odion reached into another pouch on his belt and withdrew another slip of parchment. "We're meeting with the Tavinaries in two hours, then the Kovi family after, then the Aganis, and finally the Mendels at a little after midday."

"Impressive," Thimble said. "How'd you manage all of that?"

"Not sure. I took your request to the High Inquisitor's aide and received this notice today. I can't imagine they're thrilled to be questioned again, but not many have the spine to deny High Inquisitor Rhythe. Oh, also," he reached into a small satchel to his right. "This is from the manor." He handed Thimble a small comb with the letters *EEP* burned into the back.

"Eep?" Thimble said.

"It's her initials. I imagine it was a gift from someone close to her. I tried to look for anything more substantial, but there was nothing."

"You're unnervingly reliable, Odion. Hang onto that for now. I'd like to take a decent walk around the city throughout the day though, to be more effective."

Odion nodded. "What are you planning to do with it?"

Thimble waggled his eyebrows. "Well look at that. I guess it's my turn to say *you'll see soon enough*, eh?"

Odion laughed and held up his hands. As they rose to leave, a memory flew unbidden into Thimble's head that made him start to cackle like a madman. Odion gave him a questioning look as he doubled over.

"Hah-ahaha. She said 'sweet dreams'," Thimble straightened, wiping tears from his eyes. "What a bitch."

Chapter Nine

The Old Families

Thimble spent much of that morning following Odion around the city. They began in the City Center, where the Attrangem, more massive than Thimble had guessed, rested glowing stoically as ever. The gem itself was encased in some kind of thick glass or crystal structure that matched its dimpled patterning. At a closer look around, Thimble noticed that all of the buildings immediately surrounding the square were not actual buildings, but rather stone pillars built strategically around the gem to block as much of the violet light as possible from washing through the city.

Thimble placed his palm against the crystal. "It's warm," he said. The heat pulsed with the light, not unpleasant. "Why the crystal covering?" he asked Odion.

"Well," Odion said, looking over the encasing structure. "According to the histories, one of the first people who found the stone decided to touch it. What did it say happened to him..." Odion scratched his head, trying to recall, "ah, right. 'Turned immediately into a viscous, red soup.'"

Thimble removed his hand from the crystal. "Great. Don't touch the gem. Got it."

"I find it's a good idea in general."

"Mm. So why'd it turn that person into paste?"

"I imagine you've figured out that it's this thing that's keeping the city up here?"

"Figured as much."

"Right. The theory the Readers settled on is that the Attrangem pulls everything it is near, closer to itself. The thing it is touching, the thing that's closest to it as a whole, becomes the thing that is pulled the hardest, and therefore, carries the weight of everything else on it."

Thimble narrowed his brow. "I...think I understand. So the thing closest to it now is the city, and the reason we're not being turned to sludge is because the city is supporting our weight?"

Odion moved his head side to side. "Almost. What's closest to it now is the cliffside, and by extension the mainland, which includes," he pointed toward the south, away from the sea, "all of the land for hundreds of miles in that direction. That's what carries the weight of the city and keeps it from being pulled into dust and then the city does the same for us."

Thimble's left eyelid twitched. "You know what? As long as it works, that's good enough for me. Readers, eh? What's their deal?"

"Knowledge seekers, to put it simply. They spend their time divining and discerning the ways of the world. 'As the wind.'"

"Wanderer worshippers, huh? Can you introduce me to one?"

"Probably. I don't know many, but they work out of the Archive. You've seen at least one by now though. They're the ones who operate the platforms to and from the harbor above." Odion peered out toward the horizon. "We should start making our way to the Tavinari estate. We'll pass the Archive on the way, if you want a peek at it."

Thimble tried to keep a mental image of the city layout as they made their way westward. Just beyond the central square, the first of the merchant's districts started. Thimble noted a fishery, a butcher's, a grocer, a tailor, fairly standard fare as far as he was concerned. Next was the first of the housing districts. The buildings here were quite old and close set, but appeared in fine order. Thimble spied the occasional large family emerging from a home that was definitely too small for them. He noticed more of the sluggishness, the pronounced yawns and forced sighs, given what he knew now, spread among

the populace he shared the streets with. The contrast between childrens'
bursting energy and all others' waning perseverance stood out so stark, that
he wondered how he hadn't noticed the difference sooner.

Next came a crafting district of some sort, followed by a recreational district
filled with parks and ponds before yet another merchant's district. So it went,
repeated again and again unto the edges of the city. Thimble noticed that
as they approached the outskirts the houses seemed to get larger and more
spaced while the goods on sale became higher quality and more abundant.

Odion pointed out the Reader's Archive at the end of a cross street as they
turned to head in the opposite direction. A massive structure rivaling the
Anvil headquarters, the Archive squatted at the end of a dense thoroughfare
and disappeared down multiple blocks to either side. People clad in robes of
black, purple and white streamed in and out of the building and pairs of Blue
Cloaked guards flanked both the gate and the front doors. Rows of vertical
stained glass windows flanked the entrance to either side as far as he could
see. A single window, the one immediately to the right of the entrance lay
bare. Devoid of any painted depictions.

"Impressive," Thimble said, looking up at Odion as the building faded into
the distance. "I didn't realize the Anvil also served as guards."

Odion sniffed. "We don't. Not normally, that's what the city guard's for.
But, there are certain places that require a bit...more."

"Well, *now* I'm curious. What's with the blank window?"

Odion frowned, looking over his shoulder. "An accident of some sort, I
think. They've only just managed to replace the glass. Let's hurry. We're
almost there and we do *not* want to keep these people waiting."

The Tavinari estate sat at the western edge of town. Though not quite as
massive as the de Evoire estate, humongous would still be an appropriate
description. The gate sat a bit closer to the front door, the field of a yard held
one or two less fountains. Less excess was still excess in Thimble's Mind.

"You'd better get used to it," Odion said as Thimble finished grumbling.
He waved to a guard on the other side of the gate.

The lanky man in his middle years rose to his feet. He wore simple mail and
plate armor and carried a plain spear. He squinted at the pair. "Yes?" he said

after a moment.

Odion cleared his throat. "*Ahem.* Odion Grey and Thimble Pennywhistle with the Anvil here to meet with Lady Clara Tavinari."

The guard looked from one to the other for another long minute, though Thimble suspected there wasn't much going on between those saucered ears. The guard turned, and without another word, headed for the front doors.

Before he could get halfway, the doors flew open and a man in a smooth black doublet with a pristine white ascot flowed down the front steps. A thin moustache graced his upper lip and a crown of hair clung desperately to his gleaming head. He traded a few words with the guard before sweeping toward the pair outside the gate.

"Warden Grey," he greeted Odion with a smile that didn't quite reach his eyes. "My name is Marus, Head Butler for my Lady Tavinari's estate. We appreciate your punctuality. If you would follow me." He waited long enough for the guard to open the gate before setting off toward the house once more. Thimble and Odion struggled to keep pace. Thimble moreso.

Marus led them up the stairs and into the foyer, which Thimble thought would make a fine little house on its own, and into a room to the immediate right of the entrance. The room, a small study, held five comfortable looking armchairs atop a patterned rug. One wall held a high bookshelf filled with leather bound volumes and the other, a fireplace with a painting of a tall dark tower surrounded by pink flowering trees. Thimble blinked and shook his head at the nauseating image that popped into his mind upon seeing the artwork.

"If you would wait here just a moment. Please make yourself comfortable," Marus bowed himself out of the room, closing the door as he went.

"Wow," Thimble said, looking around the room and then at Odion. "Chatty bunch, eh? Do you think he'll mind if I make myself comfortable too?"

Odion shrugged, turning away from the door and making his way to one of the chairs. "I don't see why he would. The meeting was put together last minute. I imagine they just want to get it over with."

"Mm," Thimble scanned over the books on the shelf without taking in any of the words on the spines. "Ten gold says he just went to tell his mistress she's not getting what she bargained for."

"I don't feel like losing ten gold."

Thimble snorted. He paced over to the hearth and gazed up at the painting above the mantle. Spindly branches shed pinkish leaves blown into a dance by a passing wind. From between rose a dark tower, windows on every side, ending with a terraced top. *Huh.*

The door opened and in swept Marus followed by an older woman in an expensive, deep blue gown frilled in gold. Her white striped hair was tied up in a tight bun above her head and jewels dangled from her ears and neck. She glided into the room, nose fixed firmly in the air, not looking toward either Odion or Thimble until she settled into the chair across from Odion.

Marus turned to the pair, "May I introduce Lady Clara Tavinari." He bowed and backed out of the room, shutting the door behind him.

Lady Tavinari adjusted her skirts and clasped her hands in her lap. "Warden," her voice was cool and quiet. The kind that commanded attention. "Though I have granted you this audience, know that I am rather irked by this trivial repetition."

"Er," Odion cleared his throat, "ah, yes Lady Tavinari. I understand and apologize for the disturbance, but we thought it might be useful to have another point of view to aid us in the matter, so..." he gestured to where Thimble stood.

Thimble waited a beat for Odion to continue. The young Warden's mouth worked soundlessly, his eyes darted, searching for a way to introduce Thimble.

"So," Thimble cut in. "They decided I would be that other point of view." He put on his most charming smile. "Thimble Pennywhistle, Lady Tavinari. It's a pleasure to make your acquaintance and I appreciate your time." *Might as well try to start on the right foot,* he thought to himself.

Lady Tavinari didn't avoid looking at him like her butler had. Rather, she looked him up and down as if wondering how much he would fetch at an auction. Her hazel eyes looked tired, bagged like many others Thimble had seen so far, but they pierced like needlepoints all the same.

"Mister Pennywhistle," she said. "I have not seen one of your kind in quite some time."

"Well, I'm sur–"

"And I would rather have kept it that way. Though, I thank the Weaver that you have been blessed with manners at least."

Well, that lasted all of ten seconds. A new light unfurled behind her daggered sight. "Yeah, *that's* not inherited," he muttered under his breath.

"I beg your pardon?" she snapped.

He hooked a thumb over his shoulder. "Interesting painting."

Lady Tavinari's eyes flicked over to the painting and back. "The work of Tiana Nozette. Talented woman, though a bit of a free spirit. What about it?"

"It doesn't seem a bit," he shrugged, casting a glance toward Odion who had begun the process of sinking into his seat, "I don't know...familiar?"

Lady Tavinari scoffed. "You cannot even find someone who will ask *new* questions?" she shot at Odion. "Yes, I am aware of the correlation between the painting and the tower the rabble see in their dreams. I will tell you what I told the Anvil, that painting has been in this family nigh-on three decades whereas these dreams emerged merely a month ago. Any similarity is pure coincidence. That is all."

Thimble glanced over his shoulder at the painting once more. Her reasoning was sound enough, but something still irked him. At this stage, brushing something aside as mere coincidence seemed like a quick way to run out of threads to pull.

Lady Tavinari noticed his glance. "If you do not believe me, feel free to take the painting with you. Do...whatever it is you do until you are satisfied, then sell the thing for all I care. I imagine it will fetch a price you're unlikely to have laid eyes on."

Thimble smiled at the woman, forcing it to touch his eyes. "That's alright," he wandered over to the other chair beside Odion. "What did you mean by 'the tower the *rabble* see in their dreams'?" The cushion top of the hefty chair came up to his eyeline. "Do *you* not have the dream then?"

"We did, near the beginning. We had the foresight to purchase every Draught of Quiet Slumber – *are you quite finished?*" she said hotly.

Thimble glanced over his shoulder at her, his upper half draped over the chair cushion, his legs dangling in the air. Odion shot him an incredulous look. "Almost," he grunted. He finished hoisting himself onto the chair and stood on the clean velvet. He turned back toward Lady Tavinari, "Please continue."

Lady Tavinari's right eye twitched just the once. "As I was saying, we bought every Draught of Quiet Slumber in the city and had wagonfuls carted in from the Capital. The Families distributed it evenly amongst each other with the misplaced belief that it would all be taken care of soon," she turned her glare on Odion who had turned quite pale for a bronze skinned man. "I am loath to admit that even our stores are running low, though shipments from Reiksalis should arrive any day now."

"I see," Thimble said. He tapped on his chin with a finger, shifting his weight from foot to foot. "Could you tell me what your relationship is with Lady Annabeth de Evoire and her family?"

Lady Tavinari shrugged. "Apart from being on the Council and exchanging pleasantries at the occasional gala, not much of a relationship to speak of."

"Wait," Thimble stopped bouncing. "You serve on the council? The *City Council*?"

"No, we are *on* the City Council. All of the heads of the Old Families are."

"Correct me if I'm mistaken, but isn't the role of the City Council to decide courses of action that are for the *best* of the city's population? You know, including the *rabble*?"

Lady Tavinari sneered down her nose. "You would have gotten on swimmingly with Annabeth. We the Old Families are included in the citizenry of the city are we not? As the most influential and prosperous of the citizenry, are we not then afforded greater allowances? Let's not pretend some are simply not more...*worthwhile* than others."

"Mhm, mhm," Thimble swung a leg over one chair arm and straddled it like a velvet pony. He watched a vein on Lady Tavinari's head melt into view. "I'm assuming you know what has happened to the rest of Lady Annabeth's family?"

"Of course." Her eyes softened the smallest amount. The first crack in her granite composure. What did Thimble see in that instant? Was it worry? Or pity? Maybe fear? Lady Tavinari noticed him watching her closely and recovered her mask of indifference. "Of course," she said again, steely eyed once more. "Word spreads faster than a winter cough in this city."

"Any thoughts or feelings on the matter?" Thimble asked.

"What is there to think? A disgusting act of violence against people undeserving. I would have hoped that in a city full of armor plated, faith-toting, justice harping brutes, such a thing would not be possible, but alas," she delivered the last in the direction of Odion.

Thimble watched Odion squirm for a moment. "When was the last time you saw Lady Ema in person?" he asked.

Lady Tavinari paused, taken aback by the change in tack. "The girl?" her brow furrowed. "I can't be sure. A few months ago, perhaps." Her eyes flickered to the side then back. Her mouth puckered sour.

"I see," Thimble said. He hopped off of his perch and onto the floor. "Well, Lady Tavinari, I believe we've taken enough of your time. I think it's time we take our leave."

Lady Tavinari blew a sharp breath through her nose. "Yes, I think I've entertained your questions and...antics long enough. Marus!"

The door opened almost before she stopped speaking and Marus strode into the room with a bow. "Yes, my Lady?"

"Please escort these two off the property. I will say that this has been an absolute waste of my time and my disappointment with the Anvil has only deepened," Lady Tavinari smoothed the front of her gown and turned to leave.

"One last thing," Thimble interrupted. The Lady turned fuming eyes on him, but waited nonetheless. "I actually forgot to check for a portrait while I was there, but could you tell me what Lady Ema looks like?"

Lady Tavinari shrugged. "She is a child. Twelve or thirteen years I would say. Brown hair, dark eyes, pale. Quite plain really. Unremarkable."

There it was again. The furrowed brow, the darting of the eyes to the sides and the touch of lemon drop on the tongue.

Chapter Ten

The Mendels

"What in the hells was that?" Odion's eyes looked ready to pop.

Thimble and the young Warden walked apace down a slowly busying street after leaving the Tavinari's. Thimble widened his own eyes in mock surprise. "Oh! Look who's found his tongue!"

Odion's ears turned pink. "I mean it, Thimble. You're not planning on behaving like that at all the houses are you?"

"Hey, you heard what she was saying. Those weren't exactly subtle jabs."

"I know," Odion rubbed at his temples. "I get it alright? What I'm trying to say is maybe it's not the best idea to antagonize someone when you're trying to get information from them."

Thimble sighed and held up his hands. "Alright, fair enough." The pair walked in silence for a handful of minutes, dodging through and around throngs of people going about their business. Thimble cast his eyes to the sky to get an inkling of time and felt his heart jump when he found a rolling sea staring back at him. *Gah. I'll never get used to that.* He watched a massive galleon pull slowly into a lengthy dock on the northern shore.

"Say Odion?" he said.

"Yeah?"

"What's under the city?"

Odion frowned at him, confused. "Under? Probably...rocks? Dirt?"

"No, I mean on the other side of the cliff. Is there more city or...?"

"Ah, right. Well, there's nothing up...down...over there for about half a mile. Just grassland. Then for another two miles there's range and farmland. Where a lot of the city's produce comes from. That all leads to the Whittler's Forest and further inland."

Thimble shook his head. "What an odd place. I'd want to see that at some point though."

"We're almost at the Cross Road now," Odion said, peering down the street. "I don't think we have time to go through, but it's definitely a sight."

He wasn't wrong. Their street opened into a bustling road. Carts pulled by oxen and steer tundled past in either direction. One particularly immense cart carrying overflowing crates of fruits passed by Thimble allowing a clear view southward.

You've got to be kidding. The path curved upward and bored straight into a tunnel carved into the cliff face. The tunnel must have been fifty or sixty yards tall at least. The path itself continued into the tunnel for a few hundred yards before splitting in two and beginning a slow climb up either wall before turning entirely upside down and joining once again not far from the exit. Thimble's eyes focused and unfocused as he watched man and beast alike walk along the path, apparently oblivious to the fact that up and down stopped mattering somewhere in the middle. Slack jawed, he watched a group of kids in a covered wagon sticking out of the wall to the left look up – Thimble's right – and wave to a group of horse riders going the opposite way. As if it was *normal.*

"Thimble? Thimble!" Odion snapped his fingers in front of Thimble's face.

"Huh, what?" Thimble blinked and winced at a crick on his neck. "Ow." Without realizing, he had tilted his head all the way to the side while staring down the tunnel.

"Are you alright?"

Thimble blinked a few more times. "I think I need to lie down."

Odion snorted. "I had a similar reaction the first time. Come on, we'd best get moving."

"So that would be the Attrangem then?" Thimble asked, still casting the occasional eye down the tunnel only to feel his stomach twist some more.

"Yes. The middle part is where the pull reverses and the world sort of takes over. Luckily, the change isn't sudden, at least not right away, so things like *that* are possible."

Thimble shook his head and dug his hand into his Pouch looking for the tonic he had bought the day before.

The rest of the day passed as expected. The Kovi family head, Lord Byron Kovi, was somehow even more abrasive and short than Lady Tavinari, though he seemed to be the type to dislike a bit of everything rather than just the vertically disinclined. The pair were shepherded out after a quick denial of all involvement and a threat of middling severity toward the Anvil. The meeting with the Aganis family was somehow better *and* worse. They were led into a small library off the entrance where they sat and waited for nearly two hours before being informed that Mistress Aganis was not in and would not be meeting with them that day. The pair arrived at the Mendel's just as the light began its shift into pre-dusk hues.

Thimble, who did not possess Odion's civility and had fallen into a deep slumber in the Aganis library, watched the young Warden work through his lather with an amused grin.

"I mean," Odion said, again. "Why agree to the meeting if you have no intention of *meeting*? Why not just turn us away at the door? Did it really take the maid *hours* to realize the Lady wasn't in? Do you know what sitting still in armor does to your back? *What* are you smiling at?" he rounded on Thimble.

Thimble held up his hands. "Honestly? It's really hard to take you seriously right now. You can't be *that* angry with *that* moustache. It just doesn't work." He felt another laugh bubble up and turned away.

"Oh, shut it," Odion raised his fist and knocked, hard, on the Mendel's front door.

The Mendel estate was smaller than the previous three. No gate surrounded the manor, no grassland graced their front yard, and it took a matter of seconds to walk the path to the door. Yet the manor itself stood a good three stories tall and had enough windows to embarrass a hothouse.

The door swung inward and framed a tall man in his middle years. Long dark hair flowed over his shoulders to his clavicle, framing a slender and freshly lined tan face. A thin goatee ending in a slight point enclosed a thin mouth turned up at the corners. The man wore a black waistcoat patterned with deep green flowers over a light shirt and dark trousers. He spread ringed hands wide and smiled from ear to ear.

"Gentlemen!" he boomed. "Welcome. Welcome to house Mendel."

Odion and Thimble exchanged glances out of the corners of their eyes. "Uh," Odion began. "Good afternoon. We're here to see Lord Ander Mendel."

"Ah," The man clapped his hands together. "Right, where are my manners? I'm afraid my father is quite ill at the moment and will not be able to speak with you in his state."

Odion raised an eyebrow. "Your father?"

"Yes indeed. I am Ellis Mendel. It was in fact I who accepted the Anvil's request for this meeting. How could I not when I heard who would be present! Warden Grey," he threw his hands toward Odion as if framing his face between them, "and of course Thimble Pennywhistle." He swiveled and did the same to Thimble.

"You know who we are?" Thimble resisted taking a step back from the man's enthusiasm.

"Of course, how could I not? The latest Grey undoubtedly raring to etch his mark into history as so many of his predecessors and the first Gnome to set foot on Dominion soil in a century! I'm quite unabashed to say I leaped at the chance. But! Let us retire to more comfortable surroundings. This way please." He turned and started into the foyer.

Thimble turned and spread his palms to Odion as if to say "What is going on?"

Odion shrugged in a "How should I know?" way and led the way through the door.

The trio wound their way past a narrow staircase and into a room just off a central hallway. Thimble found his attention drawn to a three paneled painted window across from the door, the middle being the largest. Swirls of color, stamps of patterned glass weaved in intricate bands and glowed in the embered daylight, setting accent strokes alight as if filled with fire bugs.

"Wow," Thimble whispered as he stepped into the room.

Ellis noticed Thimble's gaze. "Beautiful isn't it?" he said proudly. "My own late grandmother's work. A magician with glass she was. But, let's get comfortable, shall we." He motioned to a group of armchairs set by a crackling hearth.

Two of the three chairs seemed normal, the third however, was *interesting*. While identical in proportion, apparent comfort, and height, it was designed to occupy a significantly smaller body. Near the foot of the chair and a little off to the side, a small step ladder awaited, ready to assist the chair's next occupant.

"I hope you don't mind," Ellis said, taking his own seat and gesturing for them to do the same, "I took the liberty of having that procured to make our time together as pleasant as possible."

Thimble looked from the chair to Odion and shrugged. This was the most consideration he'd been given upon arriving in the city. Yet, something of Ellis' demeanor irked him. *Well, no point not enjoying it, for now.* "Not at all. Let's give her a spin." He hopped up the short step ladder and settled into the chair just as Odion did with his. The arms cradled him as if made for his own body and his legs dangled *while* his back touched the rear. "Oh this is *very* nice," he said, bouncing slightly on the plush cushion.

"Er...Lord Mendel?" Odion asked. He shot a warning glance toward Thimble.

"Please, call me Ellis, young man!" Ellis said with a laugh.

"Alright, Ellis...you seem quite well informed despite this being our first meeting."

Ellis waved a dismissive hand. "I make it my business to stay as informed as possible on the goings on of the city. How about a drink?" He clapped his hands together twice. "Mary, dear!"

The door opened and a young, dark-haired woman, about the same age as Odion walked in. She wore a light blue and white serving girl's dress and a cloth apron spilled down the front. She carried in her hands a tray with a crystal bottle of a deep blue liquid and three glasses, one much smaller than the other. She poured a quarter glass three times and handed one to each before giving a final curtsy and departing.

"Thank you, dear," Ellis said as Mary was about to shut the door. "Could you fetch Rosa for me please? Take your time. Go on then lads! Have a taste."

Thimble raised the glass, one-handed for a change, to his nose and took what he hoped was a discreet sniff. The distinct scent of citrus mixed with the slightest hint of salt and alcohol touched his nose. *Is this what I think this is?* He took a sip and felt his mouth explode into a miasma of flavor. It was as if someone had shoved an entire honey roasted orange into his mouth and topped it off with a helping of liquor. "Ah," he tried his hardest not to cough. "That's what I thought. Foof." He quickly shot a glance at Odion and saw the Warden sat frozen with the glass at his lips.

Ellis, seeing his reaction, beamed. "I was hoping you'd recognize it! The finest *Morsibol* on the continent."

Odion lowered his glass, attempting desperately to hide the puckering of his mouth. "I...ahem...I don't think I've ever heard of it."

"*Morsibol*," Ellis said, "as our gnomish friend here knows, is one of the finest drinks ever thought up in the depths of Fibgrin Town. It took quite a while and quite a lot of gold to track that bottle down."

"Bit strong for my taste. More my grampa's speed. But, appreciated nonetheless." Thimble clasped the glass between his fingers in his lap. "Shall we speak about why we're here?"

Ellis sat straight and placed his glass on a side table. "Of course. Terrible business, just terrible. We were quite close, you know, our family and the de Evoires."

"Oh?" Thimble followed suit with his glass. "Close? How so?"

"Friends. Old friends, going back when my father was my age. Even now, my Rosa is dear friends with young Ema," Ellis stared down at his hands.

Thimble glanced at Odion who seemed quite new to this piece of information. "Is that right?" he said. "Do you mind if we speak to Rosa?"

"Not at all. She should be down in a few minutes."

"Ellis," Odion said, leaning forward. A look of wary curiosity bloomed in his eyes. "We didn't know how close your families were. Would you have any idea who would do something like this? Or why?"

Ellis clenched his hands. "Ah, if I knew such a thing young man, I would bring a wrath inconceivable on their heads, but alas," he grabbed the glass and took another long sip. "Oh, Lady Annabeth, she deserved so much better. Marcos and Frilia were jewels themselves and Anton, dear Anton a paragon in the making and his dear wife Anita. And the children!" he burst out. His lip quivered, though with eyes dry.

A dull clatter against the old wood ceiling caught their attention. "Oh," Ellis waved his hand. "That would be Rosa. Girl's a bit clumsy, I'm embarrassed to admit, but a good head on her shoulders.

"Actually," he turned toward Odion. "I was wondering if the Anvil had come across any documents of bequest at the de Evoire estate."

"Documents of..." Odion shrugged toward Thimble.

"You mean a will?" Thimble asked.

"Yes, of course," Ellis said. He paused for a moment, eyes flickering between the two. "Now that no one is left to manage the estate and the family holdings...my hope is their last wishes, should any be found, be honored to the letter."

"Ah," Odion said. "Unfortunately, we can't divulge that sort of information yet."

"Also," Thimble added. "I wouldn't say *no one's* left. You're quite quick to write off the girl."

Ellis sat straighter, his eyes flickered between the two once more. "And I pray to the Forgemaster she is found safe and well."

The door to the study creaked open and in stepped Mary with a young girl no older than twelve clinging to her skirt. Her sandy hair fell in loose curls to her middle back and large watery brown eyes tried to dart every which way at once. Her frilled green dress whispered along the floor as she went.

"Ah, thank you Mary," Ellis said with a broad smile. "Come here Rosa dear."

The girl let go of Mary's skirt and shuffled her way to her father, eyes locked onto Thimble the entire way.

Ellis lifted the child onto his knee. "Gentlemen, this is Rosa. Rosa, these are the men I said would be visiting. That's Odion Grey and that is Thimble Pennywhistle."

"I've read about you," Rosa blurted, eyes still glued to Thimble.

Oh boy. Thimble put on what he hoped was a pleasant smile. "Have you?"

"Uh-huh. In *A Blue Sparrow for the Queen*, there's a Gnome that steals the queen's magic mirror and turns all the servants into rabbits with it. And in *Penelope's Private Parlor*, a Gnome hides in her washbasket and scares her grandmother to death. And in *Troubling Tales from Fibgrin to Altera,* there's this guild that's just Gnomes and they run around taking wheels from carriages and nailing them to horses," she said in one breath.

"Uh," Thimble said. "Wow. Shady fellows aren't they?"

"I dunno," she shrugged. "It gets a little old. Why can't someone else be bad?"

"Ha!" Ellis laughed, shifting uncomfortably in his seat. "She is so...*so* into her little stories. Rosa, these men want to ask you a few questions," he shot her a pointed eye. "About Ema."

Rosa stared at her father, the excitement draining from her face. "Oh. Okay."

"Rosa," Thimble said tentatively. "Do you know what's happened with Ema?"

She nodded. "Papa said she's missing."

"That's...right," Thimble said at a glance from Ellis. "And we're going to try and find her so anything you could tell us might help with that, alright?"

Rosa nodded.

"Great. Do you remember the last time you saw Ema?"

Rosa took another glance at her father who nodded encouragingly. "I...I think it was a little while ago. We played at her house."

"Did you ever see any strange people when you were playing? Anyone not supposed to be around, outside or inside?"

Rosa shook her head. "I don't think so. There was," her brow furrowed. "Her mother Anita," she ticked off on a finger. "And her father Anton. And her grandmother Annabeth. And her uncle..." Rosa paused, squinting slightly.

"...Marcos! And her aunt...Frily. I think that's all?" she said the last like a question.

"That sounds like the whole family to me," Ellis confirmed. A slight relaxing of Rosa's shoulder's caught Thimble's eye. When she turned again toward him, her eyes shone a touch brighter.

"How long ago do you think this was Ellis?" Odion chimed in.

"Oh, probably two or three months ago," Ellis said.

"Two or three...," Thimble turned from Ellis to Rosa, "Rosa, are you sure you saw Lady Annabeth there? Ema's grandmother?"

Rosa hesitated. "Uh-huh."

Thimble frowned. "How long ago did Lady Annabeth pass away?" he asked Odion.

"Just about eight months," he replied. He casually set his drink aside and sat forward in the guise of making himself more comfortable.

"Ah!" Ellis slapped a hand on his forehead. "That's my mistake. These children have so many play dates, it's impossible to keep track of. No, this would have been around a year ago actually."

"A year?" Thimble sat forward himself. "Quite a while ago for 'so many playdates'."

"Well," Ellis's ears had turned a bright shade of pink. "It has been a *very* busy year, I'll have you know and I do not appreciate this line of questioning, gentlemen!"

Rosa gasped and gripped the front of her father's coat as he became more animated.

Odion rose from his seat, his eyes set firmly on Ellis. "I don—"

"I'm very sorry, Ellis," Thimble interrupted. He shot a warning glance toward Odion. "We didn't mean to insinuate anything by our questions. It's been a difficult time I'm sure, and we all forget things. We were only wondering aloud. It helps with the process, I'm sure you can guess."

Ellis looked from Thimble to Odion and puffed out a breath. "Well. Yes, of course. Apology accepted, young man." Some of the color returned to his face. "And my apologies as well, I was a bit brash."

"Not at all," Thimble returned to the girl. "Rosa, thank you so much for answering our questions. You've been a big help. We'll do everything we can to find *Amy*, alright?"

Rosa nodded and slid off of her father's lap. Mary, who had been waiting by the door, took her by the hand. "Nice meeting you!" she said as she was led from the room.

Thimble waved goodbye and turned to Ellis. "Lord Mendel. Ellis," he slid off his own chair. Odion followed suit. "Thank you for your cooperation and for being an excellent host. The *Morsibol* was a wonderful taste of home. We won't trouble you any longer."

"Oh," Ellis stood, seeming genuinely disappointed. "Of course, any time. I do wish you could have stayed a bit longer, but I suppose you are quite busy yourselves. Would you like to keep the bottle?"

Thimble shook his head. "I couldn't possibly. Please enjoy it on my behalf."

"That I will, young man. Ha!" Ellis barked a laugh, back to his old self. "Oh, and if you do find anything at the de Evoire estate that might require the eyes of someone close to the family, do let me know."

"We will. Oh, one last thing," Thimble turned back at the door. "Could you remind me what Lady Ema looks like?"

"Oh, uh," Ellis looked taken aback. He furrowed his brow, "Young, about the same age as Rosa I think. Brown hair. Quite ordinary, really."

The pair exchanged one more round of pleasantries at the door and departed the Mendel estate into the hastily darkening streets.

Chapter Eleven

Questions

"What in the hells was *that?*"

"You know, that's getting old real fast," Thimble said.

Thimble and Odion stood in the shadows across from the Mendel manor.

"Thimble," Odion said, wild-eyed. "He was lying through his teeth! He has to know *something.*"

"You know, I never pegged you as the excitable type," Thimble rummaged in his Pouch and withdrew a tiny black twig with five curling points. "Here," he held it out to Odion. "First. Chew on this. *Don't* swallow it."

Odion took the twig from Thimble. "What is it?"

"Damirl Clove. *Morsibol* is toxic to humans, in case you didn't know. That will clear up most of the effects."

Odion blanched. "*Toxic?* He tried to poison me?" He chucked the clove into his mouth and began chewing furiously.

"No. Well...not really. Not unless you down the whole bottle. Normally, it'll leave you a bit addled for a few hours or days depending on how much you drink."

"Why would he do that? And he drank some *himself.*"

"Because, he's crazy," Thimble crossed his arms and leaned against the wall of the alley where they stood. "Not in a dangerous way, mind. More of an oddball sort of way. My guess is he likes the thrill."

Odion shook his head. "And the lying?"

Thimble shrugged. "I think he wants to make sure the Anvil knows that the Mendels and de Evoires were close. And with no one around to confirm or deny that, who's going to say otherwise?"

"I don't understand."

"It's a money thing, likely. Or clout chasing at the least," Thimble sighed. " I've seen it a couple times in Veppen. Someone worms their way into a social circle or family with not-so-great motives only to make themselves indispensable before doing whatever they intended in the first place. Never ends well. What I'm more interested in, is what the girl had to say."

"She didn't say much important I don't think."

Thimble nodded. "That's what I thought at first, but...what's the girl's name? The one we're looking for."

"Um," Odion furrowed his brow for a long moment. "Ema," he said finally. "Lady Ema."

Thimble raised an eyebrow. "Addled, remember? So when I called her Amy, I didn't expect you or Ellis to react, but neither did Rosa. Why would that be, you think?"

Odion stroked at his moustache. "Because she didn't notice."

"Or?"

"Or...or she's lying about knowing Ema."

Thimble snapped his fingers. "You're catching on quick. Normally I'd be inclined toward the simpler of those choices, but nothing about any of this has been normal. Wait, why aren't you chewing?"

"Uh," Odion glanced around sheepishly. "I swallowed it."

"You...ugh," Thimble rubbed at his eyes, tired. "Never mind. For now, I need to speak to the girl. Without the father around."

Odion gave him a dubious look. "I don't think he's going to allow that."

"No I don't think so either. So," Thimble stuck his head out of the alley and peered toward the house. He located the painted three paned window and pointed his finger to the one above it. A light flickered from within and a shadow played across the walls, moving to and fro. "That should be her room right there."

Thimble felt a hand grip him by the back of his shirt and tug him back into the alley.

"Are you crazy?" Odion hissed. "You want to climb up there? What happens if you get caught?"

Thimble straightened his collar. "I *won't* get caught, because you're going to watch my back."

"I will *not!* I'm a Warden. I can't be caught doing things like this!"

Thimble rolled his eyes. "Will you relax? I'm not going to go inside. Just one question and I'm gone. You want to find Ema don't you?"

He could almost hear the gears in Odion's head. "Fine!" he said. "Quickly then!"

"Great! I need some quiet for a minute to prepare." Thimble closed his eyes, abruptly aware that he hadn't done what he was planning to do in a while. How did it go again? He recalled his father's teaching words.

"Feel each beat of your heart. Hear its *thrum* as it guides life through your veins with every beat. Then feel that *thrum* expand. Feel it reach out and out until it finds another. The constant beat in the dark, the life pulse of the living world. Breathe. Breathe and feel your *thrum* align. Align. Until there are two no longer."

Thimble recalled the words of his incantation.

A leafy tree,
a parasol freed,
a moon between,
a bard's decree.

At the last word, he opened his eyes to a *thrum* surging down his right arm and into his palm. There it stayed for a moment of pointed burning cold. The cold blossomed in wisps of shadow and sinking light. Hues of black and darkest violet flowed from his hand. First, it formed the grip and flowed outward both directions to form the double arched limbs. Then a thin, almost invisible string of light dripped from the top and joined the other curve at the bottom.

Odion sucked in a sharp breath beside him. "Amitage's grace," Odion whispered. "You're an arcanist, too?"

Thimble examined his handiwork, pleased with himself. "Something like that," he dropped the bow to his side and walked to the alley opening. With the window on the second floor in his sights, he raised the bow and with his left hand, pulled back on the string of light. As his hand pulled further back, a feathered fletching of the same black-violet shadow formed between his fingers. The shaft followed and finally the point at full draw. He glanced at Odion, who watched him slack jawed. A shot of pleasure at his expression sent a grin spreading across his own face. "See you in a bit. *Dreics!*"

He loosed the arrow and with it, felt his body shatter into a million little black motes. The arrow cut through the night sky trailing all of him behind itself. The cold was almost unbearable. He could see the window...could he see? Did he have eyes? The window hurtled toward him too fast for panic to set in. As the arrow tip touched the glass, Thimble felt all of him collide together in a deafening rush of wind and with a *snap*, he was himself again. He reached out in a panic and grabbed the shutter edges as his feet found the narrow window sill.

"Gods," he whispered. "That's a lot less fun than I remember." Shivering, he squinted through the glass and found Rosa staring at him, mouth agape.

"Shh," Thimble lifted a finger to his lips. He pointed to her, then to himself. "Can we talk?" he mouthed, making the quacking hand sign.

Rosa inched closer to the window and unlatched the lock. She slid the window up high enough to whisper through. "Are you gonna steal something?"

"What? No!" Thimble leaned over uncomfortably to whisper through the same gap. "I just wanted to ask you something."

"Um," Rosa glanced back at her door. "I don't know if I should be talking to you without Papa."

"Well, that's probably a good point, but that's kind of what I wanted to ask about," he adjusted his grip on the shutter ends. "I know you've been asked to keep something from us, and I think it would be really helpful if we could know everything we can if we're going to find Ema."

Rosa glanced at her door again. "Papa said not to say anything more about Ema ever again."

"Um, alright," Thimble felt his knees begin to tremble with the cold and the effort of keeping himself on the narrow edge. "How about this? I'll say what I think, and you can just shake your head or nod." Rosa did neither. "Alright. I think you've never met Ema. I think your papa asked you to say that you did, and maybe pretend you were visiting her instead of one of the other de Evoire children."

"That's not all of it," Rosa's eyes lit up. "I *have* been to that house and I *have* played with the children there. There's Ira and Damin and Lescot and Sybil. That's all. There's no one called Ema who lives there."

"What's that supposed to mean?" Odion held open the door to Gloen's Getaway.

Thimble stepped through, his head in a cloud. "No idea." It was true enough. What *had* Rosa meant? That she had never met Ema? That there *was* no Ema? And why did they all describe her in such a like manner? Thimble climbed a short step into a high stool at the bar and dropped his head into his hands.

"That kinda day, huh?" Gloen's gruff voice pierced the general clamor of the guests. "Drink?"

Thimble shook his head at the old dwarf swiping a rag around a dented stein. "No. No more drinks."

"Mm. Food?"

"Why not?"

"Blue Cloak?"

Odion slid into the stool beside him. "Yes, please."

Gloen dropped the rag and stein and thumped into the back room.

Odion put his elbows on the countertop and rested his chin on his hands. "Well. What now?"

Thimble shrugged and sighed. "I don't know. What do you think? This is all new-ish information I'm guessing? Where would the Anvil go from here?"

"Is it even information? Rosa said that she doesn't know anyone named Ema. Well, what can we say from that?"

Gloen returned carrying a heavy steaming plate in each hand. "Roasted seserin chops, fresh from the butcher's." He dropped a plate in front of Odion and an equally impressive plate in front of Thimble. A huge slab of meat, fire roasted to a crackling edge and a soft pink center dominated the plate. Root vegetables surrounded the steaming meat and the whole lot was slathered in a still bubbling reddish-brown gravy.

Thimble gulped. Portion size aside, the divine scents coming from the plate reminded him of his mother's home cooking. Something he hadn't tasted in a very long while. He traded glances with Odion, and the pair fell on the food as one. It took a handful of minutes for the ravenous hunger they suddenly found themselves consumed by to settle.

"Mm," Thimble popped another chunk of meat into his mouth and settled back into his chair. "My compliments to Glena." Gloen gave a short grunt. "Alright," he turned to Odion. "I'm going to do what I was planning on anyway. You have that comb with you?"

Odion nodded and pulled the initialed comb from one of his pouches. He passed it over to Thimble. "What are you thinking?"

"Some old magic," Thimble turned the toothed piece of wood over in his hands. "If all goes well, I should be able to see roughly where the girl is."

Odion started. "What? You could do that all this time?"

"I didn't say it was going to work, but yeah."

"Then why not do it this morning?"

"Needed to see the city. Make a basic layout in my mind. What I need now is some empty space. Oh, I'm also going to burn this."

"You...you can't burn something that isn't yours!"

"Do you want to find this kid or not?" Thimble waited for an answer he knew wasn't coming. He ran through the ritual in his mind to calm himself. The ritual was simple enough, he'd done it a few times in his work, but unpleasant in the worst ways. "Let's do it in my room. I need you to make sure I don't set myself on fire."

"Ah-HEM," Gloen cleared his throat loudly just as Thimble started to move. "It's my room, and you're not setting a damn thing on fire in there. Case you haven't noticed, building's made of wood."

Thimble decided not to mention the small amount of burning that had already occurred. "Good point. We'll do it outside then."

Gloen snorted at that. "How quick do you think you'll get a boot to the head when someone sees a Gnome doing weird shit?"

"You have a better idea?" Thimble asked, irritated.

Gloen shrugged. He tilted his head back. "Everybody! Out!"

The tavern floor had a handful of occupants, all of whom turned to look at Gloen at the shout.

One mousy looking young man pointed at his table where a plate of steaming food had just been placed. "But..."

Another older man glared up from his tankard. "Got a room here!"

Gloen growled under his breath. "Take it! Come back in an hour. Now, piss off 'fore I start hucking things!"

Grumbling, the patrons gathered their things and filed out of the tavern.

"Clear a space," Gloen said to Thimble and Odion. "I'll be right back."

Odion stood and began pushing a few tables from the center of the floor to the sides. Thimble helped with the chairs. Within a few minutes, the pair had cleared a decent space from the center of the floor. Gloen returned carrying a heavy looking slab of granite. He dropped the stone in the center with a weighty *thud*.

Odion looked from the slab to Gloen. "I knew Dwarves were strong, but... *wow*."

"Gonna burn anything, burn it on that," Gloen dropped into a chair on the outside of the space.

"That works, thanks," Thimble said. "Alright. Keep an eye," he said to Odion. "This might take a bit."

He sat down in front of the granite slab and began taking components from his pouch. First, he laid a bed of flint shavings atop which he placed the comb. Next , he sprinkled a circle of kelafi spice in a tight ring around the comb. Finally, he scattered a pinch of coarse black powder over bits of all of the components, making sure to grind some into the spice, though he knew it wouldn't make it any less unpleasant. He placed a small scattering of evergreen colored grass shavings beside the slab, away from everything. He took a final pinch of firesand in his fingers.

He glanced from Odion to Gloen. "Here goes. *Salen.*" He scattered the firesand over the components with a flick of his wrist.

The black powder caught instantly, sending a puff of reddish black smoke into the air. Thimble breathed out until he couldn't anymore and stuck his head into the billowing smoke. Eyes closed, he inhaled the burning smoke, embers and all until his lungs felt aflame. The hissing and popping of the burning components faded along with the rapidly approaching steps of who he hoped was Odion. The burning in his chest lessened bit by bit until he could finally open his eyes toward the sky.

A bluish haze had settled over the tavern. He looked down at his body, hunched over in the smoke frozen mid-billow. To his left, Odion stood in an uncomfortable crouched position, his chair tipping backward, shock clear on his face. Even Gloen's eyes looked ready to pop, suspended mid-slide off his stool. Amusing as it was, Thimble hoped Odion would reach his body before he tipped into the scorching components.

Reminding himself not to breathe, Thimble raised his head toward the ceiling. With small exertion of will, he let himself flow up and out through the timber and into the open air of the city. He lifted higher and higher above the tallest buildings until the dull shape of Rardell lay bare before him coated in that same frosted light. He closed his eyes once more, focusing on the scent of the burning wood, tinged with fragrant oils that had soaked into the pores over years of use. If he'd done everything correctly, he would be able to see the owner's location as a dull glow.

He opened his eyes and froze. His heart would have leapt into his mouth if he could still feel it. A bare few paces in front of him stood a man. Long light hair flowed over either shoulder draped in a deep dark robe that covered him to the feet. Pale, long fingered hands clasped gently together in front of him. A high, leaf-shaped collar rose behind his head, casting a light shadow over an almond shaped face.

He smiled baring gleaming teeth, eyes almost closing from the motion. "Tsk, tsk, tsk." He wagged a finger with each click. "That's cheating." His voice, smooth as silk, thrummed in Thimble's mind. He reached forward, a long pointer extended and flicked Thimble on the forehead.

Thimble had no time to react. He felt himself yanked violently downward hundreds of feet, back through the city air, through the tavern roof until he found himself hurtling toward his own hunched body.

The instant of blackness was all too short. He woke, gasping as ash and smoke seared at his throat and threatened to burn a hole through his chest. He lay flat on his back, with a harried looking Odion patting at his chest fervently. He rolled over onto his side and began hacking up everything he had breathed in. "*Akh! AKH!*"

"Dear gods," Odion said, "get us some water would you Gloen?"

Gloen thumped away to return moments later carrying a sloshing tankard full of water. Thimble stopped coughing long enough to scoop up the grass shavings and dunk them into the tankard before quaffing the lot.

The burning in his chest eased ever so slightly. He glanced around at the pair gathered around him. "I *definitely* hate this town."

* * *

Endless stairs. A stone filled haze. Rising up and up and up. Thimble stopped counting eventually. What was the point? *Wait. I've been here before.* Thimble swatted at the nattering voice. "Leave me alone." Fifty thousand? Was that where he left off? *Thimble! Wake up you buffoon!* Thimble blinked. The haze swept away like a rising morning mist. He found himself standing just outside of an iron barred gate. There, at the other end of the circular room, lay the bundle of blankets. The bundle sobbed and rocked.

"Ema?" he said quietly.

The figure froze. An odd whispering came from beneath the hood.

Thimble stepped forward. "Ema? Can you tell me where you are?"

The whispering grew louder the closer he crept. "...der...under...under... under..."

"Under? Under what? Under where? Can you tell me?"

"*...under...under...under...*"

"Ema, I need you to tell me where so I can come get you."

99

The whispering stopped. A deathly silence filled the space.

"*Is someone there?*"

Chapter Twelve

Memory in Motion

The Anvil Headquarters were quite nice, Thimble noted, now that he wasn't being interrogated or threatened. He and Odion sat in chairs in High Inquisitor Samara's office mid morning, waiting for the resident herself. A desk made of some dark wood split the room neatly in half, a comfortable looking high backed chair on one side, two for guests on the other. Two tall bookshelves sat in the back corners carrying heavy tomes and scroll holders racked into diamond slots cut into the wood. Directly behind the Inquisitor's chair, a tall arched heater shield painted blue with silver trimmings and a bright coat of arms depicting the symbol of the Anvil – an Anvil – hung on the wall. A tall window to their right stood open, morning light and chilled sea breeze drifted inside in comforting amounts.

"So," he glanced side-eyed at Odion. "How'd you sleep?"

"Fine," Odion said quickly. He sat pin straight staring ahead.

"How's...how's the stomach?"

"...fine."

"Mhm, mhm. How 'bout we establish rule two?"

"...go on then."

"When someone tells you to do something, and that someone knows *more* about that something than you, let's agree to just *do it*, eh?"

"...agreed."

The door behind the pair swung open and the High Inquisitor walked in, fully armed and armored, her hair falling to her shoulders in loose ringlets. She unclipped her scabbard and leaned it against a stand behind her desk. "Warden Grey. Mister Pennywhistle." She said, taking her seat and folding her hands.

Thimble winced at the clipped formality. "Good morning, High Inquisitor," he replied, deciding not to push his luck. "How's your day going so far?"

"I just left a meeting with one of Lady Tavinari's retainers. As you can imagine, she had quite a bit to say about your visit," sharp eyes crossed between the pair.

"Um..." Thimble exchanged a side-eye with Odion. "Well...we..."

"You," Odion said pointedly.

"I..."

Samara snorted. A sound Thimble never expected from her. She leaned back in her chair and placed one foot on the other knee. "At ease, Thimble. Complaints from *that* house aren't exactly uncommon."

"Oh, well," the tension left his shoulders and he relaxed into his seat. "That's a relief –"

"Nonetheless," Samara interjected. "Let's keep the tomfoolery to a minimum, shall we? Warden, ensure it is so."

"Yes, ma'am," Odion said, inclining his head.

"Right. Noted," Thimble cleared his throat, a slight heat in his ears.

"So," Samara leaned forward once more. "You said you had some information for me."

Thimble nodded. He outlined the details of all of the events of the day before, careful to leave out the manner of his conversation with Rosa. Samara's expression became more troubled the longer he spoke and downright perplexed as he described his vision from the night before.

"Alright," Samara lifted her head from her hands. "One thing at a time," she raised a hand and extended a finger. "Rosa Mendel says she doesn't know and has never seen anyone named Ema at the de Evoire estate. I wouldn't put it past Ellis Mendel to teach his daughter how to mislead, young as she is."

"If I may, ma'am," Odion said, "she did seem quite earnest at the time."

"Mm," Samara tapped her finger on the desk. "Considering the amount of pageantry and fibbage involved in your visit, we'll err on the side of caution."

Thimble clicked his tongue. "What's Ellis Mendel's deal anyway?"

Samara rolled her eyes. "Ellis Mendel has been trying to get his hands on the de Evoire estate deed ever since the knowledge of their passing spread. Idiot.

"As to this other matter," she continued. "This man you described: tall, pale, light hair, dark robe with a high collar pointed at the back. Not exactly a comprehensive description, but I understand the limitations you were under during your...trance?"

Thimble nodded. "Something like that. Would it help if I said he had a spine jellifying grin?"

Samara crossed her arms. "I can't recall ever seeing anyone like that. We'll spread it among the patrolling Wardens to keep an eye out. *That's cheating...*" she trailed off, finger tapping away. "Thimble," she said after a long moment. "This trance of yours, you mentioned, would help locate the girl? Visually, specifically?"

"Correct. Though, in a more general area rather than pinpoint," Thimble answered.

"Would you be able to do this again?"

Thimble felt the not quite dissipated burning from his chest and held in a cough. "Not for a while at least. I've taken some quelling draught, but the ritual is a nightmare to the body."

Samara nodded, slight disappointment in her expression. "I understand. I'm beginning to think, as I'm sure you've already concluded, that this may have been our perpetrator."

"I really hope not," Thimble said. "Pulling someone out of a trance like that isn't something just anyone can do. Not to mention knowing I was doing it in the first place."

"Meaning," Odion added. "We're dealing with someone skilled?"

"Very," Thimble nodded. "A sorcerer or sage of some sort."

"One who's, at best, taken an interest in this affair, at worst, is the cause of it, and either way, is toying with us," Samara rubbed at her temples.

Thimble had only ever read about sorcerers and their ilk in books his Grampa gave him. Men and women with abilities that could quake the world and roil the seas. That power was the reason they had been hunted down and eradicated by the zealous Fribold Legion in his current homeland. And it was likely someone with that kind of power was involved here.

"What about Carrom?" Odion asked.

Samara propped her chin on her thumbs, mouth hidden by her clasped hands. She stared through Odion, lost in thought.

Thimble glanced between the two Blue Cloaks in the silence. "Carrom? What's Carrom?"

"He's a..." Odion began, "he's an...hmm."

"He's a wizard...of sorts," Samara supplied.

"Wizard?" Thimble said. "As in, someone who can cast crazy spells? Like mass dream manipulation spells?"

Samara sat back and crossed her arms, looking uncomfortable for the first time since Thimble had met her. "Yes...and no. Carrom's not the type to do this kind of thing. Hells, I doubt he's the type to do any kind of thing at this point."

"What does that mean?"

She shrugged. "Carrom's lived in this city longer than any of us. Near two centuries at this point. But, the last time he left his tower was around seventy years ago. He's...odd. But not evil. And he doesn't match the description of the man in your vision."

Thimble pursed his lips. "Still. Old and adept as he is, might be worth a visit."

"Be my guest," Samara shrugged again. "But don't expect much. Carrom hasn't entertained guests in a very long time.

"I would ask a favor of you two," Samara said. "As I said before, we will keep a lookout for the man in your vision, but I would like the matter of what he is – or may be, rather – to stay between the three of us."

Thimble and Odion traded curious looks. "As you say, High Inquisitor," Odion said.

Thimble shrugged. "I don't have a problem with that, but...wouldn't it benefit your order to know what they might be potentially up against?"

"It might," Samara sighed and leaned back, "if our assumptions are correct. If not, we would risk inciting a panic for no reason at all. You may not know much of our history, Thimble, but the last time something akin to a sorcerer showed his face in Rardell...things didn't go quite so well. So, your word if you please."

Thimble understood. At least, he hoped he did. There were bound to be many who were in the thick of the nightmare from decades past who were still living in Rardell to that day. Even the mere mention of another being such as then being back in the city could cause an uproar. Not to mention what would happen if they found out the source of the information. Thimble gave Samara a sharp nod. "You have it."

Samara gave a short sigh. "Good. Now, I think finding the girl should remain your priority, and you are welcome to try with Carrom, but–"

A sharp knock on the door cut into her words.

"Yes?" Samara called toward the door.

A young woman's voice drifted through the door, sweet and light. "Inquisitor Sheraz, High Inquisitor. Urgent request for you, ma'am."

"Enter," Samara commanded.

The door swung wide and a slip of a girl, about the same age as Odion walked through. Her hair fell in messy brown curls below her shoulders, framing a pleasantly rounded face and round brown eyes. Her silver armor gleamed with new polish, though nicks and dents were plainly visible here and there. Her blue cloak flapping about her calves showed wear and light singeing despite its tidy sheen. Unassuming to the eye, Thimble noted, but someone only a fool would disregard.

"High Inquisitor," she said from the doorframe. "Your presence has been requested urgently at..." she trailed off as her eyes found Thimble.

Samara looked at the young woman expectantly. "Well? Out with it Inquisitor."

"Um...citizen ma'am."

Samara blinked at Thimble, appearing almost dazed. "Right. Thank you,

Celia," she rubbed her eyes, "rest doesn't come easy these days. Thimble, Odion, if there's nothing else, please excuse us."

"Uh, sure," Thimble slid out of his seat and followed Odion into the hall outside of the High Inquisitor's office.

"Well," Odion said, shutting the door behind himself. "Where to first?"

Thimble didn't have a chance to respond. The door to Samara's office slammed open, barely missing Odion on the way. Samara strode out of her office with Inquisitor Sheraz in tow. "You two!" she barked over her shoulder. "With me!"

Thimble and Odion traded startled glances before hurrying behind the departing pair.

"Celia," Odion said to Inquisitor Sheraz. "What's going on?"

Celia turned disturbed eyes toward him. "That...*thing*...in the de Evoire estate. It's gone."

* * *

Less than an hour later, Thimble stood in the living room of the de Evoire estate once more. A place he was sure he would have nightmares about for a while to come. This time, he stood amidst a gaggle of Anvil paladins. Samara was present, of course, as were Celia and Odion. Kerrak and Garrett stood off to one side, accompanied by Thelia, Scar, and four others Thimble didn't recognize. All gathered stared toward the hearth.

Or, what they could see of it. The Time Anchor no longer stood barely visible on the fringes of sight. The crate-like space appeared to be filled with a muddy swirling mass of golden light, some bits darker, others lighter. Thimble thought it looked quite a lot like a vial of *Nura Amon*, or "bottled sunlight". The portrait was barely visible above the mass, but enough showed to reveal the absence of one grotesque corpse.

"Who was on watch?" Samara's quiet question tightened every spine in the room. Glances passed between the Blue Cloaks, but all remained silent.

Samara turned on her heel and surveyed her men and women with thunder in her eyes. "I will not ask again."

A wispy young man, still carrying spot scars on his face, peeked out from around Kerrak. "High Inquisitor...I-It was me."

Samara's glare paled the young Warden. She shot a glance over her shoulder toward the hearth. "Explain."

The Warden gulped. "I-I don't know what happened. When I switched off with Warden Gimaran," he motioned to a raven haired, dark-skinned young woman leaning against the wall beside Garrett, "she came inside and saw..." he trailed off, waving toward the Time Anchor.

"At the end of your watch, Ribal?" Samara snapped. "Why not sooner?"

Ribal winced. "I take my watches o-outside, ma'am. I...didn't like being in here with that *thing*."

Samara raked disbelieving eyes over the others. "How long has this been going on?"

Warden Gimaran stepped forward. Her shoulders drooped, her hands wrung together, but a glint of acceptance shone in her eyes. "Since the beginning, High Inquisitor. The blame lies with me as it was my suggestion to begin with. Alera and I agreed to it as a trade off if Ribal took longer shifts."

Thelia snorted, a disgusted snarl on her face. The others shuffled nervously as Samara swelled. "Is this a joke to you?" she said, looking to the guilty Wardens in turn.

"No ma'am," the pair intoned together.

"Do you see your orders as suggestions?"

"No ma'am."

"Do you know what would happen if this got out to the public?"

"It's a little late–" Warden Gimaran started, but was forestalled by Kerrak's heavy mitt on her shoulder.

Samara sighed, rubbing her temples with a hand. "You're both suspended," she said. "Stenzil, Hamann," she addressed the other two Wardens Thimble didn't recognize. "Take them back to headquarters. Get their reports, the full *truth*. This doesn't leave this room, understood?" she said the last to the room at large.

"Yes, ma'am."

"Yes, High Inquisitor."

"Mayane, Viros," she continued. "Find Alera. Let's hear why *she* didn't notice a missing monstrosity."

Thelia and Scar saluted and, with Thelia giving Thimble a departing acidic glare, followed the others out.

"What a mess," Samara sighed. "Kerrak I assume you're holding the connection maintaining this spell?"

"Yes, ma'am," Kerrak answered.

"I don't understand it." Samara shook her head. "Assuming they didn't shirk *all* of their duties, the connection would have passed from Ella to Alera, then to Ribal and back to Ella. That has been the rotation correct?" she put to Garrett.

"Correct, High Inquisitor," Garrett confirmed.

"Then, if we assume it was never broken, then someone would have had to come in here and take the body while Ribal was on duty *and* get away unnoticed."

"Impossible," Garrett shook his head. "No one can survive entering a Time Anchor."

"Mm," Samara rubbed at her chin. "What if the connection was interrupted..."

Thimble let the Blue Cloaks' voices fade into the background. With the room less crowded, he made his way toward the suspended spell, hoping to get a closer view. The light swirled molasses-like and an occasional shape would appear here or there that seemed familiar before fading. Thimble approached the left lower corner and crouched, lowering his diminutive form even more for a closer look. The muddied light was less present in the corners and edges, though some did stray. He poked his head around the side of the Time Anchor to get a different angle and looked up.

His blood ran cold. Gaunt and stretched, Annabelle de Evoire's decaying golden face wailed silently at him. "*OH HELLS-!*" Thimble skittered back on his bottom and pressed himself into the side of a sofa, heart hammering in his temples.

The remaining Anvil members whipped around. "Thimble? What's the matter?" Odion said. He heard swords returning to scabbards as Odion poked his head around the sofa. "You alright?"

Thimble lifted a shaky finger. "From there. Look up and right."

Odion raised a skeptical brow and bent down where Thimble had been. Thimble watched the young Warden tilt his head up, right, and freeze. "Um... you better come see this, High Inquisitor."

One by one, the others came up to catch a glimpse of what the little Gnome had seen. Each backed away with ghastly expressions. Kerrak went last. He leaned down like the rest. "I don't see anything," he said.

"Try again," Thimble said. "Up and right."

Kerrak squinted, moving his eyes as instructed. He shook his head after a minute. "Nothing."

Thimble sprang to his feet. His terror subsiding, he brushed past Kerrak and crouched to get another glimpse of the face. Except, it was nowhere to be seen.

A thought struck him. "Can I borrow a sword?"

Samara looked baffled. "A sword? Whatever for?"

"I just have to test something. Need something sturdy. Anyone?" he said looking around.

Odion drew his longsword. Taking the blade by the tip, he extended the handle toward Thimble. "Here."

Thimble stared at five feet of solid steel. "Hm. Maybe something smaller?"

Samara rolled her eyes and drew a short dagger from a sheath on her belt as Odion returned his blade to its resting place with a smirk. "Will this suffice?"

"Yes, thank you," Thimble took the dagger by the handle, its point easily cleared the top of his head by a hand. He headed to a corner where the light soup wasn't so strong and stuck the blade into the side of the Time Anchor.

Or. He tried to. The moment the blade tip passed the spell's barrier it came to an almost dead stop. Thimble pushed and wiggled the handle, yet the blade only ever inched forward miniscule bit by miniscule bit.

"*What* are you doing?" Garrett said. "I've told you what happens to objects in a Time Anchor."

"I know, I know," Thimble said. "Just give it a second...or maybe a bit more."

Eventually, the dagger submerged to the hilt, at which point Thimble began to pull. After what felt like an eternity, the dagger stopped, then reversed course. As it went, the dagger left a golden cloudy trail in the rough shape of itself behind.

Thimble left the dagger to finish coming out on its own and paced over to the increasingly impatient Blue Cloaks. As the dagger clattered to the ground, its ghostly outline began to fade as slow as it had appeared. He ran a hand through his hair, trying to stay calm. "We can't see the face from there anymore because it moved."

"What?" Samara said. "What do you mean *moved?*"

"I think the body left *on its own.*"

Chapter Thirteen

Returning Dread

"That's impossible," Garrett shook his head.

"Is it?" Thimble said. He pointed to the space the dagger had occupied. "You told me that the spell brings all objects within to a near complete stop, right? *Near?*"

"Well...yes, but," Garrett said, looking uncomfortable.

"Look at the dagger. At the trail it left behind!" Thimble could hardly contain his sudden excitement. "Every moment of where the dagger was at that point in time, within the Time Anchor, was captured like an image. A trace of what used to be there. I bet, if we tried, we could find Lady Annabeth's face again from some odd angle."

"What are you saying, Thimble?" Odion furrowed his brow.

"I'm saying," Thimble took a deep breath. Horror and excitement quickened his pulse. "If it's true that no living thing can pass through a Time Anchor, which I have no reason to doubt," he nodded toward Garrett, "*and* the link was never severed, then that leaves only two options: either something *not* alive pulled the body out of there *or* the body left on its own. Either way, I think we're dealing with—"

"Necromancy," Samara finished for him. "Oh gods." She fell back onto a chair and buried her face in her hands. Thimble watched as Kerrak closed the door to the room and placed himself in front of it. Odion and Garrett each moved to stand in front of the window looking into the room, blocking any view even without drawn curtains.

The room fell silent. The Blue Cloaks stared at the ground, each lost in his or her own thoughts. Thimble fell into his own. *Necromancy?* The thought chilled his spine. Things kept getting more and more out of his depth by the hour. He was hired to find a missing girl wasn't he? Now there were necromancers and sorcerers and gods knew what else involved? Thimble shook his head. They wouldn't begrudge him bowing out would they? Surely they would understand his position.

"Right," Samara rose to her feet, composed once more. Jaw set in grim determination. "Apologies, all. And thank you for your understanding." The Blue Cloaks each gave a respectful half bow. "Now, Kerrak," she turned toward the wolf man. "Do you have a scent?"

Kerrak gave a sharp nod. "Yes, High Inquisitor."

"Good. Find it."

Kerrak saluted and hustled from the room.

"Garrett," Samara continued. "Spread the word, we are looking for a man in his middle years, light long hair, old dark robe with a high leaf point collar. Anyone matches that description, the smallest amount, bring them in. I don't care what their station is or what power they may hold in the city, if they match, bring them in, understood?"

Garrett saluted. "Yes, ma'am."

"And there's no need to mention the possibility of a necromancer to anyone," she shot a glance at Thimble. "While Thimble's assessment is... disturbing, I do not want to cause a panic before we're certain. Once the description is out, find Warden Thelia and assist with the interrogation of the three on watch. I loath to think there might be a turncoat among us, but we *must* be sure, understood? Go."

Garrett gave short bows and followed Kerrak into the city.

Samara let out a long sigh as she, Thimble, Odion, and Celia were left alone. She turned toward Thimble with an odd expression. "I...I have to apologize, Thimble. I wasn't expecting things to develop in such a way. I will not ask you to continue any longer given the potential danger, but given how much you know and how much you've helped in this short time...I would appreciate it if you did."

This was it. His chance to walk away, freely offered. *Take it, Thimble,* he told himself. *Hawthorne's still in port. Take it and go.* But...after what Grampa Sibs told him, despite not having known his grandmother, this was personal. *She's family.* No, he would see this out. And if anything, seeing Samara in her moment of pause toughened his resolve.

Thimble shrugged. "In for a piece," he grinned. "And I remember being promised quite a few."

Samara snorted. "And then some. Right, I believe you and Odion should continue your search for the girl and this unknown man."

"We don't have any more leads, ma'am," Odion said. "Other than Carrom, which...who knows how that's going to go. Where would we even start?"

"Um..." a memory struck Thimble.

Samara raised an eyebrow. "Yes, Thimble? Do you have something?"

"I might. I have a question. Has Ema ever said anything different? In the dream?"

Odion shook his head.

"I don't believe so," Samara said. "Why?"

"She said something different last night," Thimble said.

"You're telling us this *now*?" Samara said.

Thimble held his hands up. "Hey, it's been a bit *eventful* lately in case you haven't noticed."

"What," Odion jumped in before Samara could retort, "did she say, Thimble?"

"Under," Thimble rubbed his chin. "She just kept saying 'under'."

"Under?" Samara asked. "Under what?"

"That's what I asked, but it ended there."

"Under the city maybe?" Odion supplied. "Topside?"

Samara shrugged. "It could be, or—"

"Ma'am," Celia interrupted. She had silently listened to the goings on with keen attention.

Samara turned to her. "Celia?"

"Apologies for interrupting ma'am, but there was something else I was asked to report," she cleared her throat. "The Readers have an answer for... that other matter." Thimble saw her shoot another sidelong glance at him.

Samara followed her glance. "I appreciate the discretion, Inquisitor, but I think the time's past by this point. He might as well be one of us. Report."

Celia nodded. She pulled a slip of paper from a pouch on her hip. "There were only two items taken from the archive, two tomes to be specific: The Unabridged History of Rardell by Joza Butland and Forbidden Magics of the Early Ninth Century by Clara Eddith."

Samara pondered for a moment. "Thimble, Odion, thoughts?"

"What's this about?" Thimble asked. *Forbidden Magics?* That's *not foreboding at all.*

"There was a break-in at the Reader's Archive about three weeks before your arrival," Samara answered. "It's taken a while, but the Readers have apparently realized what is missing."

"Three weeks. Almost a month. What a coincidence," Thimble said. "Do you think it might be related to," he gestured around to the surroundings, "all this?"

Samara shrugged. "Too early to tell. Odion?"

Odion stood smoothing his moustache. "Are there any copies of these tomes at the Archives?" he asked Celia.

Celia shook her head. "These volumes are not accessible to the public. They are unique for the sake of security."

"Really?" Thimble said, bemused. "A history book?"

"Joza Butland was an...interesting man," Samara said. "His opinions colored much of what he wrote and were not all too flattering most of the time. The council – the Old Families really – had the book banned for...various reasons."

"Ah, I see," Thimble said. "Politics. Of course."

"Is there," Odion paused, chewing his words. "Is there a chance the Forbidden Magics tome has mentions of necromancy?"

Samara sighed. That was the thought they had all been afraid to voice. "I'd say it's all but guaranteed, Warden. Celia. Are the Readers preparing a Ritual of Recall?"

"Yes, ma'am," Celia answered. "They should be ready within the hour."

Samara nodded. "You three, make your way to the Archive. See what you can glean from the Recall."

"Not coming with?" Thimble asked.

Samara smiled. "Nature of my position, I'm afraid. I must report to the other heads of the Anvil and there's likely a stack of papers waiting on my desk by now. But, keep me apprised of all you learn."

Chapter Fourteen

Carrom

Thimble and Odion split from Celia, agreeing to meet near the Reader's Archive after a quick detour. Odion led the way west of the crossroads, in the opposite direction from the manors of the Old Families. Thimble remembered seeing this part of the city on his first day, but had not been afforded a closer view.

The homes here were built of old wood and piled atop one another in haphazard and lopsided structures that stood tall against expectation. Thimble watched a family of six file out of one of the smaller structures; not ragged, not emaciated, but not happy.

"Here too, huh?" Thimble said, more to himself.

Odion followed his gaze and his own eyes softened. "It may be upside down, but it's still a city like any other."

"Same where you're from then?"

"I'd like to say we're different but...I never really knew enough to notice. No city's perfect, I imagine."

"Hmm."

The pair wound through cramped streets for almost an hour until, at last, the tight quarters eased and the street widened on either side. Though, as Thimble peered further down the street for a hint of their destination, the buildings appeared to close ranks once more a mere hundred yards or so down.

Odion stopped just before the center of this widened street. "This is it."

Thimble glanced around at the rundown domiciles around. "This is it? He lives in one of these?"

Odion gave him a curious look. "I thought you would have noticed. No," he stuck a finger upwards, "he lives there."

Thimble followed the gesture upward. There, about fifty yards from the ground, hung the top half of a bulb topped tower. A small balcony stuck out of the brass colored bulb where a single sheet of curtain hung from the opening. Thimble peered under the part of the tower where it ceased to exist. A spiral staircase descended into nothing and ascended into blackness, affording the smallest sliver of a view inside. He caught the occasional flash of a clothed person traipsing up and down the stairs.

"So..." he said. "Only half the tower's invisible?"

"That's right," Odion stepped closer to where the base of the tower should have been, eyes cast down on the cobblestone below.

"*Why?*"

"Because Carrom. Now where...ah, here it is," Odion stopped and dusted a particular stone on the path. He turned to face Thimble and raised his right fist to head height. "Here goes." He began jerking his fist left and right, as if shaking an invisible tambourine.

Thimble watched the young Warden for a beat. "Uh...what are you doing?"

"Shh. I need to concentrate."

A woman in her middle years with a gaggle of preteens in tow gave the pair of them appalled looks before scurrying off.

"I'm not with him!" Thimble called after them.

"Very funny–" *thunk.* Odion's fist hit something solid. "Ah, finally." He turned toward the invisible object and knocked with more purpose. "Carrom? Carrom, my name's Odion Grey. I'm with the Anvil." He stopped for a moment, awaiting reply.

Nothing.

"I was hoping you might be able to answer a couple of questions regarding some of the things happening in the city."

Pause. Nothing.

"You don't have to talk with me if you don't want to. I have a guest from abroad here helping with the investigation. His name is Thimble Pennywhistle. You can speak to him instead."

Pause. Nothing.

"I'm a Gnome!" Thimble shouted toward the balcony.

Odion spread his arms by his side. "Really?"

Thimble shrugged. "Worth a shot. Everyone else seems all hot and bothered about it."

Pop.

Between one blink and the next, Thimble stood in a cozy little kitchen with a wood stove tucked into a corner on his right and a round table squat in the middle flanked by two rickety wooden chairs. *What just happened?*

"Thimble!" Thimble heard Odion's voice carry behind him. He turned and found himself standing just beyond the balcony he'd spied earlier.

"Thimble!"

"Up here!" Thimble stepped out onto the balcony.

Odion backed up until the balcony came into view. "What? How'd you get up there?"

"I don't know. And it wasn't me this time."

"Huh. I guess it worked then. Well, best of luck. Don't be too long, they're waiting at the Archive." He stepped off the street and plonked himself down on a short bench outside a shack.

"Sure, thanks," Thimble muttered to himself, turning back into the tower. "Just teleported into some loony wizard's tower against my will, nothing odd about tha–Hello."

A man sat in one of the chairs facing the balcony. Reed thin, wild mane of a grey beard, and swaddled in a blue robe many times thicker than himself, the old man watched him through crystal green eyes, a small smile shifting his moustache to a side.

"Good morning!" the old man said brightly.

"M-morning..." Thimble pondered the likelihood of Odion catching him if he leapt off the balcony.

"Would you like some tea?" The old man's voice was thin and scratchy, yet musical.

"Uh. Sure."

"Excellent!" the old man dove from his chair and headlong into one of the cupboards beside his stove. Clanging of pots and plates and all manner of sounds echoed from the small space unlikely to hold as much. "Where is it, where is it?"

Thimble took a closer look at his surroundings. The space felt close, tightly packed, but there seemed to be more than enough room to move about. At least for someone his size, and the old man was only two feet taller than him at most. A strange assortment of decorations hung about the curving walls of the tower. A tall mirror hung near the ceiling, its bottom nowhere near low enough for either one of them to use. Further along the wall, a curving bookshelf sat empty and pristine, not a speck of dust in sight. A cloak hung from a corner of the bookshelf. A cloak made of long quill-like feathers beginning in a brilliant blue near the top and fading through the colors of winter and autumn before ending a dark reddish black near the bottom. The cloak shimmered in the noonday light filtering through the open balcony. Thimble reached out a hand to touch the brilliant surface. It called to him. It longed for him. He knew.

"Ah! Here we are."

Thimble snapped his hand away and stepped further from the cloak. The urge to touch it vanished as soon as he moved his eyes from it. *What in the world?*

The old man withdrew his upper half from the cupboard with a folded tablecloth in his arms. With a deft flick of his wrists, he spread the cloth over the table.

Whether painted or stitched, the design on the tablecloth was striking and clear. A tea set, complete with steaming kettle and assorted nibbles lay arranged in their flat plane.

Blink.

The scent of a freshly poured cup caught Thimble before the sight of the tea set, now fully realized, could register.

The old man lowered himself onto one of the chairs and poured two cups, shifting one to the other side of the table. "Sit, sit!"

Thimble hopped onto the chair and found himself within easy reach of the cup and at an eyeline with his host. *Focus, Thimble,* he chided himself. The absurdity and odd reality of the past few moments had thrown him for a loop. *You're here for a reason.* "Um," Thimble waited for the old man to take a sip before doing so himself. "Are you Carrom?"

"I am! For now, at least. And for a while, now that I think about it," Carrom said.

"Why did you let me in?"

"Well, you said you were a Gnome. I wanted to see if that was true, as I hadn't seen a Gnome in a while. And now I have! Fine day so far," he took a long pull from his cup.

Thimble sipped his own tea. A pleasant floral sweetness graced his tongue and warmed him to his toes. "Oh, that's lovely."

"Right?" Carrom grinned. "Would you believe it's just like that every single time?"

Belief went out the window a while ago. "The High Inquisitor mentioned you're a wizard or sorcerer of some sort?"

Carrom slurped from his cup. "Ah, what's one got over the other? Time, that's what. Sorcerer, eh? Not much foresight in these eyes, let me tell you. Wizard maybe, but I wouldn't go calling me a wise bastard. Ha!"

"Um..."

"High Inquisitor? Do you need to be up a pole to ask questions?" He smacked himself on the forehead. "Ah! You mean that young upstart. Slashy, stabby, screamy that one. Leave well enough alone I said. Run while you can, but did they listen? Did they?"

Carrom's eyes bored into Thimble's. "Uh...n-no?"

"No! And look where it got them. Won? Maybe. Dead? Definitely. But *why?* Just pack up and leave! I did. Well, kind of."

I think I see why Samara was hesitant about him. "Carrom," he said. "Is it alright if I ask you a few questions?"

"Already asked some. Ask more."

"Are you aware of what's been happening in the city?"

"Hmm," Carrom squinted into the distance. "I think there's a shipment of gibbler pike coming in today. I hope I can have a few brought up."

"No, I mean what's happening with these dreams. About the girl?"

"Bah," Carrom snatched a biscuit from a little plate beside his cup. "The dreams. I told those squire kids I don't get dreams about some girl. And it's not me doing it either!" The biscuit snapped as he took a hefty bite.

"Wait, you don't have the dream?" Thimble asked, leaning forward. "Why?"

Carrom shrugged. "I sleep downstairs."

"What does that have to do with it?"

Carrom shifted. It wasn't motion, not really. But something changed in the little old man's demeanor in an instant. Sharp green eyes locked onto Thimble and his smile diminished the slightest amount. "I think it's time to ask the proper questions, Mister Pennywhistle."

"Proper? What—" Carrom tilted his head a miniscule amount.

Blink.

Thimble stood on the street outside beside Odion.

Blink.

Thimble sat in the seat across from Carrom once more.

Oh. Ask the right questions or you're out. Understood. Thimble sat thinking for a long moment. Carrom didn't seem to mind. He hummed quietly to himself, eyes in the distance.

No questions about the dream. No questions about the girl. Maybe, "Do you know who killed the de Evoire family?"

"No."

Thimble bounced his knee for a moment. "Why is only half your tower invisible?"

A broad grin split Carrom's face. "Ha! *That's* a good question." He took another swig from his cup. "Let me ask you this. Why do *you* think half of the tower is invisible?"

"B—because I can't see it?" Thimble answered, feeling silly.

Carrom nodded. "A fair point. But, if it were just invisible, why couldn't your friend touch it at first?"

Thimble remembered Odion's odd dance before he was able to knock on the tower. "Because...because it wasn't there? At first."

Carrom nodded, impressed. "Bright one aren't you? Correct. For the most part. It's both there and not there at the same time. In here, it's here. Out there, it's not here, until it is, and still not completely. Make sense?"

"No," Thimble rubbed at a growing templeache. "So, where is it when it's not here?"

Carrom buttered a chunk of bread. "Where it's supposed to be, I imagine. On the eastern slope of Bren'al if my aim was right. And in between at the same time."

"Aim? Were you trying to move the tower?"

"Thrying," Carrom said through a mouthful of bread. "And failing."

"Samara mentioned you haven't left your tower in a long time. Does that have something to do with it?"

Carrom nodded. "Something like that. I believe - and I could be wrong, but the consequences of finding out are *not* great - that my proximity to the point of separation and my intimate knowledge of the tower is what's keeping it lost between both locations. In short, I leave, the bottom half goes completely. Big mess."

"So...let me get this straight," Thimble rubbed his palms against the sides of his head. "You don't get the dreams because you sleep downstairs. Downstairs is *not here*, it's on a mountain somewhere. Unless someone wants it here? Like Odion. And then it comes, but not completely?"

Carrom snapped his fingers. "Got it in one."

"But isn't that...I don't know, dangerous?"

"Why?"

"What if someone's standing right below when the bottom half gets called back?"

"Oh," Carrom nodded sagely. "That would be bad. Interesting though. Can't imagine what would happen. Well...I *can*, but the word *splat* doesn't sound descriptive enough."

Thimble spread his arms, flabbergasted. "Carrom, you live in a crowded part of town. What if some child gets squashed?"

"Bah," Carrom bit into another biscuit. "Not a problem in seven decades, boy. Won't start now."

Thimble threw up his arms. "How do you know?"

"Because most don't care, and of those who do, most don't have what it takes. And of *those* who do, most know better.

"Focus and intent!" Carrom said, loudly. "Sound familiar?"

Thimble remembered similar words his father said to him in a distant lesson. "Focus and intent. The basis for any spellcasting."

"Correct. Tough to master, eh? It's the reason most people can't shit lightning on command. Who's got the time? Anyway, same to bring my tower back. Same to cast a spell. Focus and intent. Bigger the spell, the longer the spell, the more you need."

Thimble sighed, head pounding, and sipped his still hot tea. "Why do I feel like I'm missing something?" he muttered to himself.

Carrom folded his hands and leaned forward. "Maybe you are, maybe not. You've kept up well enough so far. Learned anything?"

Thimble sat back and crossed his arms. There had to be *some* sense in all the madness, right? There's always a reason no matter the result, as he'd learned early in his line of work. *Sort it out, Thimble. Like always. One piece at a time.* "You don't get the dreams because you sleep downstairs which is not here. Then whatever is causing the dreams has a limited range. Probably fine to assume it's just this city?"

Carrom shrugged. "Probably."

"And it's been happening every night for a month. Affecting every adult mind that spends even a night here. Including every visitor on every ship that docks or every cart and wagon that rolls in from topside." Thimble looked up at Carrom who watched him like a hawk. "The bigger the spell, the longer the spell, the more you need." *Focus and intent.* Thimble shook his head. "No one can do that. That kind of power is...immense. *Ungodly.*"

"Well," Carrom stood and began gathering the tablecloth, the tea set returned back to its stoic state at a blink. "That was a fun diversion, don't you think so?"

Thimble hopped down from his seat. "Wait! That's it? Can't you help in some way?"

"No," Carrom hurled the tablecloth back into a drawer. "But," he turned back to stand in front of Thimble. "How about a fun trick before you leave? Or a quick lesson? Or both!"

"Um?"

Carrom held both of his hands in front of him, wrapping his fingers closed. "Ready? And...*look!*" he thrust his left hand out to the side and opened his fingers wide.

Thimble followed the snap of movement, to his right, expecting to see a flash of light or a random canary or something else wizardy, and found a plain old empty hand.

Crack!

Carrom's other hand connected flush with Thimble's left ear. Not enough to stagger him, but enough to leave a hot ringing for a while. "*Argh!* What the f–"

Pop.

Chapter Fifteen

Recall

The short glimpse Thimble had of the Archive the day before didn't do justice to the sheer size of the place. Steps a hundred paces across at least rose to a marble columned entrance centered by a massive golden set of double doors. Purple and black robed men and women flowed in and out of the Archive in droves. Some carried tomes and scrolls, a few heaved a hefty metal box that rattled on occasion, and a few even carried cages with odd little animals Thimble had never seen before. He was met with more curious glances here than heated ones, which was a nice change of pace.

"So, Carrom wasn't any help, huh?" Celia asked Thimble.

Thimble shook his head, ear still red from Carrom's goodbye. "I can't tell if he *was* trying to help. I'll think through that mess later."

Random Archive members called out and waved to Celia as the trio ascended the steps. "You're quite popular here, eh?" Thimble asked.

Celia shrugged. "I suppose. I spent a few years here during my time as an Initiate. Got to know a lot of people."

"Can you do whatever you want as an Initiate?"

Odion chimed in. "Not really. You get assigned to someone when you become an Initiate. Who that is determines what you'll be doing for your time. I was assigned to Warden Lomar, for example. He's in charge of all Anvil city patrols and general guard duty."

Celia winced and grinned. "Oof. Lomar? Did you manage to keep awake on duty?"

Odion's ears colored. "Mostly."

"What about you, Celia?" Thimble asked.

"Reader Brandt," she said. "He's been an archivist here for almost forty years. I shouldn't tease really, there were times I thought I'd pass on from boredom here, but he taught me a lot. Speaking of..."

The three arrived at the doors just behind the group with the box and found an older man waiting for them. His purple and black robes hung loosely on a tall frame and a white sash lay draped around his neck. A slate gray fringe peppered the sides of his head and a sparse beard framed a pointed chin.

"Ah, Celia, perfect timing, dear girl," he said, scratchy voice softened by a kind smile.

"Reader Brandt," Celia returned his smile. She gestured toward her companions. "These are Warden Odion Grey and Thimble Pennywhistle. They are to participate in the Recall as well per the High Inquisitor."

Reader Brandt scanned over Odion, then Thimble, lingering slightly longer on the latter. Again, Thimble gleaned little more than curiosity in the gaze. "Hm. Very well, very well," he turned toward the doors. "Come quickly, the Recallers are finishing their preparations now. Budge up there young'uns!" Reader Brandt bustled past the group carrying the box.

Thimble, Celia, and Odion squeezed past with apologetic smiles. Thimble felt his jaw slacken as the Archive opened up in front of him. Hundreds of feet across and many times deep, the Archive gave the impression of a small city. Massive shelves rose along the walls in columns and rows to wooden walkways a floor above where even more shelves peeked over rounded banisters. A quick glimpse beyond showed yet more floors of the same reaching up and out of sight. Oddities of all shapes and sizes accompanied innumerable books and scrolls on the shelves. Men and women of the Archive bustled about chatting in excited mutters. Thimble was surprised to see a fair number of people who seemed like ordinary citizens and even a small group of children walked about awestruck led by a chaperone.

"Thimble!" he heard Odion call. He searched around for his companions and found them heading toward a staircase near the middle of the hall where the center mirrored the floors above. Odion waved him over.

Thimble caught the three in short order. "I thought this was a library," he said, a bit breathless.

"It is, mostly," Celia answered. "It's also a vault and," she nodded toward an Archive member carrying a tall cage with an odd multicolored bird with too large eyes, "a bit of a preserve."

"Incredible," Thimble and the others followed Reader Brandt to a stairway set into the edge of the central opening. The group flowed down the first level, then the second, and finally a third before turning into a short hallway. Two blue cloaked guards stood at the end of the hallway flanking a heavy iron door. A dull orange-yellow glow seeped through the crack at the bottom of the door.

"They've started," Reader Brandt quickened his steps. The others followed suit, Thimble moreso.

The group passed through the door and let it shut behind them with a heavy thud. They stood in a small room reminiscent of an office, though rather than desks and shelves, stone tables and little bits of glass and metal equipment littered the space. The center of the room had been cleared, tables and chairs pushed to the sides and a runic circle glowed brightly on the floor. Three separate circles surrounded the center on the north, east, and west sides. Each outer circle was occupied by an Archive member, seated legs crossed and eyes closed.

To the west sat a woman in her later years. Long white hair framed a lined face and a short stubbed chin. To the east was a man of similar age. His grey hair was pulled back in a loose ponytail that draped over his right shoulder. Severe eyebrows frowned over his shut eyes as his brow furrowed in concentration. To the north sat a man younger than the other two. His dark hair flowed to his shoulders, white streaks threaded through. A long pointed chin moved in rhythm as he muttered quietly under his breath. All three wore deep blue stoles over their shoulders.

A fourth man, older than all the others, but with a shaved head and a strong jawline, stood off to one side, surveying the circle with a keen eye. He turned toward the newcomers as they entered. "Brandt," his voice set the water in Thimble's stomach to a rumble. "We are ready. Inquisitor, Warden," he inclined his head toward Celia and Odion, who responded in kind. "Honored guest," to Thimble's surprise, the old Archivist bent a short bow toward him as well.

"Um," Thimble stuttered. "Hello."

Reader Brandt greeted the old man with a smile. "Wardens, Mister Pennywhistle, this is Recaller Guimar, our most senior Recaller. That," he motioned to the woman at the west, "is Recaller Milas. There," he gestured to the man at the east, "is Recaller Kalvios. And finally," he gestured to the man at the north, "Recaller Vorst. They will be assisting with the Recall."

"Um, sorry," Thimble raised his hand. "What is this Recall you keep mentioning?"

Reader Guimar motioned them to stand at the southern end of the circle and moved into the center himself. Gathering his robes about him, he sank to the floor with his compatriots facing the south. "The Recall is an old ritual that allows us to remember, with perfect clarity, any tome, scroll, or book we've read. It comes in quite useful if something has been lost as in this case."

"Wow," Thimble said, impressed. "That's brilliant." Thimble's curiosity when it came to magic knew little bounds. Here, in the presence of new magic, his skin tingled with excited anticipation.

"Let's get started," Recaller Guimar settled into place and closed his eyes.

Reader Brandt shuffled about placing each of Thimble, Odion, and Celia in a line in front of the others. "When it begins," he said, pulling Thimble between Celia and Odion. "Ask questions related to the topic you require. Address Recaller Guimar directly. If you need to ask another question or are finished listening about something, interrupt by saying 'thank you, Recaller.' Any questions?"

The trio shook their heads.

Reader Brnadt nodded. "Very well. Any minute now." He retreated into the shadows as the glow from the runic circle grew steadily brighter.

Thimble felt the slightest tremor begin beneath his feet as the room was bathed in a bright blue light. An unseen wind whipped around the Recallers sending their stoles and robes fluttering in the draft. Thimble watched as new runes flowed from the disparate circles and joined the one in the center. The wind died away and the blue glow of the runes on the floor dimmed. As one, the Recallers opened their eyes, crackling with a brighter incandescent blue of the runes.

"Go on," Reader Brandt whispered from his corner.

Thimble, stunned by the display, had forgotten to think of any questions. To his relief, Celia had not. "Is there a mention of necromancy in the Eddith text?"

The Recallers answered as one. "*Yes,*" Their voices mingled and thrummed with an energy that made the hair on the back of Thimble's neck stand at attention.

"Could you repeat the entry from the beginning, please?" Celia asked.

"*Necromancy is an abhorrent art banned by the Concord of Diorn in the seventh century in the early inception of the Reiksall Dominion. The practice, while in its earliest stages, was used by practitioners as a means of discovering the mechanism of death for an individual, or as a way for families to have closure with lost loved ones, whereby the practitioner would breathe life into a corpse for a handful of moments to allow a sharing of final words. The practice evolved in the shadows in this way over time until the late ninth century with the emergence of the Hands of Simolg, a group of practitioners who had mastered the ability to control corpses in order to do their bidding. These mindless husks, unable to feel any pain and unburdened by conscience, were used to commit an as of yet unrivaled number of atrocities across Penosia and Lansfal over the course of five years until the Hands of Simolg were finally defeated at–*"

"Thank you, Recaller," Thimble said, causing the Recallers to fall silent at once. Thimble stood taken aback at the sudden change for an instant. "That's not creepy at all. As much as I love hearing endless amounts of history," he said to Celia and Odion, "should we try to narrow down what we're looking for?"

"Do we *know* what we're looking for?" Odion asked.

Thimble thought for a moment. It made little sense not to get to the heart of the matter right away. "Is there anything related specifically to reanimation in the necromancy entry?" he asked the Recallers.

"*Reanimation is one of the more frowned upon aspects of necromancy. In order to perform the ritual outlined below, the practitioner requires an intact cadaver, three vials of fresh mortal blood of different sources(preferably of the same race as the cadaver), and a memento of the deceased.*"

"Thank you, Recaller. Intact cadaver, eh?" Thimble said.

"A bit of a wrinkle in our case," Odion stroked his chin. "Perhaps..." he turned toward the Recallers, "...is there anything about reanimating a cadaver created as an amalgam of corpses?"

The Recallers paused for a moment. "*Within the domain of reanimation, there are practices even the most accomplished necromancer will shy away from. A Stitched Cadaver is one of these practices. When a necromancer reanimates a cadaver, they must forcibly subdue a shadow memory of the person's soul that is left at the moment of death, also known as a Soul Imprint. The Soul Imprint remembers, at least in part, the life it used to live and will resist the attempts of the necromancer to bring it into submission. A Stitched Cadaver will carry multiple Soul Imprints. This presents the necromancer with an immense challenge and can cause an arcane rebound of sorts that can severely damage the practitioner's mind. In order to ease the process by an infinitesimal degree, blood from the victims that comprise the pieces of the Stitched Cadaver can and should be used. Despite the risks, this is still only considered the second most vile necromantic practice behind the Soul Shackle.*"

"Thank you, Recaller," Odion said. "That's...worrying."

"Why's that?" Thimble asked.

"Well. It means either the culprit is extremely formidable or insane. Maybe both."

"The High Inquisitor should be notified soon," Celia said. "Should we move onto the next tome?"

Thimble held up a finger. "Hold on. I want to ask something. What is a Soul Shackle?"

"*The Soul Shackle is considered the most appalling of necromantic practices. This particular act takes the departing soul of a recently deceased individual and binds it within its own corpse. This, for reasons unknown, slows the decay of the corpse a great deal. The soul retains consciousness and is aware of actions taken and words spoken by their former body, but is unable to control or influence. There have been accounts of Shackled souls temporarily breaking through the control to speak in their own words, but this is as of yet unconfirmed..."*

"Gods," Thimble rubbed his temples. "I shouldn't have asked."

"...another report claims a Shackled victim screamed for his family to kill him before having his head—"

"THANK you, Recaller," Thimble said, a bit too loud. His fascination from before, replaced with squirming unease. The Recallers fell blessedly silent.

The trio stood quietly for a moment. Each reeling from that bit of information. Finally, Celia cleared her throat. "Should we move on?"

"Yes," Odion nodded. "Let's get this over with."

Celia addressed the Recallers once more. "Are there mentions of necromancy in the volume by Joza Butland?"

"Yes."

"Repeat the passages please."

"One of the more interesting events in the history of Rardell was the emergence and short lived reign of the necromancer Raliak the Shunned."

The Recallers fell silent. Thimble looked around, confused. "What? That's it?"

"It appears so," Celia tilted her head.

"Um. Alright," Thimble rubbed his brow. "Is there any reason to know more about this Raliak?"

Odion shrugged. "It's not exactly secret knowledge, but I guess it couldn't hurt."

"What can you tell us about Raliak the Shunned?" Thimble asked.

"Raliak the Shunned began life as Raliak Saltanis, a member of the Old Family Saltanis. At the age of fifteen Raliak was betrothed to Lady Secila Lamrose. The pair would later wed on Raliak's eighteenth birthday. Two years after the marriage, Raliak was unexpectedly banished from the Saltanis family and exiled from Rardell, bid never to return on threat of immediate execution. There are many theories as to the reason behind the banishment, the most popular being his supposed

involvement with the mysterious death of Lady Secila shortly beforehand, though this remains unfounded to this day.

Raliak returned to Rardell two decades later in the company of mercenaries known as the Broken Hamlet. Horribly disfigured, 'as if he used a campfire as a pillow', as one account colorfully put, Raliak was near unrecognizable since his departure. An altercation ensued between the guard and the company under the cover of which Raliak approached his family mausoleum. Raliak then proceeded to resurrect – in a necromantic sense – not only his late wife, but twenty generations of Saltanis deceased before laying siege to the city. Days of fighting consumed the city where the number of dead and the dead rose as one until a ragged but fortunate band of adventurers finally put an end to Raliak and his hordes.

As the city underwent efforts to rebuild, the Saltanis family quarreled over blame in regards to Raliak and his crimes. In time, the shame of one of their own committing such abhorrent crimes and bringing disrepute to the family name became too much of a burden, causing the Saltanis family to fracture. A majority of the family departed Rardell, now traveling under the surname Tolver, while the ones who remained took the name de Evoire."

"What in the hells," Thimble said, breathless, as the Recallers fell silent once more. "Did you know about this?"

"No, of course not," Odion looked almost as flustered as him. "Celia?"

Celia shook her head. "Nothing in the old records mentions this connection. Reader Brandt?"

The Reader stepped out from the corner, a somber frown in place. "There are few alive who remember that time."

"Shit," Thimble ran a hand through his hair. "I guess we know why this book was banned now. At least, *one* of the reasons. Who knows what else might be in this?"

"Wait," Odion rubbed his brow. "How does any of this help our current situation? Sure, there may be some necromantic things going on and it happens to involve an old necromancer's descendants, but Raliak has been dead for seventy years. How is it relevant to what's happening now?"

"What do you mean?" Thimble gave Odion a bemused look. "I'd say a necromancer's descendants being murdered, then turned into a walking nightmare sounds pretty relevant to me."

"Why though?" Odion pressed. "And by who? And, more importantly, why take the girl?"

Thimble started to answer, then realized he didn't have one. The list of people who could have done these things was likely short, yet he couldn't bring forth even the first name. It could be a follower, or a long lost descendant, even some sick admirer. Even with everything they now knew, it could still be *anyone.*

Thimble turned to the Recallers, a sudden thought in his mind. "Are there any physical descriptions of Raliak in either tome?"

The Recallers fell silent for a long moment. "*No.*"

"Damn," Thimble muttered under his breath.

"What was that about?" Odion asked.

"Just a thought I had."

"Reader," Celia said. "I think we're done here. We should probably report to the High Inquisitor as soon as possible," she added to Thimble and Odion.

"Very well," Reader Brandt cleared his throat. "Thank you Recallers," he said to the seated. "The Recall may now subside."

Thimble watched as the glow in the Recallers' eyes wavered and flickered before dimming to their usual hues. The seated Recallers let out identical sighs of exhaustion and began picking themselves off the floor. One by one, they filed out of the room. Recaller Guimar trailed behind and stopped by the open door.

"I hope that was satisfactory," he said to the trio. His eyes sagged and a slight slur twisted his words.

"Yes, Recaller," Odion said with a short bow. "Thank you for all of your assistance. And pass on our gratitude to the others as well."

"Mm," Guimar turned and followed the others, stifling a long yawn behind a thick sleeve.

Reader Brandt led the three back above ground and into the main hall of the Archive. The bustle of the residents seemed louder than usual after the long period in relative silence, even though the archive had cleared somewhat in that time.

"I meant to ask," Thimble said, blinking in the renewed late afternoon light. "How did someone manage to break in here anyway?"

"The old fashioned way," Celia answered. "Through one of the windows." She nodded toward the blank window they'd seen before.

"Injured themselves too if I recall," Reader Brandt added.

"I'll bet," Thimble said. "Those are thicker than pig fat, how'd they not bleed to death?"

"Surprisingly, there wasn't much blood. Though, we did find spatters of what looked like brownish water leading down into the vault where the banned tomes are kept."

"Brown...what?" Thimble was denied an answer. As if planned, every blue cloak wearing head in the Archive snapped toward the west.

Thimble bumped into Odion's calf and fell back. "Argh! What the−"

"Shh," Odion held up his hand, face scrunched in concentration.

Thimble traded bewildered looks with Reader Brandt as every other Archive goer glanced around, confused at the sudden shift. It came to him in waves. It was thin at first, barely audible over the quiet whispers. A sound unlike any he'd heard, like a far off conch shell, without the blaring start or the faltering but resonant end.

Odion shot a look toward Celia. "Is that?"

Celia nodded. "Kerrak. Let's go."

Chapter Sixteen

Painted Candles

Thimble followed Odion, Celia, and a gaggle of other Blue Cloaks out of the archive. Before long, the trio were pushing through throngs of people gathered around the central square, all craning and reaching to get a better view at what was happening near the Attrangem. Thimble saw a man lift his young son high over everyone's head.

"Look close, Morey," the father said, his arms trembling from the effort.

"I can't see da, higher!" the boy answered.

Thimble pushed and dodged through the forest of legs, his eyes glued to the swirling blue cloaks trailing from his companions. *Did Kerrak find the body? The...ugh...stitched cadaver?* He didn't know which answer he preferred.

"Is that..."

"...what's it doing here?"

"...right there, just *do* it."

The murmurs reached his ears just as Odion's cloak whipped out of sight. *Damn. Keep moving.* "Excuse me. Pardon..." Thimble squirreled through the crowd, doing his best to avoid the glares and whispers cast down from above. He ducked under a tall man carrying a young girl on his shoulders and had just caught a glimpse of Odion's head in the low light when a blow caught him hard on his side.

"Argh!" Thimble fell to the stone, clutching his groaning ribs as hot needles stabbed a path across his chest. He pushed off the ground only to feel a foot press down on the small of his back. The foot pushed him back into the grime, squeezing the air from his lungs. Panic flooded Thimble as the pressure on his back doubled. His head swam, his lungs heaved from the effort to breathe.

"ARGH!"

The pressure vanished from Thimble's back and he drew a deep hacking breath. He heard a heavy thump behind him and looked back to see a heavy-set man sprawled on his back, a welling cut already swelling on his cheek. He'd just begun to gather himself to his elbows, when he felt himself yanked into the air by his coat.

"Let go!" Thimble flailed, his fists swinging in wild panic.

"Oof. Easy, Thimble. It's me," Odion said. He tucked Thimble under his arm like a particularly heavy wheel of cheese and continued pushing through the crowd.

Shouts of "filthy pint lover!" followed them through the mass, drowned by curious mutterings as they approached closer to the center.

Panic subsiding, Thimble crossed his arms as he hung from the Warden's grip. "I can walk fine, you know," he said. An annoyed flush crept into his ears remembering how relieved he'd been to hear Odion's voice.

"Not through this you can't," Odion replied. The bulk of his armor helped part the crowd easily enough. "We'll be there in a moment."

"What's even happening?" Thimble asked.

"Kerrak found something. Not sure what yet."

"Is it the...you know..."

"Makes sense, but...we'll see."

Small bits of Attrangem glow peeked through the pressed bodies as they approached the edge of the central square. Almost as if emerging from a deep pool, the pair broke through the last of the onlookers into open air. Odion lowered Thimble to the ground just before they passed a group of guards charged with keeping the populace back. Their path was not the only one filled with people, Thimble noted, looking around. For once, almost none of the attention was on him.

Blue Cloaks stood facing away from the center in every street leading to the square, attempting to keep masses of people from pressing any further forward. He spotted the High Inquisitor flanked by Kerrak and Celia standing a few paces from the Attrangem. The three had their heads turned downward toward something near their feet.

Thimble and Odion approached the Inquisitors from behind. "Quite the party, High Inquisi–*GAH*!" Thimble jumped backward.

At the feet of the Blue Cloaks lay the decaying head of Lady Annabeth de Evoire.

"What in the world?" Thimble said, breathless.

"Scent led here," Kerrak said. His fangs glimmered through his grimace. "Felt like I was chasing my tail through half the town."

"But, where's the rest of it?" Thimble asked.

"If we knew that, we wouldn't *be* here, Thimble," Samara's words dripped with frustration. She raised her eyes to the people lining the streets. "Kerrak. Take the guard, clear the streets. Send the gawkers back on their way." She unfastened her cloak and draped the length of heavy cloth over the macabre sight. Kerrak growled under his breath and stepped away toward the ringed Wardens.

"What did you three find?" Samara asked.

Celia brought Samara up to speed on everything the three had learned in the Archive.

"Gods," Samara raised her eyes to the sea above. "This can't be happening again."

"We don't *know* if any of it's connected," Thimble said. "Not really."

Samara shook her head. "Too many things line up for it all to be coincidence. Even the biggest monsters have their followers. And this one's dangerous enough to try toying with us."

"Mister Pennywhistle!" a shout came from across the square. "Out of the way you! Thimble!" Healer Nira came shuffling toward them with a harrowed Garrett following behind.

"Nira?" Thimble said, surprised. The old healer was the last person he expected to see there. Except maybe Gloen. "What are you doing here?"

Samara glowered at the approaching Warden. "Garrett, I specifically ordered this area to remain clear of civilians."

Garrett winced, coming to a halt before them. "Apologies, ma'am, but she's...being difficult."

"Difficult? Ha!" Nira wagged a finger at him. "It is my duty as a healer to give aid to any who require it!" She rounded on Thimble, her expression softening. "Thimble, my dear, are you alright? I saw what happened in the crowd and I was so very worried."

"I'm fine, Nira, it was only–hmph" his teeth clacked shut as she grabbed him by the chin turning his head this way and that.

"At least let me get a look to be sure. That no good oaf Widlug Tchai. I'll give him a piece of my mind next time I see him, don't you worry. I've no small amount of experience with intolerant fools, have I? Seen their like all my life. Kicked my grandfather out of his home, didn't they? For what? Loving his wife? Impudent no good..."

Thimble nudged his chin out of her grasp as her rambling washed over them. "I'm fine Nira. Really."

Nira straightened, concern furrowing her brow. "Well if you're sure, dear. But take this," she pressed a vial of reddish liquid into his hand. "It's a healing draught of my own recipe. It'll take care of any soreness or bruises and the like."

Thimble palmed the vial. "Thank you, Nira. That's very kind of you."

"High Inquisitor, if I may," Celia said, returning them to the matter at hand. "Quite a few people have seen this by now. I don't think it will be possible to keep it quiet for long."

"Which is why we have to end this soon," Samara rubbed tired eyes.

"High Inquisitor!" the call came from their rear.

Thimble looked over his shoulder at an unfamiliar blonde haired Blue Cloak with anxious dark eyes hurrying in their direction. A young woman followed close at his heels. She wore a simple dark green dress and a matching kerchief held back her auburn hair.

Samara looked around, incredulous. "Am I losing my mind? Have you *all* forgotten how to follow orders?"

The blonde newcomer bowed nearly in half. "Terribly sorry, High Inquisitor. But, this young lady, Pris was it? She says she saw who left *it* here."

All eyes snapped to the young woman, who let out a tiny squeak and started wringing her hands.

"Is this true?" Samara asked.

"Y-yes mistress," Pris dipped a small curtsy. "I didn't recognise her, mind, but she were young with hair like mine, see?" she plucked at her auburn waves. "She dropped a parcel or somethin' and picked it back, but left the *thing* there, right?" Her eyes widened, a tremble crept into her voice. "I saw it then, mistress. All wrinkled and quiet shoutin' like. Never been more scared in me life."

"It's alright," Samara placed a gentle hand on her shoulder. "Can you tell me anything else about this girl you saw?"

"W-well, I..." her eyes darted around to all gathered. "She was right mean lookin', mistress. And wore a blue cloak. Like yours, mistress."

The air stilled around the group. Thimble's gaze snapped from one stunned face to the next.

"Mistress? T-that hurts, mistress," the young woman buckled the slightest bit to one side where Samara's hand dug into her shoulder.

Samara released the girl. "A-apologies," she said. "Thank you for the information. You may go."

Pris dipped another curtsy and scurried off, casting frightened eyes back over her shoulder.

"Oh dear," Nira stood eyes wide, a hand over her mouth.

Samara shot her a look and turned toward the blonde Anvilite. "Warden Rossini, correct?"

Rossini stood at full attention. "Yes, ma'am."

"Warden, please escort healer Nira here back to her abode. Immediately."

"Right away, ma'am," Rossini hurries to obey. He took Nira gently by the elbow and turned her away. "Please come with me, healer."

Nira nodded, shock evident on her face, and allowed herself to be led away without another word.

"Garrett," Samara said quietly when the departing pair left earshot. "Did you find Alera?"

Garrett cleared his throat. "No, ma'am. She wasn't at home when we checked and we were in the process of checking headquarters when we heard Kerrak's howl."

Samara ran a hand through her hair. "Celia, Odion. Go to Alera's home. Check again, break in if you have to. I want it searched top to bottom. Garrett. Have the ports and the path above blocked. No one in or out of the city until she's found. I want every available Warden and Inquisitor on the search, understood?"

Garrett gave a short bow and tore off eastward. Odion gave Thimble a nod and followed Celia out of the square.

Thimble watched the High Inquisitor pace for a moment. Her eyes darkened with each passing step. "Samara," he said. "Don't you think it's a bit drastic? Locking down the city?"

Samara shook her head and gave him a stern look. "No more chances, Thimble. Discretion has left us a pace behind and I am *very* tired."

Thimble gulped. The heat in her eyes could cow an ogre at that moment. "Um. What should I do?"

Samara's eyes locked into his, sending a tremble down his spine. She pondered for a long minute. "I need you to go to bed."

"Uh...what?"

"All of the information we've uncovered over the past two days hasn't changed anything. We still don't know who or why. As far as I can tell, the only things that are different now from a month ago are the body being missing and your dream."

"You want me to dream?"

"We both know you're *going* to dream. I want you to tell me if anything changes."

* * *

"Woof. Sounds complicated," Sibelius yanked an onion the size of his head out of the damp earth in his garden.

"You're telling me," Thimble sat on a small bench watching his grandfather work. A cool moisture hung in the air, the lingering touch of an early autumn storm. Memories of an afternoon spent merrily running from his parents in the rain came to mind. He trailed dew drops down sugar cane stalks for a handful of minutes, a bittersweet smile on his lips. "I don't know what to do next, Grampa. I'm no closer to finding the killer, much less where the girl is. Now there's a nightmare of a corpse walking around somewhere and a necromancer's biggest fan making everyone's lives miserable. What do you think I should do?"

Sibelius straightened and wiped his brow. "Honestly, Thimble? I think you should go home."

"What?" Thimble leaned forward, annoyed. "You said I should find the girl!"

"I know, I know," Sibelius dropped the onion into a basket at his feet and removed his gloves. "I may have been a bit...emotional...when we spoke last time. Truly, I want whoever this is to be caught and punished, but not if it puts you in danger, my boy. I've met my share of powerful 'practitioners', let's call them, in my day and they're nothing to be trifled with."

"Great," Thimble slumped back in his seat. "Well, there's not much I can do about it now. There's no way in or out of the city until they find that Warden."

"You think she's involved?" Sibelius returned to his harvest.

Thimble shrugged. "As far as I know, they're *all* involved. Or...maybe none? At least one. Ugh." He buried his face in his hands, unwilling to think any longer.

"Even your friend, Udon, what's his name?"

"Odion? No, I think Odion's a good man. If a bit naive sometimes. It's been a while since someone's felt like a real friend, you know?"

"Mm." Sibelius nodded. "What about the boss?"

Thimble sighed. "I don't know. Samara seems awfully eager to make sure none of what's going on gets out into the public. Losing battle if you ask me."

"Why do you think she's trying so hard?"

"Trying to keep the peace, likely. Whoever this Raliak the Shunned was, it seems like he left a pretty deep scar on the city's memory. Did I tell you?

She's the one who ended him last time."

"No kidding."

"Yeah. Well, her and a handful of her friends. None of her friends survived, though, by the sound of it."

"Interesting." Sibelius mulled a thought. "Have you considered that maybe she's trying to protect a legacy?"

Thimble raised an eyebrow. "What do you mean?"

"Well. Imagine *I* was responsible for putting an end to some villain in the past. An event significant enough to have me heralded as a hero. Now, more than a century later, it's all happening again. Not only that, the same villain's influence is likely involved. So...did I fail? All those years ago?"

"Well," Thimble shuffled in his seat. "*I* wouldn't think so."

"*You* wouldn't. And I don't believe *she* does. But it takes only a single voice to spread that doubt," Sibelius leaned against his trowel and studied Thimble's face.

"I...I *think* I understand. But, Samara doesn't seem to be the type to be concerned over things like legacies."

"What if it's not *her* legacy she's concerned with? You said her friends lost their lives fighting this Raliak? What if it was you in her place, and me or your parents instead of her friends?"

Thimble nodded, understanding at last. "I see. That...makes more sense."

"Well," Sibelius dropped his basket at the foot of the bench and hopped up beside him. "It's just a thought, really."

The pair sat facing the garden. The chirruping of out-of-sight bugs mingled with the buzz of bees as they hopped from one bloom to the next. Thimble spotted a stick bug climbing the trunk of a nearby peach tree to begin its hunting pantomime.

"What are we even doing here, Thimble?" Sibelius said after a minute.

Thimble heard the unasked question. He lowered his eyes to the damp earth and watched a worm burrow its way into the dark. "I don't know Grampa."

Sibelius sighed. He picked at the dirt smudged stitching of his gloves. "When you came to live with me, I took you in thinking I could help you...deal."

Thimble groaned. He could see where Sibelius was going. "Grampa, I don't want to talk about this."

"And you *haven't*, son. And I've respected that. But...I don't want to see you running away from this anymore."

"I don't know what you're talking about."

"It's been more than two years since she died, and you haven't spoken about it *once.* You've buried yourself in *my* work and pretended like it never happened."

Thimble slid off the bench and began to pace. An annoying heat had crept into his belly at his grampa's words. "Speak about *what?* What good would it do?" His voice came out hotter than he intended, but he found himself not caring.

"It would help you *move on*, for one."

"I *have* moved on."

"Have you?" Sibelius's eyes narrowed. "Look where I am, Thimble! You call *this* moving on?"

Thimble glanced away, shame creeping hot tendrils up his neck. "I thought you said you weren't upset."

"I'm not," Sibelius sighed. "Not about this. It doesn't mean I'm *okay* with it, but like I said before, *I get it.*" He gestured out to the horizon. "Look out there. What do you see?"

Thimble frowned at the old Gnome and gazed toward the forest. Thick fog obscured the nearest redwood until only a shadow remained. "Fog and trees." He said.

"Do you remember what it was like when we first came here?"

Thimble tried to recall. "It's...always been like that."

"No," Sibelius slid off his own seat and stepped in front of him. "*No.* It hasn't. You used to be able to see for hundreds of feet through gentle mist. When was the last time you looked up?"

"What?"

"Look up, Thimble."

Thimble stared at his grampa, a sudden cold fear in his chest. "I-I don't want to."

Sibelius placed a hand on his shoulder. "I know, son. Look up."

Thimble raised his eyes to the sky. Black clouds and muted thunder roiled in the heavens. Lightning twisted and forked, splitting a soundless sky of utter night with brilliance, only to be swallowed by the pervasive miasma churning the heavens above. The sight of it dried Thimble's mouth. Not from shock or terror. But from a piercing recognition.

Sibelius looked up as well. "There was a time when only a gloomy sky graced us." He sighed. "In my time here I've watched this place grow both more beautiful and darker than I ever would have wanted. It's like I said before, nothing here happens by mistake."

Thimble blinked as little droplets began peppering his face. He lowered his eyes toward his grampa, unsure of what to say.

"I don't know what any of it means, Thimble." Sibelius said. "And I don't think it's *for* me to know. But I know where it all comes from. I was there after all. I just hope you'll find what you're looking for." He pointed to the sky. "Before *that's* all that's left."

* * *

"*...under...under...under...under...*"

"Ema!" Thimble shielded his eyes against a buffeting gale. His coat whipped painfully at his waist. "Ema!" He pushed forward, leaning against the wind at an impossible angle.

"*...under...under...under...*"

Her voice, though still a whisper, rang in his head like a church bell. "Ema! Tell me where you are!"

"*...under...under...*"

A sharp crack and rumble thundered through the stones of the tower. With a teeth numbing grind, the bricks parted, toppling up and over in the cutting wind. Thimble tried to throw himself to the floor, but his feet left the solid stone as he was swept along, blown backward off the tower edge and away from the girl.

In his futile flailing, he turned his eyes upward.

The unfettered expanse into eternity, awash with lights dancing and fluttering upon a tapestry of magenta, violet, deepest black, and all else between spread before him. Pastel warmth and brush-stroked chill swirled in step and turned to the music of deepest heaven sent wilds. The sight of it melted his heart and chilled him to the core. As the familiar darkness came to spirit him away, for the first time, he wanted to stay.

Chapter Seventeen

Tearful Truths

Thimble thumped down the stairs of Gloen's Getaway early in the morning, his head in a fog, an annoying soreness in his back in the shape of a fat boot. He rummaged in his Pouch and pulled the vial Nira had given him the day before. He threw back the entire vial and felt some of the pain recede right away. *Cheers, Nira.* The usual muted bustle of the tavern met his ears along with a familiar voice.

"Thimble!" Odion sat at a table in the back. To his left sat a mussed and tired Celia. A tall chair awaited him across from the pair. A couple other patrons sat scattered about, fewer than usual, but not by much.

Thimble clambered up the chair and slumped into the old timber. Through his sleep-addled haze and twisting memories from the night before, he noticed two thick tomes lying open in front of the two Blue Cloaks.

"How'd you sleep?" Odion asked.

Thimble noted the pointed nature of the question and how Celia's eyes stopped moving across the pages of her tome. He could tell them of his dream, but...he barely knew what to make of what he'd seen. Was it worth it to add even more confusion to the pile they already perched on? "Fine," Thimble said. "About what you'd expect."

Odion *tsked* and Celia returned to her reading.

Thimble peered at the heavy volumes. "Wait...are those?"

Odion nodded. "Found them in Alera's attic. No such luck with the thief though."

"Shouldn't you be taking them back to the Archive?" Thimble asked.

"*I* would have, but..." Odion gave a sidelong glance at Celia.

Celia rolled tired eyes. "I thought it would be a good idea to have another look. The Recallers gave us what they could, but we could stumble on something we didn't think to ask. This seemed like as good a place as any."

"Not a bad idea," Thimble eyed the sheer girth of the volumes. "*How* long have you two been at it?"

"Not long enough. Ah, thank you, good sir," Odion shifted his volume as Gloen approached with an armful of steaming bowls.

He slid one in front of Odion, another in front of Celia, and the smaller in front of Thimble. A sweet, milky aroma tinged with light cinnamon drifted from the bowls. Odion and Celia fell on the food with ravenous efficiency.

Thimble dipped his own spoon into his porridge. "Have you two even slept?"

Celia shook her head. "No time. Took all night tearing apart Alera's house."

"How's the search going?"

"Not well," Odion surfaced from his scarfing. "She's either already out of the city, or lying low somewhere we haven't thought of."

"We'll find her," Celia said. She stared into the table grain, eyes unfocused. "We have to."

"What do you know about her?" Thimble asked. "Is there anything that says why she would be involved?"

"That's the thing," Odion leaned back in his chair and crossed his arms, frustrated. "Alera's from a farming family topside. Simple folk like most of us."

Celia snorted.

Odion ignored her. "The High Inquisitor sent a couple of Wardens to speak with them, but I'm not sure that'll amount to much."

Thimble glanced at Celia and wagged a finger at Odion. "Oh, no. We're not glossing over it so easily. What was *that* all about?"

Celia leaned back with a smirk. "I don't mean any disrespect, but the Greys are *not* 'simple folk'."

"What do you mean?" Odion said, taken aback.

Something clicked in Thimble's mind. "Oh, right. You mentioned you were from an old family."

Odion squirmed in his seat. "Not an Old Family, just an *old* family."

"Sure," Thimble nodded. "*That* made sense."

Celia leaned in, clearly enjoying herself. "Let me ask you a ridiculous question, Thimble. Do you know what one of my ancestors did two thousand years ago?"

"Uhh..."

"Yeah. Neither do I. Do you know what one of *his* ancestors did two thousand years ago?"

It was Thimble's turn to lean in. "I'm invested now. This better be good."

"It's not that important," Odion had dropped his head into a hand.

Celia snorted again. "Not that important. She only founded the bloody Forgemaster's Anvil, didn't she?"

"*What?*" Thimble turned rounded eyes toward Odion. The top of the young Warden's ears turned a bright pink.

Celia leaned back again with a laugh. "Old Katerina Grey. Great massive portrait of her in the Anvil's council chambers too. Since then, the Greys have pumped out one paladin after another, all serving the same patron, all joining the Anvil at some point. There's not an Anvilite alive who doesn't know this story."

"Wow. Didn't think you had it in you to leave the tasty parts out. Do you *know* what an old family is?" he said to Odion.

Odion surfaced and held his hands up. "Alright, I admit we've been around for a while and it's true about Katerina, but we're just Anvil paladins like the rest. There hasn't even been a Grey in one of the High Seats in generations."

"Only because your parents turned down the offers," Celia said, grin firmly in place.

"H-how do you even know that?" Odion asked.

Celia shrugged. "Your sister and I were Initiates together. She's an old friend of mine."

"You know Cass?"

"Mhm. Pretty well. She's..."

"A handful."

Celia laughed again. "I was going to say amazing, but yeah, that too. You know I once saw her shatter a man's arm with a training sword? And that attack was *blocked*? Didn't miss a beat either. Healed him up with a touch and sent him on his way."

"Yeah that's...that's Cass," Odion said. Thimble wasn't surprised by the expression of pure pride that crossed Odion's face. He *was* surprised by the tinge of apprehension.

"Also," Celia said. a mischievous glint in her eyes. "Sorry about the stuffed animals. That was my idea."

Odion groaned and dropped his head back into his hands.

Celia stopped snickering at his reaction after a minute. "All teasing aside," she said to Thimble. "The Greys *are* one of the most respected families in the Dominion and beyond I'd bet. They have a habit of wandering all over from what I hear."

"Wait, you're *all* paladins? All the Greys? Even the extended family?" Thimble asked.

Odion shook his head. "Not *all*. Every family has at least one though. Everyone in my immediate family thus far."

"And if I remember correctly, you received your visitation when you were only four, right? The youngest *ever*? Not just your family?"

Odion deflated. "Cass talks too much."

"Wow," Thimble sat back. "That sounds...wild."

Celia's eyes softened. "It sounds like a lot."

Odion said nothing. His eyes focused on his bowl.

"What about you, Celia?" Thimble asked. "Where are you from?"

"Me?" Celia leaned back in her chair. "I'm from Littleleaf town."

Odion's head snapped up. "Littleleaf?" His ears turned scarlet as he realized the volume of his outburst. "Ahem...I mean...I just have always wanted to visit, that's all."

Thimble smiled at his awkwardness. "Sounds like a special place."

Celia nodded. "You'd like it, I'm sure. *Both* of you. It's built under the last Grandmother Tree on the continent. It's a *really* big tree," she answered Thimble's unasked question.

"Well, *everything's* big to me, so I'm gonna have to ask you to elaborate, please," Thimble said.

"Get this, Thimble," Odion's eyes shone in childlike excitement. "The whole town is built *on the roots* of the tree. I've heard it takes a whole *day* to walk around the thing."

"Get out of here," Thimble gaped at Celia. "Is that true?"

"Mostly," Celia said, an amused smile brightening her features. "The town *is* built on the roots, but it takes nowhere near a day to walk the perimeter. An hour, maybe two at a stroll."

"That's something I've *got* to see," Thimble said.

"Right?" Odion agreed.

"Well, you're both welcome if you get the chance," Celia said.

"Is your family all there now?" Odion asked.

"Mhm. My mother's a baker, father's an innkeeper. I have a little sister, too. Rin. She's a handful of years older than Avra, I think. A complete hellion."

Odion snorted. "I bet she's raring to join the Anvil too?"

"Oof, not if ma has anything to say about it. Da's not too bothered but..."

Celia and Odion's chatter washed over Thimble. He sat in the bliss emanating from their smiles as they traded stories of their families.

Smiles. A wide smile, a belly laugh that tickled the humors of any that heard it. He'd grown up hearing it. Hearing both. His mother's smile flashed in front of his eyes. Her braid slung over her shoulder as she danced arm in arm with his father. His father's cackle, so much like Thimble's own, echoing through the firelit cozy little home. How long had it been since he'd heard either?

"What about you, Thimble?" Celia asked, breaking him from his reverie.

"Hm?"

"I'm curious about your family. Your parents, any sib–" she stopped short at a look from Odion.

Thimble looked between the two and heaved a long breath. "No, it's alright," he said to Odion. "Actually, I think I should come clean about something." He looked at Odion. "I told you my family wasn't around anymore and that was only half true. My dad's fine...well...I guess I can't be too sure about that anymore, really." He tapped his finger against the heavy table, unsure of what to say. An odd numbness settled into his core and words began to tumble out of him, unfocused, disjointed. "A little over two years ago, my mum fell ill. She started to lose feeling in her limbs. It was just the right foot at first. We thought it was only a sprain or maybe a fracture, but that wasn't it. It didn't take long to spread to her entire leg." His voice trembled and moisture crept into his eyes as he remembered. *What am I doing?* "She made do with a cane for a while, but...soon she could hardly walk. She was bedridden before we knew it." The general bustle of a waking tavern and town seemed to ebb away as he spoke. His vision narrowed until the memories drawn by his words played upon the grains of the table. "Months went by. We tried *everything*. My dad, my grampa, and me. We looked everywhere, sent letters up and down the country to everyone we could think of. Even sent for some of the few magical healers still in the land, but *nothing worked*. No cure. No help. *Nothing.*" Wetness streamed down his cheeks, blurred his eyes. *Stop...Why can't I stop?* "I can still see her, you know? When I close my eyes I can see her lying there, not moving, barely breathing." His breaths came ragged. Strained. His voice broke with every other word. Years of pain bubbled forth against his will. Out of his control. "She always kept a smile on her face until the end, no matter how small. For our sake. Always, for our sake. And what did I do while the woman who raised me, who loved me so completely, suffered? *Nothing.* I sat there, *useless*, and watched her waste away." A sob cut into his words. He grabbed a fistful of his shirt and scrubbed it against his eyes.

"After she was...gone," he continued. "My dad withdrew. We've spoken less and less over the years. A few months later, we found out that my grampa had fallen sick as well. Dad said it was natural, Sibs *was* pushing a hundred fourty, but I couldn't...I just couldn't. It was too soon. Too soon. I closed up my bureau. Locked up my house and left for Port Caradin. Maybe I could help my grampa, maybe I couldn't. But I had to try." He sniffed and brushed the tears away roughly. "You can imagine how that went seeing as I'm *here* of all places." He buried his face in his hands. A heat rose in his neck. "I..I don't know why...sorry...gods...stupid...embarrassing."

A heavy hand gripped him by the right shoulder. Strong. Comforting. He looked into Odion's eyes, swimming with a wetness of their own. Concern and sorrow touched the young Warden's gaze.

A pressure on his left hand made him look over. Celia sat blinking rapidly, his hand in her own. "I can't begin to understand how you feel, Thimble," she said. "Neither of us can, I think." Odion nodded. "But I know that some weights only get heavier with each step. The strongest of us crumble under it. It's only a matter of when."

"There's nothing to be ashamed of." Odion shook his head. "Nothing."

Thimble nodded. "Thank you." He didn't know why he'd opened up then. To these two. It was as if something had broken in him. Something he'd wanted to break, not that he'd ever admitted it to himself.

An hour went by, then a second before Thimble felt close to normal. The trio fell into a comfortable silence. Thimble finished up his meal and Celia and Odion continued reading.

Odion closed his tome at the end of the second hour.

"Nothing interesting?" Thimble asked, laying down his spoon.

"Plenty interesting," Odion said. "Many things that justify this being banned, but nothing we can use."

"So what's the plan for today?"

"Well," Odion said, with an apologetic grimace. "I figure we take these back to the Archive a—"

Celia shot to her feet, sending her chair clattering to the ground. Her eyes flew left to right, reading and rereading a page.

"Oi! Watch the furniture!" Gloen said from behind the counter.

"Sorry," Celia said, breathless.

"Celia?" Odion exchanged glances with Thimble. "What's the matter?"

"Listen to this," Celia said and began reading. "*After the death of Raliak the Shunned, both families, newly split, refused to accept Raliak's remains into their family mausoleum as is warranted to all members of the (then) Saltanis family. To this day, it is unclear what became of his remains with theories ranging from plausible to hilarious and outlandish. One of the more plausible theories is that he was buried on the grounds of the old Saltanis estate in a private chamber to be sealed and forgotten. While a bit of a reach, this is not entirely without merit. During the rapid reconstruction of the estate, builders were seen digging a foundation much deeper than what the newly minted Manor de Evoire would eventually sit on. Onlookers would be harshly turned away with an Anvil presence to guard the reconstruction effort, so more information on this is difficult to come by."*

Celia stopped, breathing heavily. She stared a hole through Thimble.

Odion eyes darted from her to Thimble and back again. "Am I missing something? He's buried under the manor, right? How does that help?"

Under...under...under. A light flared in Thimble's head. "No...*no!* All this time?"

"We need to go," Celia grabbed both tomes into her arms and made for the door without a second word. Thimble and Odion hurried to catch up, the latter stopping long enough to replace the tipped chair.

"Celia! Wait!" Odion caught up to Celia and Thimble. "Can you two tell me what's going on please?"

"Thimble, tell him. I'm going to report to the High Inquisitor. I'll meet you at the manor," Celia broke into a run and turned down a side path.

"Wait!" Odion called.

"Don't go down there without us!" she shouted over her shoulder before disappearing around the corner.

Odion threw his arms up at the departing Inquisitor.

Thimble tugged on the Warden's cloak, part excitement, part terror quickening his heart. "Come on, I'll tell you on the way."

Odion gave a frustrated sigh. He looked up and down the street before jerking his head opposite the direction Celia had departed. "This way."

The pair took off at a brisk pace, Thimble on the verge of a light jog.

"Alright, so," Thimble began as they wove through the early risers. "Those books were taken for a reason, right? The Forbidden Magics book had these descriptions on completing necromantic rituals and resurrecting cadavers and all of the other awful things it said. Then we had the Unabridged History book which, aside from an entry into Raliak, didn't seem like it connected, right?"

"Sure," Odion said, pushing past a cartload of cabbages.

"Well Celia just found a possible connection. Raliak's burial site."

"Isn't that just a rumor though?"

"That's what I thought. But then I remembered my dream. Ema keeps telling me 'under'. What if she meant under the manor? Under her home?"

Odion gave him an incredulous look. "You're basing this on rumors and dreams? That's crazy!"

"*Crazy?* Have you been paying attention? The whole city dreams about a missing girl stuck in a tower every night. *Every single one* of the de Evoire family is dead *and* their bodies have been turned into a reanimated monstrosity which is *still* missing I'll add. Someone broke into an Archive guarded by the Anvil itself *and* there's likely a necromancer running around toying with you lot for gods know what reason. It's been crazy since minute *one* and I left out about four things!"

"I...I guess I hadn't thought about it all together before," Odion's brow furrowed and his steps quickened causing Thimble to break into a jog.

"Benefit of fresh eyes, eh? Don't worry, I know how batty it sounds. It's something to follow up on at the very least and *oof*–" Thimble ran smack into Odion's armored right leg. "*Ow!*" he rubbed his nose. "Stop *doing* that!" He looked up at the young Warden.

Odion's eyes were fixed to a point beyond a fence Thimble couldn't even dream of seeing over. A mixture of anger and confusion warred in his features. Thimble glanced toward the fence without much hope and found himself staring at the bordering barrier of the de Evoire estate. The entrance they had used a few days before lay open around fifty paces further down the street.

"Odion? What's going on?" he asked. An odd sense of foreboding had settled into his gut at the expression on Odion's face.

Without a word, Odion continued down the street, his eyes fixed on something beyond the fence. The pair arrived at the gate, affording Thimble a view into the courtyard. A person stood at the center of the path to the manor. Auburn hair, tattered blue cloak, shredded sleeves, Alera stood facing the gate, her expression blank, stoic.

"Alera!" Odion's voice thundered across the empty courtyard. He pushed through the gate and advanced up the path, his right hand firmly on his sword hilt. "You have a lot to answer for."

Alera said nothing. She drew her rapier with a smooth motion. Thimble noticed a long patch of brown on her sword arm as she unsheathed the weapon.

"Don't be a fool," Odion said. His steps slowed. "The High Inquisitor will be here soon. Come quietly."

"Odion, stop. Stop!" Thimble yanked on his cloak.

Odion barely flinched, but did come to a stop ten paces from the other Warden. "Stay out of the way, Thimble."

"Wait!" Thimble held his hands up, urging Odion back. "Something's not right." He peered at the odd discoloration on the girl's arm. It was faint, but even in the dim light the diamond shaped scales stood out in layered patterns.

"Thimble?" Odion glanced down at him.

Thimble addressed Alera. "It doesn't work as well on cold flesh does it? Dracolisk skin?"

Alera stared straight ahead, not focusing on anything in particular.

"You see," Thimble stepped to the right to get a better view, "once it's applied, the skin needs constant heat to stay grafted. Torches and candles can help for a while, but it'll eventually start to brown from the flame."

"Thimble?" Odion said through gritted teeth. "What are you on about?"

"I guess nature will do what it will, eh? Everything decays eventually," he looked deep into the glassed over eyes of the former Warden. "Alera? Are you still in there?"

Alera's lips parted the slightest amount and a deep reverberating rattle escaped her throat. "...I'm...sorry..."

"Gods," Thimble closed his eyes. This was beyond evil. "How long have you been dead?"

"...weeks..."

"*What?*" Odion's voice wavered.

"...here...she's...here...go...please..."

"She?" Thimble said. "Who's she?"

"...Mum...Da...I'm...sor−" a sudden inhale cut through her words and rocked her head back. As she turned her eyes back toward Thimble, her face was once again stone-like. Her mouth turned up at the corners the slightest amount. She raised her sword and lunged.

"Oh..." Thimble watched the rapier approach his eyes through a detached calmness. He knew he should move, he knew he probably could move, but his legs didn't feel like his own at that moment.

A shower of sparks snapped Thimble out of his stupor as Odion's blade swung up and crashed into Alera's rapier mere inches from his eyes, pushing the slender blade up and away. Odion twisted on the spot, dragging Thimble by the collar behind him until the pair stood opposite where they had started. Alera lunged once, twice more, each thrust aiming for either Odion's head or groin. Twice more Odion deflected the blows with his longsword if only by a hair.

"Stay back!" Odion pushed Thimble toward the front doors and away from the fight.

"I can help!" Thimble shouted back, untangling himself from his coat. He clenched his fist, mind racing through his list of incantations, trying to find one that would help.

"No!"

"But..."

"Rule two, Thimble!" Odion barged shoulder first into Alera, sending her sprawling on the stone path. He straightened his stance, loosening his shoulders with a roll. He raised his right fist and punched the open air, hard. A sharp *click* resounded from underneath the shield on his shoulder as the rounded metal flew down the groove on his arm, latching itself firmly to the hook on his elbow and coming to rest on the center of his forearm.

As Alera rose back to her feet, her movements choppy yet quick, Odion raised his sword and touched the flat against his forehead. "My lady," his voice was no more than a whisper, yet it thrummed and crackled with an energy that set the hairs on the back of Thimble's neck to attention. "Pray, allow me the strength to return this wayward child to the path, so she may rest in deserved peace." A gentle glow suffused the length of the blade, cascading down in strands of glacial blue light to dissipate upon the ground as Odion readied his stance. The glow reflected in spots and drops where water had begun to condense against the flat of the blade.

The pairs' next clash reverberated through the air. Thimble felt the strike and crash of sword and shield deep in his gut. The flashes of light with each swing of Odion's sword stung at his eyes. The sight was mesmerizing. He watched Odion, this naive cherub of a young man, swing five feet of steel with deadly accuracy and intense strength. Each movement flowed with liquid ease and sword and shield danced in tandem partnership. Alera struck and struck again, but whatever power moved her limbs couldn't resurrect the girl's own ability.

As Odion began to overpower Alera, Thimble turned toward the manor. *She's here*, Alera had said. Who? Thimble couldn't begin to guess. But if whoever they were after *was* here, then there had to be only one reason: Raliak. Thimble pelted toward the front door, leaving the clash of steel behind. The door lay the slightest bit ajar and the morning light from the rising sun made it difficult to see inside. Thimble peered through the crack, resting a trembling hand on the handle, prepared to slam it shut at the first sign of movement. The interior lay still. Motes of dust floated up from the rug covered foyer, twirling in the slim beam of light from the door. He waited for a beat, willing his heart to quieten, his breaths to slow, ears open for sounds of any movement. Hearing nothing aside from the distant sound of clanging steel, Thimble squeezed through and into the manor.

He stood in the darkened interior, letting his eyes adjust. Though he'd seen it in passing, the foyer, even with its random selection of tapestries, gold inlaid drawer stands, and ceremonial vases three times his height, seemed hollow. A sudden chill took hold of him. Not the kind that comes with a draft or a sudden shade on a sunny day, but a chill that comes with knowing something one should not. An odd sensation of drawn attention pressed in on him. He shook himself, trying to blot out the clawing memory that nine people had been murdered here in the not too distant past.

He crept away from the front sitting room to the left. He'd seen that place enough times to last his lifetime. To the right sat an open dining room. The widest and longest table he'd ever seen dominated much of the room. A heavy cabinet with carefully arranged porcelain plates sat against the back wall and another set of the same with silver cutlery sat ready at every place on the table. Thimble glanced over the room looking for signs of anything moved or jostled or out of place.

Finding nothing, he moved toward a closed room near the start of the main hallway. As the door turned in with a slight creak, a faint sweet scent, like the blossoms from a peach tree caught his nose. The door opened to a small room, the floor covered with a thick, dark carpet made of the fur of some immense, shaggy animal. Here and there, he saw a doll, a tiny ship with cloth sails, even an intricate carved figure of a sword wielding warrior, and other toys scattered across the carpet, with more spilling out of a hinged basket against the right wall. On the far wall hung a portrait: a quartet of very young children wearing gaudy uncomfortable looking vestments stood scowling at the painter. Thimble shut the door. His breaths came in shallow gasps, his hands trembling on the handle.

"Easy...easy Thimble. Deep breaths."

Thunk.

His head snapped to the right, toward the sound. A solitary door stood at the end of the hall, the sound had come from behind. His heart hammered a mile a minute and his feet felt rooted to the floor. He waited, motionless, a minute...then two. The manor lay silent once more. He willed his feet forward toward the door, each step placed with the utmost care. He pressed his ear against the door. Part of him wanted to hear something. Anything. Somehow, the silence made things much worse.

Hearing nothing, he eased open the door. Inside awaited a lightly furnished study. A desk sat against the back wall, a bookshelf stood to its left. Along the right wall, built into the old stone was a fireplace, cold and empty. At a closer look, the fireplace was missing a back wall. A light draft wafted from the opening and what sounded like a soft *tap...tap...tap* echoed through the opening.

"Well. *This* might be the dumbest thing I've ever done," Thimble slipped through the opening.

Chapter Eighteen

The Well of Stars

Thimble emerged from the opening into a narrow, dank corridor of stone that spiraled down and out of sight with little steps carved into the stone along the way. A distant sound of soft shuffling echoed up the stone passage along with the same tinny *tap...tap...tap.* Thimble padded down the steps, ears twitching at every sound.

The path leveled off sooner than he expected. The stairs ended at the beginning of a short hallway. An arched opening sat at the end of the hallway, though in the place of a door, was an odd swirling wall of gentle luminescent smoke tinged a light blue-grey color. Thimble crept toward the wall of smoke. The tapping and shuffling ceased as he set foot in the hallway, and utter silence reigned once more. He peered at the smoke wall, hoping for a distorted glimpse at what lay beyond, but was met with an opaque mass full of false shadows. He waved his hand around and through the wall to no avail.

Let's be smart about this. He reached into his Pouch, hoping he had remembered to pack a vial of corrosov powder. To his relief, his hand closed around a single glass bottle. He withdrew a small vial half filled with a bright white powder, uncorked it and held it within the smoke wall for a handful of seconds. He pulled the vial back out and held it up to his eye. The white powder remained unchanged, stoic. He corked and tossed the vial back into his Pouch and stepped through the smoke wall.

He expected to walk through a barrier into some sort of a chamber. Instead, he was met with more voluminous odorless fog that obscured his vision almost entirely. He reached to his right, hoping he hadn't wandered too far from the opening and found solid rock against his fingers. He reached left, then directly behind and was met with more impassive, damp stone.

"You know what I love *most* about your people? Your infinite curiosity." Thimble froze. The voice was familiar, though he couldn't quite place it. He turned towards the source. His fear and curiosity warring and clouding his mind. "Honestly, if there was a massive glowing sign saying 'Don't come here! You'll probably die!' you'd still dive headlong wouldn't you?"

Thimble jumped as something unseen whipped itself around both of his feet and arms, rooting him in place. He struggled and pulled at the bindings.

"Ah ah, none of that! Be a good lad and stay still would you?" His bonds tightened and pulled, dragging him to his knees.

"Who are you?" Thimble broke his silence.

"Really now?" the voice sounded offended. "And after I invited you to tea?"

The smoke in the chamber began to dissipate. A spacious rounded cavern with dipping stalactites and odd rock formations opened in front of Thimble. An earthen path surrounded a massive pit in the center, framed by sharp rocks jutting in every direction. Small cages and barrels sat on the outskirts of the cavern and here and there, little bundles of candles or dim sconces gave off a flickering golden light. Above the pit hung a massive single stalactite from which a chain dangled, rigid and taught. From the chain hung a massive stone sarcophagus, lashed and tied tens of times by yet more metal fastenings, suspended above the pit. A small path extended from the left side of the chamber to end at a circular disk suspended near the center of the pit, within touching distance of the sarcophagus.

Upon the disk stood an old woman. Ample hoops on her ears, bug-eye like spectacles, colored ribbons tied through her stormy hair, bangles clanging on her forearms. She held in her hand a corked bottle of bluish liquid, a wicked smile crossed her lips. She flicked a finger against the bottle: *tap...tap...tap.*

"Wait...*you?*" Thimble stood flabbergasted.

"Me!" Nira stowed the bottle and bounced happily.

"But...*why?*"

"You know," she tapped her chin in faux thought. "I would love nothing more than to tell you everything, but," she jerked her head toward the sarcophagus, "I don't have a lot of time. Grandfather's been waiting long enough. So, if you wouldn't mind, please sit there. Quietly."

A vine snaked its way up Thimble's torso and bound itself tight around his mouth. Thimble struggled and seethed. An unknown anger at being bound bubbled forth.

"There we are!" she turned toward the sarcophagus. Thimble watched her fumble with something on her belt. She withdrew an armful of thin vials of dark liquid and tossed them one at a time into the pit. Thimble expected to hear chattering glass as the vials met stone, yet no sound emerged from the pit. She held up a final vial and peered at it closely. "Do you know how hard it is to extract blood from a decaying corpse, Mister Pennywhistle?" she asked. "Very. It took almost a month and this is all that's left of dear Annabeth." She flipped the last vial into the pit.

Nira turned to her left, to the opposite corner of the cavern from Thimble. "Go on then. In you get!"

Out of the shadows lumbered the headless stitched abomination, each step sending tremors across the cavern. Bloated, disfigured, dripping with residue and holding a rancid heavy basket, the Stitched Cadaver tipped itself over the side of the pit. Again, no sound, no wet thud or cracking of bones came from the pit.

Nira raised her arms above her head. "Blood of our blood, flesh of our flesh, family ties, soul bound. Open the path of spirit stepped climbs to beyond and beyond. Accept this sacrifice of mortal frailty and let one drink from the Well of Stars!" Her voice echoed around the chamber as she finished.

A single beam of light, thin and insignificant rose from the center of the pit to alight the bottom of the suspended sarcophagus. Ever so slowly, the column of light began to expand. Nira sighed, her expression one of relief and triumph. She lowered her arms and sank to her knees.

"It works," she whispered. She turned toward Thimble. "And now to wait. Isn't this exciting, Mister Pennywhistle?"

Thimble glared. His eyes darted toward the light, now encompassing the entirety of the sarcophagus with no indication of slowing. *Stop it. How do I stop it?* He brought an incantation to his mind out of pure instinct, but as the point of heat blossomed in his palm, the vines around his shoulders tightened painfully, pulling him to his knees. The incantation faded, lost to the pain.

"Oh, this is no fun," Nira snapped her fingers. The vine binding Thimble's mouth fell away. "There we are. I'm sure you've got oodles of ques–"

"Where's the girl?" Thimble said, trying to steady his breath.

Nira's eye twitched at the interruption. "Ah, ever the gallant investigator. Not here."

"Where is she?"

"Not. Here." She shook her head. "Honestly, all that's happening in front of you, and you're worried about one silly child?"

"Is she alive?"

"Probably. I don't know. Look!" She sprang to her feet. "You'd better ask something less *boring,* or I'll toss *you* in next!"

A part of Thimble wanted to needle her to the point of breaking. The same part that hated how he was being held. The manic glint in Nira's eyes held his tongue. "What's happening down there?" he nodded toward the pit.

"Ah, finally," her face relaxed into a smile once more. "Have you ever heard of the Well of Stars?"

Thimble shook his head.

"A myth. A hearthside tale passed down from one mage to another for ages. Legends say it's a portal. A gateway to the place souls reside when they leave our plane."

"So what? You open this Well and bring back dear old Grandfather? That's the plan?"

"Oh ho ho!" Nira clapped and bounced some more. "Clever boy aren't you? Then again, of course you are! Those cloaked buffoons would never have found me on their own."

"Why though?" Thimble asked. He tested his bindings, but they only dug further in. Maybe if he kept her talking, he would still be alive by the time the Anvil showed up. "Why bring him back at all?"

"Why?" she snorted. "Because he asked me to, silly boy."

"Asked?"

"Well...really he only asked me to take the girl but," she tapped her nose. "I understood all too well. Ah! It's time!"

The light reached the very edges of the pit. The chain holding the sarcophagus trembled, then rattled as sharper jerks and twists from forces unseen unsettled the massive tomb. The noise from the chains and stone reached a crescendo to the point of paining Thimble's ears.

A blinding explosion sent shards of stone and metal hurtling in every direction. Stars swam in his eyes and a loud ringing assaulted his ears. He coughed at a dull pain near his stomach, trying to blink sight back into his eyes. The cavern came into focus in waves and hues and the ringing lessened bit by bit. The sarcophagus was nowhere to be seen. What remained of the chain hung limply from the stalactite. In its place, hovering in the still air before Nira, was a man.

An emaciated corpse of a man with visible bones and barren skin, but a man nonetheless. Long wisps of white hair tralied down his back and bits of cloth hung from his hideous form in places. The man raised his hands in front of his eyes, the movements slow, grating. Bit of dust and skin flaked at his movements.

"I...am...alive?" his voice was no more than a rattling whisper.

"Yes!" Nira clasped her hands together, tears brimming her eyes. "Yes, Grandfather! You have returned to the world of the living."

Raliak lowered his hands and turned his eyes toward Nira. "I...need... sustenance."

"Of course, Grandfather," she gestured toward Thimble. "There it is! A life's worth of time."

Raliak turned his head toward Thimble. A pair of sunken black hollows stared through him. Raliak raised a hand and the vines holding him melted away. He gathered himself to his feet and felt a searing pain near his chest as he straightened. Before he could look, he felt himself yanked off his feet by an invisible force. He flew through the air toward Raliak's outstretched hand, unable to resist in any way. As he passed over the lip of the pit, his eyes turned downward, and was greeted by a familiar sight that chilled the marrow.

A tapestry of hues and twinkling candlelights.

"Humph," Raliak caught him by the throat, fleshless fingers digging in with an impossible strength. The dusty stench of decay assaulted his nose.

The old husk of a necromancer peered at him through sunken hollows, his granddaughter watched awestruck over his shoulder. Raliak's eyes moved down his body and stopped near his chest. "Waste."

Thimble pulled at the skeletal hand on his throat and found his movements sluggish, labored. He managed to shift his head down far enough to get a glimpse at what Raliak had noticed. There, just above his topmost right rib, protruded a shard of shattered sarcophagus, buried deep into his torso. Blood flowed from the wound, hot and quick, dripping from his toes.

He heard Nira utter a vile curse and took some morbid amusement from her annoyance.

Raliak turned over his shoulder. "Heal."

Nira glanced about frantically. "I...I can't. He's lost too much blood and I don't have any of my potions with me. Wait here, Grandfather. I will fetch someone at once." She turned on her heel to leave.

"No," Raliak raised his other hand. Nira lifted mid stride into the air and wafted toward him. She grappled with an invisible force around her throat, spittle flying from her gasping mouth. "No...waiting."

For the first time, an expression of terror gripped old Nira. Her legs thrashed about and her eyes looked ready to pop out of her head. Raliak took a deep rattling breath. Motes of light emerged from Nira and flowed down Raliak's throat. Thimble watched as the old healer withered in front of his eyes. Her skin turned to ash, her bones to powder. Not even a scream escaped her lips before she was nothing more than dust on the wind.

Raliak turned his attention back toward Thimble and, to his horror, gazed at him with shriveled, dry excuses for eyes where once only pits of darkness remained. He watched as the eyes slowly filled in and the skin of Raliak's torso stretched over his protruding bones.

Raliak took another rattling breath, though this one rattled less. "That's better," he peered closely at Thimble once more. "Such a shame. No matter. The time will come elsewhere."

Thimble felt the grasping hand release him. He let his eyes close of their own accord. He was tired. So tired.

And the fall brought an odd comfort.

Chapter Nineteen

The Keeper of Dreams

Thimble felt the cool caress of water embracing him head to toe. The slightest ghost of a tremor touched his lungs... a far off cry from when it mattered. His arms and legs, had they the strength, would rip and tear towards an unseen surface, he imagined, but no such desire took hold of him. He would drift here, in this weightless, comfortable bliss he had woken to. For as long as time spanned.

His eyes fluttered open, and for a moment, he saw nothing. As the smallest breath escaped his lips and the tiny bubbles crept past his eyes with the faintest touch, he realized the enormity of the watery void he wafted in. To his mild surprise, no fear gripped his senses. No dread sent spines of ice through his bones. He felt serene, at peace. He stared out at the endless abyss, content.

Except, something was changing. It came in waves; the blackest void gave way to frigid midnight, then steely cobalt, into piercing sapphire on and on it came. As azure faded, he raised his eyes to the approaching luminance. He felt the top of his head breach a surface. Not sudden or dramatic, but slow and deliberate. A sickly pain seared where his skin met air, and a gentle breeze – warm and soothing – whisked it away. So it went as he rose from the water, knit together by this harsh yet tender new world.

Thimble stood transfixed upon this surface, unbelieving of all his eyes saw. The water below his feet rippled a lazy wave at his step, but slowly as if made from sap and only as far as his arms outstretched. Upon the surface of the water, scattered about in little clumps or vast fields glided small spaded pads of vibrant green, each topped with a beautiful white bloom. From amid the littered pads slowly rose globes of gentle luminance from the water below. Lights flickered and played within each globe, images and colors indiscernible to his eye flashed and faded in instants. His gaze followed the sea of bubbles up and beyond. To a sight he expected. The expanse called to him. A dulcet melody of tinted shades meant for him, and countless others.

"A sight beyond words...isn't it?" the voice seemed to emanate from the heavens. A glimmer flitted through one bubble after another until their own luminance seemed diminished by comparison. Thimble watched as a man stepped around the closest globe, and an infinite more appeared beside their own. The man smiled at Thimble. His pale, pointed features warmed at the gesture, his deep violet eyes crinkling at the corners. He wore a robe of purest, starlight white trimmed in gold and sapphire thread. A high collar rose above the top of his head where a sheet of snow cascaded down beyond his shoulders.

"I almost envy you, you know," the man said. "To behold such a wonder again and again as if for the first time..."

"You..." words evaded Thimble's tongue as if determined not to be spoken. "I've seen you."

The man nodded. "You have. Ah, please excuse me for a moment." The man peered into the shimmering orb beside him, seeing something within its faded flashing images. "Hmm, so it is...for the moment," he muttered to himself. The man lifted a slender finger and gently drew it over the surface of the orb. The bubble rippled and warped in the wake of his touch, then sank slowly back into the depths below, dimming and fading as it submerged.

Thimble looked about at the other hims and watched as they followed suit, some for longer, some less so. With a touch globe after globe sank back into the water, but once in a long while among the endless sea, an orb pulsated and grew in its luminance. Thimble watched as a handful of these orbs rose ever so gradually up and into the expanse above, growing ever brighter before joining the field of lights as a companion. He lowered his gaze back to the man closest to him as the rise and fall of lights continued beyond them. "Who are you?" he croaked.

The man smiled. A warm and inviting sight. "I am the Keeper of Dreams."

Thimble gazed around, not quite looking at anything. He wrung his hands together. "Keeper of...right...am I dreaming then? *Ow!*" his wrist clipped against something on his chest, sending a spear of white hot pain through his person. He looked down and found the shard of stone still protruding from his body.

"Not quite," the Keeper withdrew his hands from his robe sleeves, producing a small clay cup. He knelt and scooped a cupful of water from below and held it out to Thimble. "Here. This should help."

Thimble took the cup in trembling hands. Flares of colors and lights and sounds flashed through his mind in discombobulated patches. He shook his head, trying to rid himself of the dull pain creeping up the back of his neck, and took a sip.

The cup fell from his hands as the cool liquid snaked its way down his throat. He doubled over, a gripping agony bloomed at the base of the shard and grew with each beat of his heart. He dropped to his knees, unable to utter a word as all breath left his body from the sheer torment. The shard dropped into the water with a thin *plop.*

"Hah! Oh..." Thimble rolled onto his back, his head sinking an inch into the water. He touched the space the shard had fallen from and found his skin intact, if a bit raw. Images came flooding back in a rush. Memories of what had happened a few moments ago. Had it been only a few moments?

"I...um...I'm pretty sure I died," Thimble said.

The Keeper chuckled. He lowered himself to the water beside Thimble and crossed his feet. "Not quite," he said again. "You, my friend, were cast into the Well of Stars. A stroke of luck indeed for you would have perished otherwise."

Thimble considered the strange man. His eyes were gentle and his smile, almost apologetic. "Have I been here long?"

The Keeper shook his head. "A handful of minutes have passed in your world since your arrival. And more will continue to, but you are welcome to rest here. Though, I'm afraid you cannot stay long."

"Where *is* here?"

"This," the Keeper swept his hand across their view, "is the During and After and that," he lifted a finger skyward, "is the Beyond."

"Uh-huh," Thimble hauled himself to a seating position. "That's not really an answer."

"It's the simple truth."

Thimble nodded slowly. "And...why can't I stay?" He felt an odd comfort in this place. A strange nostalgia.

The Keeper smiled. "Because it's not your time," he reached into the water below and scooped a smoky orb from the depths. He held the orb out toward Thimble as lights and shadows danced within its core. "And because you are still needed."

The flashes and patches of dark resolved into a crystal clear view of a sweeping street. Dim violet light spilled from the left of his sight and people of all shapes and sizes ran and screamed. Shambling, rotting corpses pursued the fleeing citizens, battering down doors with relentless ferocity and tearing into flesh like warm pastry. Here and there whirling blue cloaks and their keepers cut down one shuffling monstrosity after the next, steel glowing sunlight gold in their fists. Yet more came in droves, pushing back the Anvil's warriors through sheer numbers.

The image zoomed into a narrow alleyway where a grey haired matron and a young green eyed woman fought back to back, their weapons gliding through swaths of undead. He shouted out as Samara missed a block by a hair's breadth. The monstrosity dug a hand into her left eye and pulled away, a gout of blood spurting from the injury. The image zoomed away as Samara screamed and Celia turned to cover the High Inquisitor.

The city flew by in a whirl of color and sound before stopping above the city center. A man stood before the Attrangem. Shoulder length black hair fluttered in the sea breeze, and a maniacal gleam in his eye matched the twisted sneer on his lips. His hand lay open, outstretched in front of him where a young man, no older than twenty, hovered flailing above the ground.

Thimble watched the young man age into dust. Raliak drew a long breath, savoring every moment. He raised his arms as his body lifted to hover above the gem. He bent his head, and began to chant. The image zoomed away until only dull smoke remained.

The Keeper lowered the orb back into the water, and watched Thimble with a curious eye.

Thimble sat breathless at what he'd seen. "What in the hells is happening out there?"

"It appears this Raliak has decided to continue his trek of terror," The Keeper said. "It's a shame. Not many receive second chances. He has squandered his," he tilted his head, "what will you choose to do with yours I wonder?"

Thimble ran a hand through his hair. "I...I don't know. What *can* I do? You saw what he did to Nira, to all of those people. Look at me. I'm not a fighter. What can someone like me even do here?"

The Keeper smiled once more and placed a hand atop Thimble's head. He leaned in close until their faces were level. "I think you are capable of *so much*, Thimble Pennywhistle. I believe you will surprise us all."

The Keeper pushed hard against the top of Thimble's head, plunging him into the depths below. Thimble cried out as a force pulled him deeper into the darkness below and a torrent of water filled his lungs.

Chapter Twenty

The Ticking Clock

"Gaah!" Thimble broke the surface of the pool in a panic. He flailed wildly in the water trying his utmost to kick in futility toward an edge to grab onto all the while his body bent and wracked with coughs.

"Thimble!" He felt a strong hand grab his arm and yank him out of the pool. He landed on stone and earth, cutting his palms on the rough floor, but thankful to be out of the water.

"*Akh! Akh!*" Water fled his body in buckets.

"Thimble! Thimble, what happened? Are you alright?" Odion's voice cut through his own raucous hacking.

He lifted his head to see a concerned and battered Odion kneeling in front of him. Cuts leaked from his cheek and forehead, and a few more bled through his side not protected by heavy plate.

"Wow," Thimble said between gasps. "You look like hell."

Odion gave him an annoyed frown and pulled him to his feet. "Turns out dead people don't get tired. She pushed me all the way out to the street. Thought I was done for, but she just flopped over all of a sudden. I saw..." his eyes held no small measure of fear. "I saw someone...some*thing* come out of the house. Was that..."

Thimble nodded. "Raliak."

"Gods," Odion pulled on his moustache. "He flew...*flew*...towards the city center. Thimble, what *happened* here? And what in the world is *that*?" He pointed toward the pit. The well had stilled, its surface a mosaic of twinkling stars once more.

"Complicated" Thimble made for the cave entrance.

Thimble didn't know what he expected upon leaving the manor. Buildings aflame? Streets running with blood and gore? What he found was what he had left, a bright day in the rich part of town. Somehow, that was even more unnerving. The pair hurried from the compound and back into the approaching street.

Alera's corpse lay on the side of the street, one arm twisted under her chest, the other splayed out, rapier lying a few inches from stiff fingers. Matted hair and the cobblestone below hid most of her features, though through a part in her locks, a glassed over eye peered into nothing.

"Gods," Odion stared at the young Warden, pain in his eyes.

"We'll come back," Thimble tore his own gaze away and started towards the crossroads. "We'll come back. Send her off properly."

"Right," Odion turned to follow.

Carnage awaited at the crossroads. People ran though ruin strewn streets. Some screamed, others didn't. Men and women and children lay scattered throughout the streets, their bodies torn apart by blade or by hand. As they watched, a handful of bodies twitched and rose to their feet, heads lolling with an absent laziness. As one, the fresh risen corpses turned and sprinted toward the pair of them.

"Oh sh−" Thimble faltered and stumbled.

Odion swept past him without pause. Shield deployed, blade singing, he cut down three of the risen corpses in an instant. Thimble watched the heads roll down the street with no small measure of awe. Odion sheathed his blade and turned to rejoin Thimble, when a fourth undead lurched forth from the dark interior of a shattered smithy just out of his sight.

"Odion!" Thimble shouted. The Warden reached for his blade, but the thing was upon him in an instant.

A blinding flash illuminated the space where Odion stood, forcing Thimble's eyes away. Thimble blinked at the image of a forking bolt of golden lightning imprinted in his vision. Odion lay stunned on his back a few feet from where he had stood. Where the undead corpse had been was nothing more than a smoking crater and a ring of ash.

"What kind of idiot sheaths his sword in the middle of battle, Warden?"

Thimble turned toward the speaker, his eyes slowly adjusting to normal. Staggering up the street with a limping Celia over her shoulder and a thick, bleeding bandage wrapped around half her head, was the High Inquisitor Samara Rhythe herself.

Odion picked himself off the street. "High Inquisitor?"

"Give us a hand Odion," Samara nodded toward Celia, "It's her leg."

"Of course," Odion rushed to relieve the High inquisitor of her burden and sat Celia gingerly down on an intact crate. She winced and held her leg off the ground. Blood ran free down the back where a nasty tear bled just above the calf. Thimble joined Samara and the others at the crate.

Celia hissed as Odion laid a hand on her wound. "*Sssha!* Easy!"

"Sorry," a gentle glow gathered around his palm and seeped into the wound.

Samara addressed Thimble. "Celia filled me in on some of what's been going on. I would appreciate the rest."

Thimble nodded. He informed Samara of everything that had happened since their split with Celia, careful to omit all that transpired within the Well of Stars. "We didn't know what else to do with her. She's still by the manor."

Samara heaved a heavy sigh. "Poor girl. Her...*gods*...her family...and...*Nira?*" Her eyes darted about as she tried to comprehend all she'd heard.

"I know it's a lot," Thimble said. "And I might have a bit more. But for now, Raliak is in the city center. I think he's planning something with the Attrangem."

"The Attrangem?" Samara's brow furrowed. "What could he..." her eyes darted around as her mind rattled off possibilities. She shook her head. "It doesn't matter. We stop him now." She turned toward Odion and Celia. "Inquisitor? Status."

Odion gave Celia a nod and stepped away, allowing the woman to raise gingerly to her feet. Celia tested the injured leg. "Mobile, ma'am."

"Good," Samara turned back to Thimble. She opened her mouth to speak, but a loud crash halted her words.

Pushing through and over the wreckage of a cart that had barricaded a side alley, two dozen new corpses forced their way into the street. The one in front, a young man wearing a dark blue waistcoat with the buttons undone where his stomach was ripped into, whipped toward them and bellowed a gurgling cry. As one, the undead turned and began sprinting in their direction.

"*Kazeh*," Samara swore in dwarvish. "Celia left, Odion, right. I'll take the center. Not a step back, understood?"

Celai and Odion drew weapons and moved to obey the High Inquisitor.

"Thimble," Samara's deep blue eyes shimmered with an apologetic sheen. "I would offer you an escape from this, but I'm not sure if anywhere is safe at the moment. If you want to run, run. I will not begrudge you and will consider our contract fulfilled. If you wish to help...then I would ask you to reconsider. I would also be eternally grateful."

Samara turned and joined the other Anvilites. Thimble stood chewing his lip furiously. He could run, but where to? Where in the city could be safer than with these three? The Keeper believed he could help, but...*how?* Light from the three blades bathed the street in multihued radiance, framing the trio against the onrushing death.

He couldn't run. Even if he wanted to. He *liked* these people. Even saw them as friends. And what would Mum, Dad, and Grampa think of him if they knew he turned his back on them? "Ah, *Screw it!*" seizing on all of his terror to quicken his steps, he charged headlong into battle alongside the three-wide wall of paladins.

Crash and spray,
  rigid display,
  alight a way,
  moment of day.

"Right!" the stings and bites of fingers of jagged light snaked up his arm and snipped at his cheeks as he drew back on his roiling thundercloud of a bow. Blue-purple light crashed from between his fingers, snaking their way up the bow arms.

Celia's steps faltered and she swiveled to her left just as Thimble's arrow forked within a hair's breadth of her face. Her inevitable swear was cut short by the sharp peal of thunder as the arrow...missed.

"*Dammit!*" Thimble ducked back behind the advancing holy trio. The undead poured forth. In lines, in groups, in droves, on and on they came. He flinched as a snarling head snapping toward him was bisected by a flash of Samara's sword.

"I know you're trying to help, Thimble," Samara shouted through the din. "But could you *please* hit something?"

Thimble threw up his hands and ducked as Celia's boot caught another undead crawling toward him square between the eyes. "I'm sorry, *High Inquisitor*. My targets don't usually have *faces!* Oh. Also, I'm *terrified!*"

Samara looked over her shoulder into his eyes. "They're gone, Thimble. *They're gone.* The kindest thing we can do for them now is to put them down. Let them find peace."

Her words, strong and clear, rang in his ears. *Gone. That's right. Like the stitched cadaver. Not people anymore.* He took a deep breath and brought up his Storm Bow once more. The string came back smooth, the arrow formed in one fluid motion. His bracing arm steady, he fired.

The bolt slammed into the nearest shambling horror, arcing between it and four of its compatriots, rooting them to the spot and sending convulsions through their bloodstilled veins. Thimble whooped in surprise and relief.

Odion and Celia made quick work of the stunned combatants and returned to their places in the little circle the paladins had formed around Thimble.

"Not bad," Odion grinned.

"Nice shot," added Celia.

"Thanks," he gave Samara a grateful nod. "How much further?"

"Two streets," Samara answered. "Not far now." Her breathing came heavy, tired. As did the others'. The foursome had fought their way through wave after wave of undead, some fresh, some nothing more than sinew and bones. The armored ones were the trickiest. The fallen city guard.

"There!"

"To the High Inquisitor! Quickly!"

Thimble chanced a look over his shoulder toward the new voices.

In a blur of light and steel, Anvil paladins cut a swath through the horde in their direction. At their head, a furious looking Kerrak swung blade and claw alike with unbridled ferocity. Within seconds, the brightly armored warriors had pushed back the tide and formed a protective barrier around Thimble's group.

Thimble's arms sagged with relief. His fingertips tingled with the sustained effects from holding his Storm Bow for so long. Every now and then, his right arm jerked to a random side.

"Kerrak," Samara rested her blade point down on the ground. Sweat plastered locks to her forehead. "Status."

"Awful," the Gougen growled. He brushed past them to the building at their backs. Once what looked to be a grocer now sat barren with shattered windows and ruined stalls. Kerrak held what was left of the door open. "Inside please. I need to show you something."

Samara swept through without a word, followed closely by Thimble, Odion, and Celia. Odion stopped to lean against a countertop. Catching his breath, he turned a questioning look toward Thimble.

"What?" Thimble said.

"You've really never shot anyone before? In your line of work?"

Thimble shrugged. "Magic, especially my kind of magic, is *very* illegal in Dunalis. You need a special license from the Empire to practice openly. In a major city like Veppen, I could get thrown into prison. For a long time. I practiced in secret. On dummies in my basement, or disks when I'd visit my parents and had someone – who wasn't likely to turn me in – to throw for me."

"What a strange place," Odion said.

"Don't I know it."

"Odion, give me a hand," Kerrak called from further in the shop.

With an assist from Odion, Kerrak righted an upturned table and dragged it to the center of the room. "Gather round," he spread a heavy map over the

177

wooden surface. Thimble hopped onto a chair for a better look. A large violet circle in the center marked it as a map of the city.

"Most of the fighting is focused here," Kerrak jabbed a clawed finger at the center. "There's a mass of them blocking any approach to the Attrangem. That's where *he* is." He swept his finger an arms length to the right. "Whatever he's doing, it's affecting people a thousand yards in all directions. Not to mention three Old Families all have mausoleums within the area."

"Gods," Celia whispered. "A thousand yards? So everyone..."

Kerrak shook his head. "Not everyone. Anyone who enters the field has roughly one minute until they're dead and another before they've fully risen." He nodded toward Samara. "Thanks to your message, we were able to mobilize every Initiate, Warden, and Inquisitor to clear the surrounding homes. Unfortunately, the ones closest to the center were the hardest to clear and the most densely packed. So, as I said, not everyone, but too many still."

"Why aren't we affected?" Odion asked.

Kerrak shrugged. "Whatever spell Raliak is weaving, it is the antithesis of what we stand for in the Anvil. I believe our blessed patrons convey some manner of protection for us against this magic."

"Message?" Samara ran a hand through her hair. "What message? I never sent you a message."

Kerrak looked between the other three Blue Cloaks. "Your message, High Inquisitor. About Raliak's return. You told us about this spell, and ordered us to get the people away."

"Show me this message," Samara held out a hand.

"Uh..." Kerrak shuffled uncomfortably. "Actually, High Inquisitor, I was going to ask how you managed it, but..." he raised a hand to his temple and tapped, "We heard it here. Your voice, giving the orders. All of us. At headquarters anyway."

Samara rounded on the other three. "Did any of you hear this message as well?"

The trio shook their heads in unison.

Thimble felt a slight chill run down his spine. He had a small inkling of who the true messenger may have been.

Shall we tell them?

Thimble let out an involuntary squeak at the voice in his mind not his own. The others snapped their attention to him.

He shook out his hands. "Sorry! Residuals from the Storm Bow. Should pass soon."

Is this...is this the Keeper? he wondered to himself as the others returned to their strategizing.

Yes indeed, Thimble. I apologize for startling you but, there's not really a subtle way to mention you're in someone's head.

How long have you been in there?

Since our meeting. I am quite curious as to how this turns out.

"Hold on," Celia turned back toward Thimble, breaking him from his internal conversation. "I've got a question. Are you a paladin or a priest of some sort?"

"What? No." Thimble answered, taken aback by the sudden question.

"Then why aren't you affected by the spell?"

"Um," he said aloud.

I'm guessing you have something to do with that? he said in his own mind.

Of course, the Keeper answered. *It would be unfortunate for you to end at this juncture.*

He shrugged. "No idea."

"Curious as *I* am, I hesitate to count our good graces given the situation," Samara strode to the shattered window. She stood peering through to the open street where a dozen Blue Cloaks stood at the ready. The carnage of the battle remained strewn across the street. "Oddly quiet out there. Warden!" she called to the closest Blue Cloak who turned and saluted. "What's the situation?"

"No threats in the immediate area, ma'am," the Warden responded.

"Odd," Samara turned back to the group. "It feels like we've been fighting for hours. Why stop no–"

"*Brave, strong, and immensely stupid,*" the terrible voice, different from all Thimble had heard till then, rang through wood and stone. The Blue Cloaks swiveled their heads, searching for a source. The voice laughed, leaving a hollow chill in the pit of Thimble's stomach. *"That is the Anvil I remember. Come then. Come to me and I shall reward your tenacity with a swift end before sending this city to where it belongs."*

The ground heaved beneath their feet, sending them to the floor. Outside, clanks of steel and grunts resounded from the present Blue Cloaks. Old planks and cross beams above buckled under the strain as shards and splinters rained down on their heads.

"Out!" Samara shouted into the racket.

Thimble scrambled after the others, his feet landing awkwardly as the earth shifted where his mind thought he would step. With a final leap, he pushed into the open air of the street just as the old grocer's collapsed behind them.

Thimble picked himself off the street and dusted himself off. His eyes roamed over the wreckage of the surrounding abodes. His gaze turned upward to the crashing waves high above as the words "where it belongs" clicked into place and the Keeper spoke in his mind.

Clock's ticking, Thimble. What are you going to do?

Chapter Twenty-One

Fistful Reprisal

Thimble heaved and stopped himself from gagging aloud. The stench assaulted his nostrils and coated his gums. His eyes watered from the effort.

"Why are they just standing there?" he whispered through his sleeve.

It hadn't taken Thimble and the Blue Cloaks long to find where the rest of the undead had gone. Taking their adversary's invitation, the group of paladins had advanced on the city center from all sides. The leftover horde stood crowded around the Attrangem, shoulder to shoulder, front to back, an impassive wall of puppeteered flesh.

Raliak himself hovered above their heads, near the crown of the Attrangem. He held one hand extended toward the gem, and the other held a struggling black haired young woman.

"Release her!" Samara's command resounded through the square.

Raliak pitched a sneer in their direction. His eyes alighted on Samara and paused. "I...know you. Why?"

"Allow me to remind you!" Samara extended a hand with two fingers pointed in Raliak's direction.

Raliak wasn't dead. Not anymore. But...was he still a person...after all he'd done? Thimble's Storm Bow leapt into his hands and an arrow streaked toward the hovering necromancer before he even realized what he was doing.

As one, Thimble's forking arrow and Samara's conjured bolt of divine fury from above crashed into Raliak's still grinning form. The roaring thunder was met with a greater clamor as the undead flew from their statue-like postures into a full assault on the surrounding Blue Cloaks.

Metal sang and spells dazzled the eyes as the Anvilites responded in kind. Unarmed and unarmored citizenry fell to the Blue Cloaks assaults in droves, while the armored fallen guards proved a challenge. Thimble, Samara, Odion, and Celia stood back with a few others. The Wardens and Inquisitors formed a protective guard around their High Inquisitor.

Thimble's gaze remained locked to the space the bolts had crashed, sending a plume of blackish smoke in all directions. The smoke cleared, bit by bit. *Please be gone,* he hoped. *Please be gone.*

His grin hadn't changed.

The young woman dissolved into ash to drift away with the clearing smoke. Raliak threw back his now smooth face and laughed, the sound swallowed by the din of the battle.

"Damn!" Thimble punched his own leg with frustration. "What now?"

"Keep up the pressure!" Samara pointed at two bow wielding Wardens firing into the crowd of undead behind her. "You, you! I want constant fire on him. Now!"

The pair of Wardens nodded and loosed light infused arrows towards the necromancer. Mere inches from Raliak's body, the arrows shattered against a barrier visible for the briefest moment on impact. Raliak paid them no mind and returned his attention to the Attrangem as more arrows and spells thudded against his barrier.

"What in the hells is he doing?" Odion shouted, kicking an armored torso back into the melee.

"I think he's trying to break the gem!" Thimble shouted back. He shot his own storm arrows into the crowd and sent the occasional bolt toward the ambivalent necromancer.

"What? Why?"

"How many people do you think will die if all of this falls into the sea?"

"Everyone," Samara answered. "There's no surviving that."

"Why would he do such a thing?" Odion said, horrified.

Thimble threw up his arms. "I don't know! You're welcome to ask him!"

The ground rumbled and heaved. A massive fissure appeared in the crystal surrounding the gem.

Thimble regained his footing and cast an eye at Raliak. *There's got to be a way through. Hey! Keeper! Any ideas?*

Silence.

"Great," Thimble muttered under his breath. A sudden flash caught his eye as a dense ball of flame streaked out of the battling throng toward Raliak. The necromancer leaned away, letting the fireball pass harmlessly between himself and the gem.

Worth a shot I guess, Thimble lamented. His eyes scanned the battlefield, looking for something, anything that would give them a chance. *Wait,* Thimble turned back toward Raliak who had returned to his chanting. Still, spells and arrows bounced off of his barrier in droves. *Then why...* Thimble let his Storm Bow dissipate into nothing and stripped his gloves from his hands, a new incantation returning to his mind.

Earth a-run,

Midsummer sun,

A top undone,

A peppered tongue.

Thimble hissed as a searing spot bloomed in the palm of his right hand. The spot blossomed outward, trails of bright reds and oranges carved rivulets halfway up his arm as his skin split and blackened.

Thimble grunted a breath through his teeth. *Just breathe, just breathe,* he thought. *You're the master. Tame it.*

The throbbing agony lessened bit by bit, ages it felt like, but he knew only seconds had passed. He clenched his blackened, now fire-dripped fist around the cinder in his palm. The bow bloomed from between his fingers, flowing lava and rock locked in their metamorphing dance until the glowing weapon pulsed gently in his hand.

Thimble puffed rushed breaths as sweat streamed down his face from the heat and effort. He looked up to find all of the surrounding Blue Cloaks' eyes locked to him.

"Lumenal's grace," Samara whispered. Her eyes held both awe and bewilderment in equal measure. "You're just full of surprises."

"Well," Thimble shrugged and winced. "Guy's gotta have hobbies right?" He turned toward Raliak. "Watch close!" Thimble took aim and drew back the luminous bow string until a volcanic arrow sent hopping embers stinging into his cheek.

The arrow loosed, leaving rippling waves of heat in its wake, streaking toward its target. Raliak turned at the last moment and shot upwards, dodging the projectile by a hair's breadth. He snarled down at Thimble who didn't wait for a response. He loosed arrow after arrow, each one aimed dead center on the old necromancer's torso. Each one dodged without effort.

"Look!" he shouted. His focus was beginning to slip. The pain returned in waves of needling cold and blistering heat. Too much longer and the fire would consume his arm. Permanently. "Look at what he's doing!"

"What?" Samara watched Raliak duck and weave. He snarled unheard words and sent a bolt of purplish light Thimble's way. The spell descended, preparing to ensnare him in its shadowy malice.

With a screech, the void-like bolt slammed into Odion's shield and faltered at the radiant surface. Odion grunted as the blast pushed him back a handful of feet.

"He keeps dodging!" Thimble nodded thanks to Odion, who dropped to one knee to catch his breath, and returned to his firing. "Why is he dodging my arrows and nothing else?"

"I-I don't know," Samara said. "What are you thinking?"

"I don't know either. But he dodged the fireball earlier too. I think it has something to do with fire."

"Celia," Samara gestured to the young Inquisitor.

Celia stepped forward. Hand clenched to her side, she muttered words under her breath. At the last she thrust her hand forward and sent a gout of flame streaking toward the agitating necromancer.

Raliak twisted and shot further into the air. "I've had enough of your impudence!" he shrieked.

Samara ignored him. "Fire! Use fire! Arrows, spells, hells throw torches if you have to. Take him down!"

A volley of flaming projectiles erupted from the Blue Cloaks not engaged in combat with the remaining undead. Raliak rose ever higher in his attempts to avoid the assault. He raised a hand toward where they stood. "*Shiraz Muluk!*"

"Oh, that doesn't sound good," Thimble said.

"High Inquisitor! Behind!"

The group whirled at the shout just as the litter of dead surrounding them began to rise once more. Thimble heard screams of agony as Blue Cloaks were taken by surprise at their once defeated foes' fresh assault.

"*Garrett!*" the shriek from an unfamiliar voice pulled Thimble's eyes. He looked into the face of the serious young Warden, his coiffed hair a mess, his eyes clouded, a bloody tear where his throat used to be as he was dragged into the resurging group of undead.

"Regroup!" Samara belted. "Clear the middle! No strays in the ranks!"

Steel and spells flashed in unison as every Blue Cloak struggled to comply against the re-risen horde. Thimble put an arrow between a closing undead's eyes before sending two more toward Raliak, who rose higher out of reach. His eyes scanned the crowd for Garrett, wishing what he'd seen wasn't true. He saw only more death. "This is bad!" The heat from his Volcanic Bow had begun to poke through his focus. He gritted his teeth against the throbbing pangs of searing flesh.

"No kidding!" Odion snarled back, splitting a headless torso down the middle. "Any ideas?"

"Not really!"

Celia pulled her slender curved blade out of a struggling undead's head. "As long as he's alive, they won't stop."

Thimble snarled up at the hovering necromancer. His sneer returned at their struggle and his eyes focused on the Attrangem once more. *There's got to be something. A little help please!* He thought in desperation.

He's awful high up isn't he? replied a voice not his own.

What? What does that mean?

Silence.

"Damn it all," Thimble said through gritted teeth. He cast his eyes back up. "Awful high...what?"

He glanced past the necromancer to the roiling sea above. The place where, if they let Raliak have his way, they would all be resting for eternity. Maybe some would make it, but not him. He couldn't even swim.

"Celia!" he shouted. "Odion! How high does the gem's pull go?"

"How high?" both intoned.

"Yes! How high? When does the pull reverse?"

Odion shoved a corpse off of the Blue Cloak beside him and shrugged a free shoulder, trading bewildered looks with Celia. "A-a hundred or so yards above the tallest building," she said. "I think!"

"How close is he?" Thimble jabbed his bow toward Raliak. He chanced a glance at his flaming arm. It was still there, attached, blackened, running with liquid flame. Though he could no longer feel it. *No time for that now. Focus.*

"Close," Celia answered.

"Help me!" He raised his numb arm and loosed toward Raliak's feet. "Send him up! Higher!" Celia complied without hesitation.

Streaks of fire hurtled toward Raliak from the pair while the others held off the surrounding undead. Higher and higher the necromancer went, agitation evident on his pointed face. Thimble aimed a shot directly at his groin. Raliak snarled and shot upward. Then stopped. Surprise crossed his face momentarily, before he was once again buffeted by the hail of flame. He continued to dodge, though only side to side.

"There! Keep it up!" Thimble let the Volcanic Bow fade. The feeling in his arm did not return and, though he could still move his fingers, it seemed almost involuntary. "Kerrak!" his terror for his arm pitched his voice higher as he bellowed toward the fighting Gougen. "Kerrak! Come here!"

Kerrak turned bloodlusted eyes toward him as another Blue Cloak stepped across to take up his fight. He thundered up to Thimble, who felt his knees give a little. "None may command me but the High Seats, boy!"

Thimble raised his arms. "I'm sorry. I need your help. Please."

Kerrak's eyes lingered on his blackened arm and softened the tiniest amount. "Hmph. Go on then."

"I need you to throw me at him," he pointed at Raliak.

Kerrak gaped at him like he had lost his mind. "Throw?"

"As hard as you can."

"What are you on abou–"

"Kerrak, just do it!" Samara shouted from behind the pair, her sword locked with a risen Guard's.

"Fine!" Kerrak snatched Thimble from the ground by the collar like an oversized doll. One hand on Thimbles collar, another latched to the hem of his pants, Kerrrak began to spin him like a sack of potatoes.

Thimble could barely hold his eyes open as the world went by in a dizzying blur. "I'm beginning to think this was a bad idea!" Kerrak let go. Thimble sailed through the air faster than he could have imagined. Above the Attrangem, above the stone pillars shielding the city from the gem's light. Higher he rose until he began to slow. The throw wouldn't let him reach. Then again, it wasn't meant to.

With as much focus as he could muster here, hundreds of yards above a city hanging from the bottom of a cliff, he conjured his void bow once more. Taking aim, he loosed a final shot toward the necromancer's head.

"*Dreics!*" He felt himself shatter apart once more. The speed of his thrown momentum and the pull of the void arrow sped his granular body toward the stunned murderer. He came together just as he hit Raliak square in the face, and held on for dear life.

"Argh! You filthy..."

Thimble wasn't listening. He felt the pull of the gem fade as their collision sent them past the point of no return. The world beckoned in that moment. Thimble shoved his mangled hand into his Pouch and withdrew a fistful of powder.

"Hey!" Thimble shouted in Raliak's face. "This one's from my Grampa! Have a little *Taste of Gnome!*" he shoved his powdery fist into the old necromancer's mouth and dumped the entire fistful down his gullet.

Raliak sputtered and coughed as Thimble withdrew his hand. "*Akh...Akh!* What...*akh*...what did you..." his words were cut short as his throat seemed to close in on itself.

As the pair fell, Thimble watched the terrible necromancer writhe and twist as every part of his body shrank and shrank. Raliak screamed and thrashed as his bones and joints popped and twisted, forming into their new size before slotting back into vacant sockets. His newly acquired clothes swallowed him whole, wrapping around him like a silken cocoon. Thimble pulled the new Gnomish bundle close and wrapped both arms and legs around him.

Raliak wailed and thrashed, bound as he was. "When I get out of this, your whole lineage will feel my *agh*!" Thimble squeezed where the sound was coming from.

He looked up, toward the rapidly approaching sea. "Unfortunately, neither of us is getting out of this," he said. He brushed aside the mild shock at how calm he sounded. How calm he felt. "There's something you should know about Gnomes, now that your body will be one for the next day or so." An involuntary laugh bubbled from his throat from the absurdity of it all. "We can't swim."

Chapter Twenty-Two

Irises and Orchids

Old and half rusted, the lock to *Penny's Watching* fought Thimble as always. A recently passed storm hung in the air, the scent of clean mist mingling with fresh mud and damp stone. The lock clicked shut with a final almighty wrench. Thimble shook out his stinging hands and yanked the key from the lock. The bureau was well overdue for a makeover. *Soon, old girl*, he patted the old sodden wood.

Penny's Watching sat at the southern edge of town between a stable and a smithy. An awful location for a business for any outsiders looking in, but Thimble didn't mind. Better here than in the bustling heart of Veppen with its scraping spires and throaty hawkers. He figured he might get more business further in, but the thought of all the noise sent a shiver down his back.

"Mister Pennywhistle!"

Thimble dropped the key into his Pouch and turned toward the familiar caller. Theo Cantle was a slip of a young man. Barely out of his teens and all gangly limbs and freckles, Theo was the very image of a farm lad lost in the big city. He stopped in front of Thimble, huffing and puffing from a long run.

Thimble eyed the young Human bent double. "You know, you don't *have* to run to every delivery?"

Theo straightened, clutching a stitch at his side. His blue and white courier uniform hung from his frame, a size too large. "I-I know, sir. Takin' more jobs. I could u-use the extra coin," he said between breaths. He reached into the satchel draped around his shoulders and pulled a small pouch with an attached letter from the depths. He knelt and held the items out. "For you."

Thimble took the pouch. The smooth rounded edges of coins pressed into his palm through the velvety cloth. Interested, he folded open the letter and read. "Ah," he said as he reached the bottom. "It's from Alma Tredd. Looks like she made it to Ballum safely."

Theo tilted his head. "Tredd? The lady with the diamond buttons?"

Thimble nodded and opened the pouch. "All the best to her, then." He grabbed a handful of gold. "As long as *Mister* Tredd never finds out. Here." He held the gold out toward the young man.

Theo balked. "W-what? I can't take this!"

"Yes you can. I wouldn't have gotten her out of the city without your help. And consider it a thank you for not turning me in." Thimble dropped the coins into Theo's hand.

Theo's eyes shimmered as he looked from the gold down to Thimble. "Turn you in? N-no, sir, I'd never. Not on my life."

"I appreciate that." Thimble dropped the rest of the gold into his Pouch. "Also, it's probably best if you forget what you saw. *All* of it." With a final nod, he turned down the street.

Theo caught up after a moment, hurriedly stuffing the gold into his pockets. "Forget? Sir, I *never* wanna forget. The things you can do−"

"*Shh!*" Thimble hissed as they passed a clump of chattering housewives.

"Sorry," Theo dropped his voice. "I just...I've never seen nothin' like it. Not even in my dreams. I was hopin'..." Theo chewed on his lip, "I was hopin' you'd teach me how."

Thimble stopped in his tracks. "Are you crazy? Do you even know what you're asking?"

"I know it's dangerous−"

"I don't think you do." Thimble ducked into an alley between a grocer and a barber, away from wandering ears. Theo followed, a sheepish expression on his face. "It's *beyond* dangerous, Theo. If the Suppressors caught wind of what I can do, they wouldn't just come for me. They'd come for my whole family, do you understand? We'd spend the rest of our days in a cell, or worse on some lost cause front-line to the west. What you saw was me making a *very* stupid decision and getting lucky that no one *else* happened to be watching at the time. That's all."

Theo frowned at the dirt between his feet. "I understand, sir. I do. I just..." He blew an impatient sigh through his teeth. "I don't wanna be runnin' letters my whole life. It's just me and my sister now, and we're already scrapin' the barrel. I just wish I could do *more. Be* more." He sniffed and glanced out into the street. "I'd better get on to my next delivery. Thank you for the money. It means more than I can say."

Thimble rubbed his eyes, mulling over the terrible choice he knew he would make eventually. "Alright, *alright.* Give me a couple of days. I'll think about it."

Theo's eyes shone like midsummer starlight. "Really? Oh, thank you! Thank you, sir!"

"Hey, I'm not making any promises here."

Theo backed out of the alley, a childlike grin splitting his narrow face in two. "You won't regret it, sir. I promise." He turned and dashed off into the street.

"I haven't said yes yet!" He called to the retreating figure, who threw a hand up and waved as he rounded a corner. "And stop calling me sir!" *Oh boy. What have you done, Thimble?* Thimble shook his head and stepped out of the alley.

A few streets over, he turned into *What in Carnation*, a florist he'd begun to frequent in recent months. The shopkeeper, a rotund woman with the broadest smile he'd ever seen, beamed at his approach. "Mister Pennywhistle, so good to have you back. Will it be the same again?"

Thimble tried not to stare at the enormous daylily tucked behind her ear. "Ah, yes Miss Pick. Thank you."

"Sure, sugar, just a minute." Miss Pick busied herself among her bunches of colors and thorns and returned with a gnome sized trimmed bouquet of violet irises and pink orchids. "Here, y'ar, hun. The best I've got." She stooped to hand Thimble the bouquet.

He dropped a few coins into her palm as she straightened. "Thanks again, Miss Pick. Till next time."

The first rays of sun poked through the departing clouds as he stepped from the shop. He turned eastward, toward his parents' home. His steps slowed and his breath quickened whenever his mind turned to that place. Squat on a hill at the eastern edge of town nestled within a gnomish neighborhood, his old family home had so often been a place to escape from the madness of the city. A place of peace and warmth, where he could just *be*. Even more so than his *own* home. Those days, it was an effort to even think about. An effort that brought its own serving of shame.

"Thimble!" The call roused him from his thoughts. He looked to his right. He'd passed in front of the only Gnome sized eatery in this part of the city and Thimble's daily lunch stop. The mobile shop had its large wheels anchored by bricks, its front shaded by a spotless red and white awning. Four stools sat on the serving side, their occupants tucking into bowls and plates of this or that.

Thimble spotted the caller and waved. "Hiya, Nel."

Nel leaned over the counter top. She'd tied her dirty blonde hair back into a tail, but loose strands fell into her eyes with the motion, like always. "Argh, dammit!" She blew the hair out of her face. "Plate of the usual for you?"

Thimble's stomach rumbled at the familiar smells. "Not today, Nel. Thanks, though." He turned to continue on his way.

"Oh! Thimble wait!" Nel whipped around the little kitchen sending a pan clattering to the floor. Angry shouts between her and the owner echoed out into the street before she spilled out of a side door. "Give me two minutes, Boba! I'll be right back!" She snapped the door shut and hurried toward him. She stood of a height with Thimble, if a hair taller. Her cheeks, stained with a light streak of grease flushed in the sudden cold of the open air.

"Hey, um," she began, rubbing her hands together. "Lily and I and a couple of the guys were thinking about going for a few drinks later. I was hoping you could come."

"Oh...um," he cleared his throat. "Sorry, I-not today."

"Come *on*, you never come out with us. Just this one time."

Vibrant green eyes watched him expectantly. "I...um. Nel, I'm not too good in—"

She held up her hands. "I know, I know. You don't like crowds. Not to worry, it'll just be the five of us. We'll get a private booth. No crowds, no noise. Okay, maybe a little noise. They have these great big battered fried balls filled with dunomo cheese that melts in the mouth and *oh,* I'm drooling already. C'mon it'll be a good time. I promise. Please? *Please?*" She wrapped her hands together and smiled. His ears became hot enough to steam.

"Ahem," he shuffled from foot to foot. "That *does* sound like fun. Um, maybe next time. Today's..." his eyes lingered on the flowers in his arms.

Nel followed his gaze. "Are these for your mum?" She leaned forward and took a scent of the flowers. "They're beautiful."

"Yeah, they are," Thimble breathed as she straightened, his mouth suddenly dry. He shook himself. "Um, the Leighis are here today."

Nel's head rocked back, her eyes rounded in shock. "The *Leighis?* From Greater Baisti? H-how'd you manage that?"

"My dad knows some people."

"Thimble," her eyes shone and she laughed as she took his free hand in both of hers. "That's *amazing* news!"

"I-um...yeah it's..."

Nel studied his face and her smile slipped bit by bit. "What's the matter? If anyone can help, it's them, right?"

Thimble gazed at his hand, still locked firmly between hers. "I hope so. That's what I'm nervous about. I mean, if *they* can't, then what? We've tried everything else, even reached out overseas and nothing else has worked. It's...terrifying. The thought."

"Hey." Nel pressed a soft, gentle hand into his cheek and raised his eyes to hers. "Have a little faith, hmm? Everything will be fine. I'm sure of it."

Thimble couldn't help but return her smile. His heart still skipped, but no longer at the doubts that had eaten away at him. For an all too brief moment, the world faded away around them.

"*Nel! Get back in here!*"

The pair jumped in unison. Nel turned over her shoulder. "I'm coming,

Boba! Gods!" She turned back toward him with a mischievous grin and inviting eyes. She tapped him twice on the cheek and broke away. "I'll let you off the hook this time, Thimble. Next time, you're coming along. No buts, got it?" She turned away and hurried back toward the cart, her soup stained apron swishing along with her skipping stride. Thimble smiled, watching her go. The gentle scent of daffodils lingered in her wake.

* * *

His steps echoed heavily as he ascended the stairs to the front porch. Something wasn't right. Where were the carts and carriages full of Leighis? Where was the bustle and buzz of a place at work? A place infected with the verve of hope? The windows of the house lay dark. Only the occasional lantern flickered behind the frosted glass.

Thimble pushed open the door. Some part of him hoped he'd missed something. That sound and activity would envelop him as he entered. None came. He stood alone in the dark entryway. In the quiet. He kicked off his boots and padded further into the house, bouquet gripped in his arms.

The hallway opened into a living area to the right and a kitchen and dining area to the left. Sofas and seats lay scattered about and in one of the longer ones sat his grampa and his dad. Grumble sat with his head in his hands, not moving, not speaking. Sibelius sat beside with a hand on his son's back, eyes in the distance.

Sibelius glanced over as Thimble entered. "Thimble...my boy."

Thimble eyes darted between the pair. "Grampa? Dad? W–where is everyone?"

Sibelius shook his head. "They're gone, son."

"Gone?" Thimble stepped shakily toward them. "What did they say?"

"I'm...I'm sorry, Thimble. They couldn't do anything."

All of his fears rushed forth at once. His breathing came sharp, quick. "What do you mean they couldn't do anything?" His voice rose out of his control. "They're the greatest magical healers on the continent, aren't they? *What do you mean they couldn't do anything?*"

"Give it a rest, Thimble. It's *over*," Grumble said without looking up. Thimble stared at his father in disbelief. "Over? How can it be over?"

"We've tried everything. *Everything.*"

"Dad. We can't just give up!"

"What would you have us do, huh?" Grumble shot to his feet. His shout echoed through the silent house. "What *haven't* we done? They tried, Thimble. They tried and they failed! *Just* like us."

"That's enough." Sibelius laid a hand on Grumble's shoulder. "Enough."

Grumble sucked in a rattling breath, his red and puffy eyes widening for an instant. He gave a defeated sigh and brushed past Thimble and out the front door.

Thimble stood leaned against the wall. His eyes unfocused. His mind in a thousand places at once. How could they give up? There had to be something, didn't there? How could there be *nothing?*

"Thimble." His grampa's voice snapped him back to the present. Sibelius stood in front of him, eyes drooping with sorrow. "Go on up, son. She'll be glad to see you."

Thimble sniffed and scrubbed at his eyes. His feet carried him toward the stairs, though when or how he arrived in front of his parents' room door, he hardly knew. His hand trembled on the handle as it had so many times before. He hated walking through this door. Hated seeing what lay beyond. Hated himself more for feeling this way. He turned the handle and entered.

"Ma?" he said, shutting the door behind him. He heard her before he rounded the short hallway into the bedroom. Her breathing had become more ragged, more strained in recent weeks. Now, the breaths barely came at all. Whispers, they sounded like, to Thimble's ears. "Ma? It's me."

She lay propped up on a pillow, her head tilted back, her eyes barely open. "...mble?" she whispered.

"That's right," he smiled. Her eyes found him after a moment, sunken as they were. Her cheeks were gaunt and hollow, her skin stretched and pallid. Her hair, thinning and frayed as it was, appeared combed and tidy. "Brought you some flowers. Let's get these old things out of here." He plucked the wilting stems from the vase beside her bed and unwrapped the fresh bouquet into the water. He busied himself replacing the dwindling candles around the room.

"Remember the button lady I told you about?" He spoke as he worked. "The one running from her slimeball husband? She's safe and sound in Ballum now. Theo was a big help, too. You were right about him, of course." He closed and shuttered the only window in the room. "Nel invited me out again today. Gods, I feel like such an *idiot* when I'm around her, I don't know why. Well...I know *why*, it's just...you know."

"...Thimble..."

"Yeah?" He lit the last candle and turned back toward the bed. Candlelight glinted off streaks of wetness from her eyes. Thimble's heart sank as he hurried to her side. "Hey, Ma. What's the matter?" He pulled a clean handkerchief from his Pouch and dabbed at her eyes.

"...don't...fight..." her breath escaped in a quiet sob and tears redoubled from her eyes.

Oh, you giant moron, Thimble. "D-don't worry about that Ma," he said, his voice breaking. "You know me and Dad are the biggest knuckleheads in the world, right? We'll be okay, don't you worry."

"...I'm...*sorry*..."

"No no no," his own eyes welled over as he dabbed at hers. "This isn't your fault, Ma. None of this is your fault. Screw the Leighis. We'll keep looking. We'll find *something*, I promise." Her fingers twitched on the covers. He took her hand and pressed it against his cheek like she used to when she could. Her fingers were cold, motionless except for a gentle tremble. "I promise."

"...my...boys..."

"We're here, Ma," he sobbed into her palm. "We're right here."

"...please...live."

The trembling stilled. The whispers hushed.

"M-ma?"

Silence and stillness reigned as his world crumbled around him.

Chapter Twenty-Three

Muted Victory

Thimble held tight. Something squirmed in his arms. In the cold. In the dark. Until it didn't. He sank. Down, down further than thought. Past any feeling, any want or need. This place was familiar, if it was a place at all.

His eyes felt heavy. Color and motion danced behind leaded lids until dark soothed them away. Sound touched his ears in whispers and muffled thrums, but never long enough to matter.

He was warm. So warm. The cold, a distant memory. Who was he again? Why did he matter?

Thimble awoke bundled in sun warmed sheets. His protesting eyes fluttered open to blurred haloes clouding his vision. He blinked away the nagging coronas and tried to sit up. Every fiber of his being screamed in protest. He gave in, flopping back into his inviting chrysalis.

When next he opened his eyes, the lights glowed softer. He groaned as he pushed himself upright.

"Hey! Easy," a gentle voice sounded somewhere to his left. A strong hand found the small of his back and tipped him the whole way up.

Thimble pushed himself back on the seat of his pants until his back found a blessedly soft purchase. He sighed as his body relaxed from the exertion and took in his surroundings.

He lay on a bed too large by ten. Spotless white sheets graced a plush bedding and little knobs of wood poked up by the corners. He himself was clothed in what looked to be a child's nightgown. To his left sat a concerned looking Odion, flanked by Celia, who studied him intently. To his right sat Samara, the right side of her head wrapped in clean bandages and off the foot of the bed stood Kerrak. Against the back wall of the lengthy room stood Thelia and Scar.

Thimble, surprised, lingered on them for a moment. Thelia caught his eye, turned a light shade of pink, gave a stiff nod, and stalked off. Scar took a longer moment to dip a small bow in his direction before following.

The surrounding Blue Cloaks had ditched their namesake adornments and armor and instead donned simple cream colored clothing embroidered in thin gold thread around the edges and down the sleeves. The gathered smiled down at him, all touched with sadness.

"Well," Thimble cleared his throat. "I'd hoped the afterlife would be a bit more...uh...attractive."

A quiet laugh rippled through the group and a few shoulders seemed to relax if only a bit.

"How are you feeling?" Samara asked.

Thimble blew out a breath. "Like death. Who, I'm guessing I was pretty close to meeting face to face?"

"About as close as you can get," Celia said.

"How'd you get to me fast enough to pull me out?"

"We didn't," Odion answered. "We found you at the end of a pier with a note beside." He reached into a pocket and unfolded a rumpled slip of paper. "'*I told you nothing good comes with mingling with that lot.*'"

"Aha," Thimble recalled the words said to him by a boorish Captain. "I was going to ask what kind of person leaves a note next to a corpse, but never mind."

"An old friend?" Samara asked.

Thimble shrugged. "Something like that." He left it at that. The Blue Cloaks didn't press.

"By the way," he said, eyeing them up and down. "Is this a new uniform? I like it."

"Mm. No," Samara said, her smile sad. "Today was a day for farewells. This is the Anvil's traditional wear."

"I see," Thimble could still see Garrett's lifeless face every time he blinked; could still hear the screams of the falling Anvilites. It wasn't something he was likely to forget soon. "How many?"

"Too many...and more."

Thimble nodded. "What happened with...you know. Him."

"Funnily enough, we found him right next to you," Samara answered. "Bundled in what was left of his clothes. He was long gone before you were ever pulled out of the water."

"Good. Though...it's not the first time he's been 'gone'."

Celia shook her head. "We gave him a more traditional sendoff. I daresay even the gods would have trouble putting his ashes back together."

Thimble let go of a tension he hadn't realized he was holding and sank further into his seat. "There's that at least." He reached over to scratch at his right arm at the mention of 'ashes'.

His fingers reached through open air.

Thimble closed his eyes as his heart sank. *Oh no. Oh...oh no.*

He opened his eyes and forced himself to look. A wrapped stump of a limb hung limply, severed clean at the elbow. "Ahh...damn it."

Samara laid a hand on his shoulder. "I'm sorry, Thimble. We tried to save it but...it was too far gone."

Thimble stared at the space his arm used to be. He swore he could feel an itch, just above the missing wrist. Pangs of grief rippled through him. Odd...that he would feel this way after losing a limb. *It's just an arm,* he thought. *Isn't it?* He grabbed the front of his nightgown and scrubbed at his eyes.

"Yeah, well," he said after a moment. "It's not like I didn't know what I was doing. Still...guess my archery days are over." He choked on a stifled sob.

Samara gave his shoulder a gentle squeeze and sat back in her seat. "I don't know how we can ever thank you, Thimble. You risked everything to save this city. Us," she glanced around the others, "Words can hardly convey our gratitude, but it's no excuse to not say them. Thank you." The other Blue

Cloaks echoed the sentiment.

Thimble was never great at taking compliments or praise. He felt his collar heat up under all of the gazes and scrambled for something to say. "Well. Let's not get ahead of ourselves. I never did find the girl."

The Blue Cloaks traded confused glances. "What girl?"

Pop.

"WAH! Stop! Stop! It's me!"

Thimble hardly registered the appearance of the old wizard before he was pinned to the ground by Celia. Odion, Kerrak, and Samara all stood at the ready, Samara with a lithe dagger in one hand.

"Carrom?" Samara and Thimble said together.

"Yes! Hello!" Carrom grunted from the floor. "If you could release my arm, young lady, it doesn't quite bend that way anymore."

Celia glanced up at Samara. "Ma'am?"

Samara nodded. "Ease off, Inquisitor. He's not a threat...are you Carrom?"

Celia stood back, allowing Carrom to gather himself to his feet. He wore the same thick blue bathrobe and had donned a shady pointed purple hat. "No, no. Of course not," he dusted himself off and waved a hand. "I only came to see the boy."

"Carrom," Thimble said as the little old man bustled around the foot of the bed to his right side, watched closely by the Blue Cloaks. "What are you doing here? What about your tower?"

"Oh that old thing?" Carrom stood over his bed peering down at him through round spectacles. "I brought it back. Well, the rest of it."

"Brought it back? What, it's whole now?"

"That it is!" he leaned close. "Between you and me, I was trying to take the rest of it with me. All the ruckus going on in the city. But, I saw something that changed my mind." His face returned to that stoic, almost frightening mask he'd shown before. His eyes bore through Thimble. "My boy, had I an iota of your bravery, this entire mess could have been avoided. The last time...the first time. But I am, and have always been a coward." He placed a hand on Thimble's shoulder. "For that. For this. I am sorry." He took his free hand and gripped Thimble's bandaged stump. Hard.

"*Gah!* What –" A blistering pain, too familiar, shot up his shoulder and rang his bells. He writhed in agony as the pain crawled its way back down his arm. Though he knew it wasn't there anymore, he still felt the heat cut its way down where his forearm should have been, past his absent wrists and to the tips of his late fingers.

"Hey! Let him go!"

Samara reached for Carrom. Each Blue Cloak moved as if to spring at the old man, but their movements slowed, molasses like. He looked back at Carrom and found the old wizard's eyes boring into his own.

"My apologies once again, Thimble Pennywhistle. And my thanks. Whenever you need it. You will have it."

Pop.

The pain vanished with Carrom. Samara and the others stumbled, her hand snatching at the air where the old man had been moments before. "Argh! That...piece of..." Samara snarled, scanning the room to see where Carrom could have gotten to.

"Um...Thimble?" Odion gawked at Thimble. He gestured to his right.

Thimble followed his gaze toward his missing arm and let out a yelp. The stump was still there, as were the bandages. But, just below where once had been empty air, a shimmering pale blue translucent arm poked out of his sleeves. As he watched, the shimmering ceased and the blue faded until all that was left were thin lines of blue luminescence that traveled up and down in the shape of his arm in strange patterns and dances. He flexed his fingers, feeling the shift and tightening of tendons and joints he knew weren't there. He squeezed his fist tight and felt invisible fingernails cut into his palm. The lines brightened and sped as he moved and flexed and relaxed along with him.

"What in the world," Odion whispered. The Blue Cloaks stared with wonder at Thimble's new appendage.

"When I need it..." Thimble muttered to himself. He let his new arm fall limply to the bedding. The lines slowed and grew still, until with a last flicker faded entirely, leaving nothing but air in their wake. Thimble waved his left hand through where the arm was until moments ago and felt nothing. He lay back, breathless. "Odion, hand me a glass of water would you?"

Odion started from his awestruck staring and poured Thimble a glass with a brass pitcher beside his bed. "Here," he held it out to Thimble.

Thimble reached across with his right. *When I need it.* Thin blue lines erupted from the point his phantom fingers found the cool glass and snaked their way down to his elbow, forming the new spellwoven arm.

"Oh shit."

Chapter Twenty-Four

Inheritance

The next few days passed in a blur of color and noise. The Anvil's head physician insisted on keeping Thimble for longer, no doubt to continue poking and prodding at his new arm, which could still feel pain and cold and heat, as it turned out. She would have succeeded as well, had Samara not stepped in.

"He's not some experiment you can toy with to your heart's content, Deacon Mazlen!" She thundered down at the cowering bespectacled woman. "You *will* discharge him. Now."

"Y-yes High I-inquisitor. A-as you w-wish ma'am."

The first blast of cool, fresh sea air wrapped Thimble like a favorite coat. Mid morning sunlight glimmered off the quiet sea above, gentle waves lapping against and rocking docked ships filled with goods and people alike. The peaceful scene felt almost out of place, after all that had occurred only days ago.

What girl, eh? Thimble had prodded over the last few days, desperate to find what they had meant. The truth found its way to him eventually. The dreams had stopped the day after Raliak's defeat. And with it had gone the memory of Lady Ema de Erek Profs. Careful not to come off like a nutter, Thimble had pried from his friends the whole story. There had only ever been nine members in the de Evoire family, including the late Lady Annabeth. Not only was there no Ema, the surname de Erek Profs didn't exist either.

"Thimble," Samara joined him on the last step of the Anvil's Infirmary. A new oiled leather patch covered her left eye. "I'm sure you have a lot on your mind. But, I was hoping you could spare me a bit more of your time. There's something I'd like you to see."

Thimble had planned on journeying to the only place he could hope to find answers, but he was in no hurry to dunk himself headlong into another pool of water. "Of course."

Samara led him through to the crossroads. The streets were not so busy as he remembered, though a steady stream of comers and goers made their way by foot or by wagon through the topsy tunnel. Thimble followed Samara toward the city square where the Attrangem stood, stoic as ever. Here and there people waved toward them as they passed. Most smiled, most sad. It took a while for Thimble to realize they were waving at *him*.

"So," Samara said. "Word of your deeds may have spread quicker than I thought it would. Though it may not touch the most ardent of naysayers and old-wayers, I daresay you've changed a few perceptions. For the better."

"Oh...great," Thimble returned a nervous wave to a small child waving with her entire body. "Now I get to decide which is worse: being ignored or being noticed."

Samara snorted. Their steps took them to the mid city sections where most of the fighting had taken place. The hum and bustle of a place usually filled to bursting with life fell into a somber hush. Ruined homes yet lined the streets, though groups of Blue Cloaks along with City Guard and citizenry worked to clear the rubble. Here and there, sounds of hammers on nails echoed through too empty streets.

"What's going to happen to all of this?" Thimble asked.

Samara surveyed the working Anvilites. "We save what we can. Families of the fallen, the ones who made it, should have what closure they can," she heaved a heavy sigh. "Then, we tear it all down and start anew. Better, this time though. With more mind paid to those with less."

Thimble nodded. "That sounds nice."

Samara lowered her eyes to the cobblestone. "It's unfortunate that it takes a tragedy to remind us of what's really important. May we not forget any time soon."

What's really important. Thimble mulled over the words as the pair walked in silence. The city center hadn't changed much since that day. Once or twice, Thimble shook himself at the images that came to mind as he studied the mostly empty square. Images that would plague his dreams for a while.

Ladders and scaffolds leaned against many of the tall stone walls surrounding the square. Workers stood on almost every level with a hammer in one hand, and a small chisel in the other.

"Here. This one's complete," Samara beckoned him over to one of the walls closest to the crossroads entrance. "Take a look."

Thimble stepped in front of the wall and peered at the strange carvings studded into the old stone. It took him too long to realize what he was seeing. "Are these...names?"

Samara nodded. "Every person who fell that day will be remembered on these walls. Anvilite, guard, citizen. Everyone. It's with a heavy heart that I believe every inch of these stones will be covered by the time the work is done. But, as I said, we cannot forget.

"Ah! Speaking of forgetting," Samara reached under her cloak and pulled a jangling pouch from around her belt. "This," she dropped the *heavy* pouch into his arms. "Is the rest of your pay. And a little extra as thanks. From the city."

"Wha—" Thimble struggled under the weight of the thing. "I-well-h-hold on, help me would you." He handed the satchel of gold back to the amused High Inquisitor and withdrew his Almost Unending Pouch of Things. Stretching the opening wide, he watched Samara drop the mound of gold into the inert darkness.

"Handy that," Samara said, impressed.

"An old gift from my mum." Thimble cinched the opening shut once more and stared at the little pouch. "Are you sure this is alright? Doesn't the city need it for the rebuild?"

Samara waved a hand. "The city has more than enough, believe me. You've earned every piece."

Thimble stared at the old Pouch a moment longer. "Can I ask you something, Samara?"

"Of course."

"What's really important? To me?"

Samara blinked, bemused. "I...think the best person to answer that would be yourself, no?"

"Yeah...*yeah*, of course," he shook his head and tied the Pouch back onto his belt. He looked up into the High Inquisitor's face, her expression curious and concerned. "It's just...the last month...the last *while*, really. It's. It's been a lot, and um..." he rubbed at his eyes, words finding no purchase on his tongue. *Not again. Hold it together, Thimble,* he chided himself.

A light clinking of armor in front made him look up. Samara knelt on one knee, her eyes, touched with a gentle sorrow, level with Thimble. "I recognize the torment of loss all too well, Thimble," she said softly. "I saw it when we first met. It's only grown stronger since then. And I understand. I do. I've been there myself. Too many times in my years." She placed a hand on his shoulder. "I don't know if I can tell you what you need to hear. If I could tell you the fastest way out of that shadow infested mire, *gods* I would, but...I'm afraid there is no shortcut. But, I'll tell you this. Don't use your memories of the departed as a path into deeper sorrow. That's not what they would want, is it? Instead, use those memories to bolster yourself. Remind yourself that they were here, right beside you once, and left their indelible marks upon you as a person. Now, it's your responsibility to carry those marks in a way that would fill their givers with endless pride." She squeezed his shoulder once and sat back. "Does that make sense? I'm not the best with words."

"It does," Thimble nodded, a lump firm in his throat. "It does."

Samara smiled. "I'm glad. As for what's really important? Well, once you have space in your mind, in your soul, I have faith the answer will come to you. It may not be today or tomorrow or for a while yet, but it will come. And when it does, it will be so simple, you'll kick yourself for not realizing sooner."

Thimble smiled at the last. *What's really important?* He still wasn't sure how to answer the question, but the High Inquisitor's words eased his mind a blessed bit. He watched Samara rise to her full height with a groan. Answer or no, he was grateful, immensely so, to have met the people he had on this journey. He looked down at his right side and made his new arm appear for a moment with the smallest exertion of intent. *Even the crazier ones.*

"High Inquisitor!" a familiar voice boomed across the square.

Samara gave Thimble a long pained eye roll. The pair turned as one toward the newcomers and found Lord Ellis Mendel strutting in their direction with Lady Clara Tavinari in tow. The two were accompanied by an older man and a middle aged woman Thimble didn't recognize, but their clothing marked them as a similar ilk to the Tavinaris and Mendels.

"Speaking of kicking," Samara said, low enough for only Thimble to hear. "Lord Mendel," she said aloud. "Lady Tavinari. And Lord and Lady Aganis and Kovi as well. What a...pleasant...surprise."

Ellis Mendel stopped a few paces from them, his hair rumpled and angry sweat beading his forehead. "It would not have been a surprise had you heeded our summons, High Inquisitor. I know you've been avoiding us."

"Avoiding?" Samara narrowed her eyes, causing Ellis to pale the slightest bit. "I avoid nothing, Lord Mendel. As you can plainly see, the Anvil has been quite busy with reconstruction efforts, thanks of course to the Families and your generosity." She dipped a smallest of bows toward the Lords and Ladies.

The older man, Lord Aganis, pulled a handkerchief from inside his silken coat and dabbed at his upper lip. "You are well aware that we had little choice in the matter, High Inquisitor."

"And yet you chose anyway, Lord Aganis. Again, I am very grateful."

Ellis waved his hand impatiently. "Yes yes, that's all well and good. What about the estate, High inquisitor. The *estate*."

"Yes, do resolve this matter, Samara," Lady Tavinari added. "At least to cease young Ellis' incessant blubbering."

Samara rubbed at her brow. "As you are all well aware, the de Eviore estate should pass to the closest living relative of the de Evoires. We do indeed have word that none of the remaining Saltanis family want anything to do with the place–"

"Then?" Ellis interrupted. "That's it isn't it? Council bylaw states that any vacated estate gets auctioned and any citizen of the city may participate."

He spread his hands by his sides. "And seeing as I am the only bidder worth a damn, I suggest you hurry this along. Unless you think one of *these*," he looked around at no one in particular. "Can give more."

Samara's scowl could have withered the sun into early retirement. "You are correct in your assertion, Lord Mendel. We have done our due diligence and agree that you are probably the only choice in this matter."

"Wait!" Thimble said. Five heads snapped in his direction.

"It speaks?" Lady Kovi's slurring accent dripped with disgust. "How vulgar."

"Yes, do keep quiet when those of import speak, Gnome," Lady Tavinari added. "You allow this even in your presence, High Inquisitor? Hmph."

Samara ignored them. "What is it, Thimble?"

How could he have forgotten? His heart skipped against his chest as it all came rushing back to him. "Um...well...actually..."

"Out with it!" Lord Mendel snapped.

Oh he would relish this moment for years to come. "I'm Lady Annabeth's grandson."

The silence was deafening. Thimble looked from one stunned face to the next, soaking in the disbelief.

"Absurd."

"What a load of crock."

"The audacity! You should be clapped in chains for that!"

"Horseshit stinks less!"

"Thimble?" Samara studied him, bewildered as the Lords' and Ladies' tirade washed over them. "What are you saying?"

"I know it sounds crazy. But it's true."

"Why haven't you mentioned this before?"

Thimble shuffled uncomfortably. "I...ah...I kind of forgot."

"Forgot!" Ellis Mendel's eyes looked ready to pop out. Spittle flew at his every word. "Of course you forgot! Oh and what a convenient time to remember, isn't it! I harbor no ill feeling toward your people, young man, but a wilder tale I've not heard from even the Drifters!"

Lady Tavinari cleared her throat. "Surely you aren't entertaining this drivel,

Samara? I had no love for Annabeth, but *she* at least knew her station."

"Thimble, are you absolutely sure? How do you know this?" Disbelief and excitement warred in Samara's expression.

Thimble shrugged. "My grampa told me."

"Your *grampa*, is it?" the scorn in Lady Kovi's voice would strip the hide from an aldgoat. "Another Gnome is he? *Fel manus iztna malercia!* Liars and cheats the lot!"

Thimble spread his hands to his sides. "We can go to your circle if you like?" he said to Samara.

Something glimmered in Samara's eyes. "I don't think that'll be necessary. I believe you."

"Believe!" Ellis had turned a shade of red not named in the common tongue as of yet. "Necessary! It is absolutely necessary! Take him there, we will all go. Let the circle lay bare his lies!"

"I have a better idea," Samara turned on her heel. "Come!" she sped off down the street. Thimble chanced a cheeky grin at the Lords and Ladies before taking off after the departing High Inquisitor.

Samara led them through narrow alleys – for which the gentry were none too grateful – straight to the Reader's Archive. The first floor of the archive had its usual bustle of citizenry along with the occasional Blue Cloak Initiate poring over one tome or another.

Samara hailed a passing blue stoled Reader. "Recaller Guimar!"

The Recaller stopped and turned their way. "Ah, High Inquisitor," Guimar's soothing baritone was touched with a smile. "And Mister Pennywhistle. To what do I owe the honor? I see you've brought...guests." The lords and ladies arrived huffing and puffing while trying to maintain their demeanor. Thimble stifled a laugh.

"Recaller, there is a matter we need your assistance with. Are you familiar with the linking of lineages?"

"Of course, it is a speciality of mine. Whose lineage would you like to confirm today?"

"Lady Annabeth. I assume there is still a sample of her blood within the archives?"

"Of course. And with whom are we comparing?"

"Mine," Thimble said.

Recaller Guimar's eyebrows would have climbed into his hair if he had any. "Is that right? Fascinating. It would be my pleasure to assist. This way please."

Up two flights of stairs and down a long corridor, Guimar led them to a small room adorned much like a writing room. He ushered the lot in and bid them wait. Not too long after, the Reader returned carrying a small vial of reddish brown liquid and a thin coin sized saucer.

"Just a moment while I prepare," Guimar pulled an assortment of materials from within a large writing desk that dominated much of the room. He placed the saucer in the middle and tipped in a few drops of blood from the vial. He surrounded the saucer with a few tufts of red clover and strips of sage and biloba.

Placing the last of the leaves, Guimar beckoned Thimble to join him. He drew a small penknife from a drawer as Thimble approached. "I'm afraid a bit of blood is required for the ritual, my friend."

Thimble glanced down to his right. With the bandages removed, he hadn't quite gotten used to the abrupt end of his arm. He shook himself of the feeling and extended his left to the Recaller. "What's a bit more, eh? Have at it."

Guimarn pricked the tip of his middle finger and gathered a few drops of blood into a separate clean vial. With a soft whisper and a touch, he closed Thimble's cut and released his arm. "Now," he said to all gathered. "I will tell you what is to be expected. Shortly I will mix the two sources of blood into one. Then, I will begin the incantation that will determine the connection. I will not be able to see what is occurring as I will have my eyes closed. Please remember, green is a distant relation, gold is a direct blood relation, and black is no relation, understood?"

Thimble and Samara nodded.

"Yes yes!" Ellis snapped. "Get on with it!"

Guimar gave him a disapproving look before tipping Thimble's blood into the saucer. The two liquids merged into one until indistinguishable from one another. Guimar lowered himself onto the chair behind the desk, clasped his hands and closed his eyes. He began to chant under his breath.

Thimble stood on his tiptoes to peer over the edge of the table. What if it turned gold? What if it *didn't*? He couldn't decide which outcome was better. He glanced around at the beady, hungry eyes of the Lords and Ladies. *Never mind. I know which one's better.*

The blood swayed with the rhythmic chanting, undulating and twisting with a depth unbecoming. Gently, the liquid rose into the air, spinning faster and faster forming into a tightly packed orb. The glow started deep within the little globe. Dim white at first, then flashes of blue and green.

"What is this? What are we looking at?" Lady Tavinari said.

"Shh," Samara put a finger to her lips. Lady Tavinari's face soured, but she held her tongue.

The little orb pulsed with swirling hues until finally, the colors stilled. The surface of the orb lay golden, shimmering. As they watched, the orb scattered in motes of brilliant light as if eased apart by gentle wind, until nothing remained. Guimar heaved a sigh, his work completed.

Thimble's heart hammered in his chest. He looked toward Samara and found the High Inquisitor's face lit by the biggest, toothiest grin.

Chapter Twenty-Five

Back Under

The key turned. The lock clicked. The door swung forward to a place Thimble had hoped he would never return. And now, it was his. The foyer lay as dark as ever, a reminder of all that had occurred. A bit of him hoped the family had found some small measure of peace at last.

"Thimble?" Odion said from the doorway. "Remind me again why I'm here. I'm not too fond of this place, you know."

"You and me both. But I need someone I can trust to make sure I don't drown. Again." He turned to face the young Warden. "Besides, you've already seen it, so that he–! *What* are you doing here?"

Celia poked her head over Odion's shoulder. "Hello."

Thimble spread his arms by his side. "Um...Hello. Were you following us?"

"Uh-huh. For a while actually."

"Why?"

Celia shrugged. "It's my day off. I was bored. Saw you two sneaking about. Got curious. You've got to work on your awareness, by the way. I wasn't exactly hiding."

"We weren't *sneaking* anywhere," Thimble crossed his arms. "This is my house now, you know."

"Oh ho! I know," Celia pushed past Odion and welcomed herself in. She peered around the dim interior. "I think *everyone* knows. Well done by the way. I hear Ellis Mendel hasn't left his manor in almost two days." She cackled into the dark.

"Well," Thimble gazed around himself. "I still don't really want it. But I couldn't let it fall to those clowns."

"Mm. What are you two doing here anyway? Grand tour?"

Thimble traded a glance with Odion, the question unsaid and obvious: "What do you think?"

Odion shrugged. "We've been through a lot together."

Thimble nodded. It was true enough. He gestured for both Odion and Celia to follow. "Come on then. And not a word to anyone else, yes? Not even Samara."

Celia faltered a step. "You're keeping this from the High Inquisitor? Why? She trusts you, doesn't she? Is she not afforded the same?"

Thimble shook his head. "It's not about trust. She would have questions about what you're about to see. Questions I don't have answers to. I'd rather not get her involved until I have something to say. Let's make it quick."

* * *

"What in the world?" Celia breathed.

The trio stood at the edge of the Well of Stars on a path leading down to the surface Thimble hadn't noticed before. The surface lay glass still, twinkling in torchlight.

"Apparently, it's called the Well of Stars. That's what Nira said anyway." He shook himself of a ghostly allure that pulled at him upon seeing the Well once more. "Do you have the rope?" he asked Odion.

Odion nodded and pulled a heavy length of rope from a satchel on his side. He handed an end to Thimble. "I don't know about this."

Thimble took the rope and began fastening it around his waist. "Neither do I. But, if this works, we'll know a bit more about what happened here."

"Wait, wait," Celia rubbed her temples. "Are you planning on going *in there*? Have you lost your mind?"

"I don't think so," Thimble stretched the last knot tight. "Listen. I'll explain everything once I'm out. Hold this," he handed Odion the other end of the rope. "If I'm not out in, say, ten minutes...pull."

"Ten minutes!" Celia gave him a disbelieving look. "Didn't you *just* survive a drowning?" She looked at Odion. "How are you going along with this?"

Thimble raised his hands. "Hey. I'll ask you the same thing I asked Odion. Can you please just trust me on this? I know it's odd, and I promise, I'll tell you all I can when I'm back." He turned toward the Well. "Also, don't follow me down there. I don't know how he'll react."

"Who's he?" the Blue Cloaks said together.

Thimble jumped.

Chapter Twenty-Six

To End the Unending

Thimble stood staring out at the field of pads and bubbles once more. The swirling tapestry above glimmered brilliant as ever. A familiar serenity surrounded him. The Keeper of Dreams drifted towards him in his sweeping robes and high collar.

"Ah," he spread his arms wide. "The victor returns. Welcome back, Thimble."

"Uh...hello," the Keeper stopped a few paces from Thimble, looming over with this impressive height.

The Keeper scrunched his eyebrows together. "Hm. I don't really see myself as the looming type, actually. Wait, I have an idea." He raised a hand and snapped his fingers. In a puff of wispy smoke, the Keeper shrank until a Gnome sized version of him stood in front of Thimble, sweeping robes and all.

The Keeper examined his new form. "Not bad, if I do say so myself. What do you think?"

Thimble snapped his teeth shut. "Y-yeah...that works." Thimble couldn't remember the last time he'd seen a Gnome that wasn't part of his family. So used to craning his neck to taller speakers, the relief of looking a standing person in the eye caught him by surprise.

"By the way," The Keeper pointed to the rope tied around Thimble's midriff. "That's adorable."

Thimble examined the rope and found a severed end trailing in the water below a few paces behind him. "Oh."

"Not to worry. I'm sure you'll be back with your friends in no time. Meanwhile," he leaned in. "I *know* you've got some questions for me. Let's chat."

Thimble put the cut rope out of his mind. He hoped Odion and Celia wouldn't do anything drastic. Something about the Keeper's mannerisms unnerved him. He was...different from before. "Right. Questions. Nobody in the city remembers the girl. It seems like any memory of her went with the dreams. Your doing I assume?"

The Keeper smiled a broad toothy grin. "One of the perks of the role."

"So she *isn't* real?"

"Never was."

"What was the point of the dream then?"

The Keeper shrugged. "Just something to keep the dogs chasing their tails really."

Thimble scratched his chin, confusion mounting. "Who sent the letter? The one I received from her?"

"Ah yes, the letter. That was me as well. Or, technically, that was me through dear old Nira."

"Nira sent the letter?"

The Keeper nodded. "She did indeed. And with zeal."

Thimble rubbed his brow. "I don't understand. You told her to? And she just went along with it? Why?"

"Because she received a vision of her dear old grandfather in a dream one night. He congratulated her on snatching away the youngest daughter of that detestable family. All that was left was to send one measly letter and go about her business. She was all too happy to believe it because," he tapped the side of his head, "she wasn't all there. And oh my did she *hate* her family. The kind of hate that...well...you saw what she did to them."

"Go about her business? Then what about the rest? Everything that happened after?"

"All her idea. Every. Last. Thing." The Keeper threw his head back and laughed. The sound rippled the water below in angry ridges as little waves crashed and foamed the once mirror surface. Thimble winced at the pulse between breaths, the sound sheared against his eardrums like a steel toothed brush. "I do admit I nudged her along here and there, but truly, I think she was waiting for *any* excuse to swan dive off the deep end." The Keeper flourished his arms above his head into a diver's pose.

"I can't imagine the kind of hate that would make her do the things she's done." Images of the Stitched Cadaver forced their way into Thimble's thoughts. What a mask Nira wore to hide hatred of that kind. Or maybe, he hadn't been paying enough attention. The thought annoyed him to no end.

"Can't you?" The Keeper lowered his arms and raised a brow. "I'd say such feelings are quite common amongst mortalkind. Then again I *have* been around for a *long* time."

Thimble thought back to the last time he'd seen Nira in the city center. "She said the family exiled Raliak for 'loving his wife'. Is that why?"

The Keeper smirked. "That would be the start of it I suppose." The Keeper drew a long breath and tapped a finger against his chin, his eyes distant, recalling. "Young Raliak and his wife Secilia had a tiff, you see. She had caught him practicing his 'necromancy' - if you can call it that - and was horrified. The young lady pleaded for him to stop, to give up his pursuits lest his family discover him and ostracize them both. Raliak refused and in the ensuing bit of weeping and arm grabbing, lashed out at the poor young woman. The blow wasn't meant to be harsh, only enough to remind her of her place, or so Raliak intended. She toppled backward and cracked her skull open on one of their bedposts." The Keeper sighed, a glint of pity in his eyes. "A stupid mistake from a bullheaded young man. Funnily enough, I think Nira was right. Raliak truly did love his wife, and it's what he did next out of that love that led to his eventual banishment. He called on the only real knowledge he had and tried to bring her back."

"He tried to resurrect her?"

The Keeper nodded. "He managed only to shackle her soul, the poor thing.

217

Her body stood, her eyes glass as her powerless spirit despaired from within a husk awaiting commands from an inept master. His wails shook the walls when he realized what he'd done. Mind broken, he was soon discovered and...well you know how it went from there. Raliak was exiled, Lady Secilia put down once more, and their baby girl - barely a handful of months old - sent to an orphanage far, far from the city. The taint of the family excised with ruthless efficiency."

Thimble listened with breathless attention. The pieces slid into place in his mind one piteous click after the next. "The baby...Nira's mother?"

"Correct. Sent to fend for herself in a harsh world, ripped from everything any mortal could want, and none of it her fault. I believe Raliak tracked her down a few years before his rampage, when she was in her late teens and Nira, just old enough to understand. Told them the truth of it all, *his* truth anyway."

Thimble stared at the Keeper. Under his ceaseless incredulity bubbled a seething heat towards the godly figure he'd never felt in all his years.

The Keeper examined Thimble and held his hands over his chest in mock offense. "Oh you wound me, Mister Pennywhistle. What did I do to deserve such daggered eyes?"

"You...preyed on a broken woman," his voice shook, the words forced through clenched teeth. "You fed into a lifetime's worth of resentment and sat back as innocents paid the price." Disgust and fury warred in his eyes. "Aren't you a god? How *could* you?"

The Keeper rolled his eyes. "I didn't *make* her do anything, Thimble."

"You enabled every last bit!" Thimble shouted. "Do you think any of this would have happened if you'd just left her alone? Or heavens forbid, *stopped her* before all the murder started?"

The Keeper scoffed. "Stopped her? What for? My opportunistic ploy had taken a most amusing turn of events. How could I not see it play out to its end, eh?"

"Amus−" Thimble gaped at him. "People died! Innocent people!"

"Thimble...people die *all the time!*" the Keeper's voice thrummed through the water, agitating the surface. His grin had vanished; his eyes, round and popping. "That's. What. You. Do." He spread his arms and raised his face to the stars above. "Look! See for yourself! There they are, in all their glory! For eons I've ferried people to the Beyond. For ages I've watched them all come and go. The sick, the healthy, the good, the evil, the rich, the poor, the deserving and not. They all came, they all went, and more often than I'd care to remember, they did it to themselves, to each other! So what's a few more?"

The Keeper looked out across the unending stretch of luminant bubbles, his expression serene, eerily so. "Do you know what these are?"

Thimble's voice caught in his throat as he tried to answer. The Keeper's sudden outburst had caught him off guard. At the moment, the skinny, frail looking robed being had seemed colossal in presence, if not size. Thimble suppressed his urge to run. He cleared his throat. "Dreams?"

"Correct," the Keeper nodded. "Dreams of the living. Dreams of the dying. So many. I've seen so *many*. Do you know what most people dream about?"

Thimble shook his head.

"The future. Not just any future either. But one where they're happy. Where they've succeeded at everything they struggled with. One where they didn't make the mistakes or choices that drowned every minute of their waking lives in misery. One that isn't plagued with ups and downs and rights and wrongs. Where they can simply sit and smile. Just be." The Keeper reached out a hand and caressed a bubble. The globe shivered, then rose into the sky. "I find myself envious of these. To see the Beyond is one thing. To go through the veil... So many times I've envisioned myself passing through. Alas, it is not the way of a god."

"Why?" Thimble's voice was hardly above a whisper. He tried his best to stop his knees from trembling. "All the death, all the pain. What was it all for?"

"Ah, now that's the real interesting bit, isn't it?" The Keeper tapped his chin. He looked Thimble up and down like a cut of meat. "You know, I see a lot of old Raliak in you."

Thimble's blood ran cold at the words. "What are you talking about?"

"*Tsk tsk.* Let's not pretend we don't know. It was a *genius* bit of magic I must say. And to pull it off on your first try? Bravo!" The Keeper clapped, slow, sarcastic. "I didn't think you had it in you, honestly. Trapping your own grandfather's soul in a corner of your mind to prolong his existence *without* his approval or consent. My, my what a *naughty* little boy." The Keeper giggled. "And all because you couldn't let go. Touching really. But you crossed a line, Thimble. You meddled in *my* world."

With a snap of his fingers, the Keeper returned to his full size. "So I sent for your grandfather knowing your guilt and shame and oh-so-present desire to run away would bring you here. Into my little game. And how well you've done! You've proven as resourceful as I'd hoped and completed my puzzle, which admittedly became a much bigger puzzle, with flying colors. You even managed to throw a wrinkle my way that I had to *personally* address. To think, all my innumerable powers turned toward making a simple comb. It's quite funny really.

"Ah! In my excitement, I've neglected to answer your question. My apologies. Why? What was it all for?" The Keeper leaned toward him. "Well Thimble," he stopped inches from Thimble's face, eyes boring into him. "I need you to do something for me that I do not think anyone else can."

"No one else..." Thimble swallowed, his mouth barren. "What if I refuse?"

"You will not. I have something over you that I do not have with any other person in this world..." he tilted his head to the right, "...leverage."

Thimble screamed. His head felt as if it had been wrenched in two by a force unimaginable. He doubled over, his throat tearing as his voice clawed its way out with reckless abandon. Tears streamed down his face as he wished for death.

He heard a loud splash beside him as the pain vanished altogether. He stood gasping, willing air back into his lungs. He wiped at his eyes and glanced to his left, and felt his heart stop.

Sibelius Pennywhistle, stark as his name day, lay in the water. His terrified eyes darted around, frantic, desperate.

"Grampa?" Thimble rushed to his side and laid a hand on his shoulder. Sibelius jumped and yelped at the touch. "Grampa, wha– how?"

"Thimble?" Sibelius touched his arm. His voice came weak, thready. "Thimble, what's going on? Where are we?" He looked toward the Keeper.

"Who is that?"

Thimble knelt in the water. "It's okay. It's gonna be okay."

The Keeper smiled at the two Gnomes. "Sibelius Pennywhistle," he shook his head. "It's a pleasure to finally meet you, although under different circumstances than what was *meant* to be."

"What is he on about? What are you on about?" Sibelius said louder to the Keeper.

"He knows about the ritual, Grampa," Thimble whispered.

Sibelius' face fell. His gaze roved over the Keeper, to the horizon and finally to the sky above. A flame of understanding flickered in his eyes. "I don't know who or *what* you are," he gathered himself to his feet. "You leave my grandson alone. It was *my* fault he came across that spell in the first place. If there's a price to be paid, I'll pay it."

"Grampa, what are you saying?" Thimble asked, panicking. "Hey!" He shouted at the Keeper. "I'll do whatever you want, just send him back!"

"Mm no," The Keeper moved toward the pair one deliberate step after the next. "In fact, I think I'll keep him here with me." The Keeper raised a hand and snapped his fingers.

A bubble formed around Sibleius, knocking Thimble away. "Thimble!" Sibelius yelled as Thimble splashed into the water on his back. He pushed himself onto his elbows, heart hammering and met the old Gnome's eyes. "It's not your fault, son." Sibelius said as the bubble snapped shut and dragged him below the surface.

"Grampa!" Thimble fell on his hands and knees where the bubble had disappeared. The water lay still once more with no trace of his grandfather anywhere. "You're sick!" he spat at the Keeper.

"Maybe so," the Keeper stood over him. "But I'm afraid you don't know the meaning of that just yet. Not to worry though. He will be fine as long as you do what I ask. Succeed well enough, and we'll talk about his eventual destination."

Thimble gathered himself to his feet. A burning hatred for the Keeper seared at his chest. "What do you want?"

The Keeper straightened and folded his arms in his sleeves. He looked down his slender nose at Thimble. "First, let me ask you something. Why did you take this job?"

"What?" Thimble was hardly listening anymore. His anger outweighed his fear and sense tenfold.

"The job, Thimble. Why did you take the job when Samara offered it to you so many nights ago?"

Thimble's mind flashed back to the night he'd dived headfirst into the nightmare. The answer was obvious...wasn't it? "I thought I could help. And...the money, I could use it for the Penny and my–"

"NO!" The Keeper's shout shook droplets into the air for miles around. "No, no, no! Lies, Thimble! Lies you told yourself in the moment. You and I both know better, don't we?"

"I don't know what you're talking about." Thimble's fear took hold once more.

"I think you do," The Keeper's eyes, two points of frigid scrutiny pressed down on him. His voice, a whisper. "I think you do. Shall I remind you?"

Thimble inched back, away from this overwhelming pressure. The Keeper didn't move. No closer, no further, despite how many steps Thimble took. "I don't know what you're talking about." His voice trembled, his whisper near silent.

"It was a distraction, wasn't it Thimble? As much as running to your dear Grandfather's all those years ago. One you latched on to with nary a thought. The desperate attempts of a flailing will, eh?" The Keeper's eyes narrowed. "How long do you think it would have been, hm? A few months? Years, maybe? How long till you climbed a ladder to that knotted, twisted visage of release? Or maybe a nearby cliff would do. Or a midnight swim?"

"You don't know what you're *talking about!*" Thimble's scream faded quickly in the vastness. His breathing came shallow, rapid as if standing in a room with thinning air.

"Oh, but I do," The Keeper's eyes grew wide, manic. "The same way I knew you would take the job. Because I knew you would run from the alternative. But, you see, the alternative is the whole *point*. Except, unlike you, I'm desperate for it. I will do *anything* to get it. I need a key to the door, Thimble.

I need a part in this veil. What do I want?" The Keeper smiled down at him, teeth gleaming in the starlight. "I want you to find a way to kill me."